THE UNIQUE MAGAZINE   ISSN 0898-5073

Summer 1990   Art by Frank Kelly Freas

Weird Tales® is published quarterly by the Terminus Publishing Company, Inc., P.O. Box 13418, Philadelphia PA 19101-3418. (4426 Larchwood Ave., Philadelphia, PA 19104-3916). Second class postage paid at Philadelphia PA and additional mailing offices. Single copies, $4.95 (plus $1.00 postage if ordered by mail). Subscription rates: One year (4 issues) for $16.00 in the United States and its possessions, for $20.00 in Canada, and for $22.00 elsewhere. The publishers are not responsible for the loss of manuscripts, although reasonable care will be taken of such material while in their possession. Copyright© 1990 by the Terminus Publishing Company, Inc.; all rights reserved. Reproduction prohibited without prior permission. *Weird Tales*® is a registered trade mark owned by Weird Tales, Limited. Typeset, printed, and bound in the United States of America.

THE EYRIE

Concerning the Uniqueness of **The Unique Magazine**: There's been a lot of talk about categories in the field recently, among fans, professionals, and critics; and much of it hasn't been very enlightened talk, along the lines of: "Well, *horror* is noble stuff which sears the depths of the human psyche, while . . . ugh, *fantasy* is all adolescents in capes and brainless escapism . . . but only *science fiction* can be the true, relevant literature of the 20th century, since anything else makes hopeless compromises with the nature of reality, and doesn't have enough computers in it anyway. . . ."

Our general impression is that, for all that it sells well, *fantasy* — that is, the imaginary-scene, magic-and-dragons sort of fantasy — has gotten the short end of the stick, and is very, *very* looked down upon by practitioners of others kinds of imaginative fiction. ("The nigger of fantastic literature," as one critic we know so tactfully put it.)

Indeed, of the three basic types of non-realistic story telling — fantasy, horror, and science fiction — fantasy does seem to be in the weakest position right now. It has no organization of professional writers, like the Horror Writers of America or Science Fiction Writers of America. It has — and this is an unprecedented situation — no critical journal, with the possible exception of *Mythlore*, which deals with Tolkien, Lewis, Charles Williams, and the Inklings; and only incidentally with anything else. By contrast, science-fiction journals flourish: *Foundation, Science Fiction Studies,* and the newly revived *Science Fiction Review.*

There are more magazines of news and reviews and analysis of horror fiction than we can hope to keep track of. A few that come to mind are *Afraid* and *Scream Factory* and *Midnight Graffiti.*

And the fantasy fiction market seems more bloated than healthy: there are precious few outlets for a seriously intended, adult-level fantasy short story; and most of the novels seem to be formula trilogies. We cannot think of any particular line of fantasy books to which we can reliably turn for quality, the way you can turn to, say, Bantam Spectra Special Editions for quality science fiction. The Ace Fantasy Specials seem to have been an attempt in that direction, but there haven't been many of them of late. We hope the line hasn't been canceled.

But all too many people — readers, editors, critics, and even writers — assume that fantasy novels (usually trilogies) are just cookie-cutter junk, akin to nurse novels. They assume this without having read much in the field, and then dump on *everything.* Such charges are grossly unfair, not only when dealing with works by established masters, such as Gene Wolfe's *Soldier of the Mist,* but those of ambitious newcomers, such as Ellen Kushner's *Swordspoint.*

Admittedly there are a lot of books out there — and even more covers, if you judge books that way — which give such an impression; but the horror fans should remember that the science-fiction fans are saying the same things about horror, and the mainstream critics and academic establishment are saying the same thing about

4

all of us. (And in retaliation, some of us are saying that all "literary mainstream" consists of second-rate Updike imitations about fornication in suburbia.)

Possibly this isn't a good idea. The uniqueness of *Weird Tales*®, dubbed The Unique Magazine by its original publishers back in the 1920s, is that it *isn't* hopelessly bound by categories. The present editors are much more interested in a story being *good* rather than it being in a specific category.

We see no virtue in narrowness. It seems more likely that a reader who only wants to read one kind of story all the time has immature tastes. For the rest of us, isn't it likely that one Hideous Horror followed by another Searingly Hideous Horror, followed by another Hideously Searing Horror, every story in every issue, is going to make a magazine a trifle monotonous? Strictly all-horror magazines have a very poor record of survival in this country, and we think the reason may be sheer lack of variety in the scary-cum-gory fare. In such a context, even a very good story can lose its effect: if the reader *knows* that every story in the magazine is a horror story, how can an author surprise anyone?

We've got nothing against horror, surely. You will continue to see the best short horror fiction we can acquire, by both famous names and talented newcomers. As this is being written, we have just acquired a splendid, very intense horror novelet from Chet Williamson, which will be the centerpiece of our special Chet Williamson issue. And we're particularly proud of some of the horror stories we've published in the past, such as Brian Lumley's award-winning "Fruiting Bodies" and Alan Rodgers's "Emma's Daughter." (Alan's story has recently been anthologized, in Marvin Kaye's *Witches and Warlocks*.)

If a new Poe or Lovecraft came along — or, optimistically, *when* one comes along — we'd like to think that *Weird Tales*® would be just the magazine to showcase his (or her) work.

But we'd also like to be able to accommodate a new Clark Ashton Smith. Smith, a *Weird Tales*® regular of the '20s and '30s, wrote some of the most intensely morbid, grotesque horror fiction ever, but he tended to set the action in the far future, on the Earth's last continent of Zothique, or in pri-

Editors & Publishers:
Darrell Schweitzer
John Betancourt
George H. Scithers
Assistant Editors:
Leslie Smith
Dainis Bisenieks
Diane Weinman
Michael W. Betancourt
Circulation Manager:
Richard Kabakjian
Computer Consultant:
David J. Williams III
Of Counsel:
Yale F. Edeiken
Photographer:
Advanced Litho, Inc.
Typesetters:
The Twin Company, Inc.
Campus Copy Center
Wildside Press
Printer:
Malloy Lithographing, Inc.
Hard-cover Binder
Hoster Bindery, Inc.

SUBMISSIONS?

Like most editors, we get unsolicited manuscripts, *lots* of them. We survive, as do other editors, only by imposing Rules.

Yes, we read unsolicited manuscripts — *if* they are in proper manuscript format. Each must arrive with a self-addressed, stamped return envelope big enough to take that manuscript back to you, or with a stamped, addressed, business-letter-sized envelope *and* instructions to dispose of the manuscript if not bought. And no, we will not read manuscripts in unacceptable format.

This proper format is described in numerous reference works. One of them is *On Writing Science Fiction: The Editors Strike Back!*, by George H. Scithers, Darrell Schweitzer, and John M. Ford — which also goes into the whole art and practice of writing and selling fantastic literature. *On Writing* is available for $19.50, postpaid, from Owlswick Press, PO Box 8243, Philadelphia, PA 19101 (if you live in Pennsylvania, add $1.17 for sales tax).

mordial Hyperborea, or in the (imaginary) medieval French province of Averoigne.

But according to present-day categorizations, Smith would be a Fantasy writer, not a Horror writer, since *horror* seems to preclude historical settings prior to about 1800, or imaginary settings altogether. Most of the horror anthologies and small-press horror magazines today would probably not know what to do with such Smith tales as "The Dark Eidolon," much less "The Vaults of Yoth-Vombis," which is a classically creepy horror story *set on Mars.*

But *Weird Tales*® would. We think our greater flexibility is one of our strongest assets, as it always has been throughout the history of this magazine. Consider Seabury Quinn's famous "Roads" (January 1938), which manages to combine an immortal adventurer with the crucifixion of Jesus Christ and the legend of Santa Claus. It was definitely "unique" when it appeared, but it was hardly a conventional horror/fantasy story, or a conventional Christmas story. Only *Weird Tales*® could possibly have published it.

A more recent, less extreme example is Gerald Pearce's "Kindred of the Crescent Moon" in the present issue. We doubt any other magazine in the field would have been able to use this story, despite its obvious excellence. Is it a Fantasy, in the commercial, generic sense? Only marginally, and no one is publishing Fantasy novellas anyway. A historical story? There are even fewer markets for that? Horror? Well, there *is* a supernatural element, but this is hardly what we expect to be issued in a limited edition from Scream Press.

So the only way this story can reach an audience is through *Weird Tales*®, which alone has the editorial flexibility to cross over every generic boundary there is — or ignore them altogether — in the pursuit of excellence.

We'd like to keep it that way.

The Eyrie needs letters! There used to be an old fannish joke: how to get published in *Weird Tales*®? Simple: write a letter to the Eyrie.

It happens to be true. We do want to hear from you. We'd like to publish and discuss your opinions. We want you to let us know what you think of *Weird Tales*®, its ap-

pearance, its fiction, its policies.

Should we, for instance, run serials? This idea has been discussed. The two sides of the argument are that it's a buyer's market for serials (since there are far more novels out there than anyone can serialize), so a serial insures a large chunk of great writing by a top name. Then again, some people prefer to just wait and read the book, and have those pages filled up with short fiction. What do you think?

John Bracy of Tempe, Arizona, would seem to agree with us, sort of:

First, I'd like to stress that I want Weird Tales® *to survive and to remain "different." I also have a theory that says the philosophy of printing a name instead of a story was instrumental in the demise of both* Night Cry *and* Twilight Zone. *I, for one (and I'm not alone), don't give a fig about who's on the cover as long as what's inside will take me for a float down-stream. I mean, it's the actual words* on the page *that I'm purchasing, right? Moreover, some of the "innovation" running in* Asimov's *and* The Horror Show *could make a blue nun barf green Jello. It is really too bad. And it's only a matter of time before* Weird Tales® *is left to stand alone — but with a subscription rate of two hundred thousand.*

Anyway, you've stated in the Eyrie that you welcome readers' comments/opinions, and while my brief familiarity with the mag can't grant me critical notoriety, here goes:

— But wait. I should first admit that I've never been a big fan of the "sword" story, and laughable as it may sound, I didn't know who Robert E. Howard was until about four months ago when I met someone who worships every line he ever wrote. I myself grew up on Tom Swift, golden age SF, and Edgar Rice Burroughs (who did, come to think of it, employ vast sword-play in his Venus/Mars series), but I just never got around to Howard. In short, what follows may be retrogressive insight.

It is my impression that Weird Tales® *studiously uses a lot of swords; this might be by virtue of the school's popularity (and you quite rightly want to please the vogue readership), and/or because — as you've already mentioned — Weird Tales® has used swords from the beginning. It's tradition. But I have no complaint on this point; even nonfans like*

me can be entertained by stories like "Three Heads for the High King." Actually, I don't have any complaints. Concern would be a better word. You see, when someone who doesn't go out of his way to read swords embarks upon reading a mag like Weird Tales® *and find it's the very swords that he doesn't go out of his way to read which consistently end up near the top of his list, he begins to wonder if he's acquired a modified disposition, or if the contemporary stories included might be just a tad impoverished.*

Are solid, contemporary, horrific/weird tales hard to come by? Or is everything, in reality, excellent, and it's simply a format thing? Or, then again, am I vacationing on Planet X?

Well, John, we have nothing against vacationing on Planet X, as long as *Weird Tales®* is distributed there. But seriously, your letter states both the problem and the solution.

If the trends in both anthologies and small-press publications are any indication, the "vogue audience" does not like sword-and-sorcery at all, but modern-scene horror of the King/Koontz/McCammon type. Much of the best imaginary-scene fantasy, such as "Three Heads for the High King" or "King Yvorian's Wager" (which we note you voted for in first place) is getting lost under what is at least packaged to look like a deluge of imitation Tolkien or imitation Piers Anthony trilogies. We're glad you actually do like the examples of such fiction we've published, even if you don't normally read that kind of thing. Possibly we *are* slowly altering your disposition. Meanwhile we hope that fans of such stories learn to come to *Weird Tales®* for the *best.*

But a magazine of nothing other than swordly stories would be just as monotonous as one of 100% horror. That is why we would like to preserve our diversity.

The *best* of anything is always hard to come by. But there are lots of modern-scene horror stories being written today. Possibly we have to compete a little harder to get them (against the high-class, invitational anthology market, books like *Prime Evil* and *The Book of the Dead*) than we do for imaginary-scene fantasy (for which in novelet and novella lengths at least, there is *no* competition, no other professional market), but we remain confident that we can get

good material. We're paying competitive rates, and there are only so many anthologies a year. A top name writer might sell four or five that way, but anybody who writes short fiction regularly will inevitably, we hope, turn to *Weird Tales®*.

We can't really agree with your estimations of the other magazines. *Isaac Asimov's SF Magazine* must be doing something right because it keeps selling, and stories from its pages dominate the Hugo-award voting. *Night Cry* sold well on the stands, but perished because its publisher regarded it as merely an experiment and refused to back it. *Twilight Zone* hung in there for eight years, and so most have managed to acquire something of a following. It was always an uneasy mix of movie material and fiction, which may have been a factor. But we have our own (unconfirmed) theory: Subscription copies of *Twilight Zone* were sent through the mails unwrapped, with just a label attached. Such arriving copies as we ever saw looked like they'd been through a shredder. Our guess is that *TZ* readers got sick of this and let their subscriptions lapse. Nothing will kill a magazine faster than subscribers who do not renew.

Which raises a point, Dear Readers. Have you renewed your subscription yet? Remember that *Weird Tales®* comes safely wrapped in plastic, and so, as best as the Postal Service can manage, tends to arrive in one (untattered) piece.

Debra Weaver of Shallotte, North Carolina, suggests that maybe writing isn't a disease after all:

Reading Koster's letter (#295) which compares writing to struggling against cancer, and your analogy which equates writers with Olympic contenders, I offer another comparison. We (writers) are like parents who strive to prepare our children/stories for acceptance in a cold world. They are tidied up, hair combed, shoes polished to the best of our ability, only to return rejected (often with no explanation), being merely told that they are "not right." We wonder what we've done wrong, where we've failed, and worst of all, like children after our own heart, we feel that they are *right.*

And for those that stay away and fret great lengths of time, we worry and fret. Are they all right? Have they gotten lost or perhaps merely shoved to the side? And if that child/story is accepted, oh, do we cheer! Not because we receive money, but because the time, effort, and worry actually proved emotionally rewarding.

These are just metaphors, but we think that the hair-combing and shoe-shining are analogous to the correct *format*. Beyond that, combed-hair/neat-typing or not, the child/story has to have the right number of limbs and organs and be *alive*. So possibly writers are more like mad scientists sewing little bodies together and sending them on their way . . . Where did we go wrong, Igor? Maybe if the eyes had been in the *front* . . .

Peni R. Griffin has a first-place vote:

Best story, Winter '89: "The Lady of Belac." I am continually, if mildly, irritated by characters in historical fiction who are gifted by their authors with inappropriately modern attitudes — presumably because modern audiences cannot be expected to sympathize with people who hold "wrong" opinions. The life of an ordinary medieval gentlewoman looks so unbearable to a twentieth-century woman, that we refuse to believe they did bear it — forgotten the automatic mechanisms with which we all bear the unbearable in our lives. I wonder which of our unthinking assumptions are going to be unthinkable to our descendants. Will they regard as intolerable the situation of parents forced by economic necessity to spend the bulk of their time working outside the home rather than raising their families? Anyway, "The Lady of Belac" is wonderful; a tour de force of character (in a genre supposedly devoid of that quality), striving valiantly to reproduce the viewpoint of a long-ago and voiceless generation.

Don Edwards of Montebello, California, offers these thoughts on the nature of horror:

Horror is a genre of fiction or film embracing the very space and darkness we see our names upon. However briefly, however real, clearly, we see our own deaths, or own wonder at life itself, when the tight mask of horror breathes in our face.

Horror is the unknown undefined. *It is most frightening when the symbolic mask is formally brisk and in place, when that which is beneath is unseen and not understood. Blood and guts and salty ketchup membranes all over the quivering theater screen or snow-white printed page are patently unnecessary and bordering on the mood-breaking obscene. (As a struggling writer, I put blood, splatter, violence in my stories sometimes because many editors want it. I want to sell, and I want to eat.) Mood-breaking because the most effective, beautiful, memorable horror excursions rely almost totally on a tightly constructed atmosphere and well-drawn, well-defined characters. Only as a last-resort 'climax' to a story plot should such dubious violent elements be utilized, and rarely and briefly as a sort of 'orgasm' to the earlier occurrences in a story. I despise censorship, emphatically. But mood and atmosphere in a horror tale are everything. Break this fragile environment with premature ejaculation of blood and guts, and the story is virtually lost in a tangle of torn mood fabric; and it's time to start over, if you can find your way.*

When I was a little boy, in my neighborhood (and probably yours), there was a forlorn old house, in disrepair, badly in need of paint, grass unwatered and eight inches high, shutters leaning on hinges. All the kids in the neighborhood thought it was haunted. When we eventually discovered that an elderly woman was living there, naturally we assumed she was a 'real' witch. Nothing, before or since, has equalled the heart-racing excitement and thrill of wobblily standing in front of her ancient wood-frame abode in an eerie brown October twilight, in a brash, exotic Halloween frame of mind; with that energetic sense of wonder and youthful imagining. Imagine! What clipped black wings! What stroked and strange macabre things went on inside her marvelous cobwebbed black dwelling! Candles moved at hazy windows! Creaking doors squeaked. Porch swings swayed, rattled, and seemed to speak! What queer and miraculous cloven-hooved dreams were root-cellar spawned and mushrooming?

When she invited us in to her house two weeks later for hot apple cider, popcorn, and Trick-or-Treat, the bubble burst. She was just an ordinary nice old lady now. See? Horror loses everything, its thundering supernatural sense of wonder, its snakes, pumpkins, and windy midnight broomstick

THE EYRIE

rides, when it is exposed, when the blood and guts are seen naked, in puddles, in the harsh yellow light of day. The bubble pops. The dream sours.

Let's keep horror magical, special.

Well, we hasten to add that the bubble *really* popped for you when you found out that there was no *menace*, that the old lady was just a nice neighbor. But if you *had* seen blood and guts in there, some child from the neighborhood chopped up on a cutting board, with eyeballs floating in the sink . . . well, it would have been quite a memorable occasion!

It might not have made the best story. We tend to agree with you on gore-for-gore's sake. Our own feeling is that gore *is* permissible in a story as long as it is there for a constructive purpose and not merely as a substitute for plot, character, action, atmosphere.

The Splatterpunk authors object that you can have just so many M.R. Jamesian stories of elderly clerics who get a fright from a rippling curtain seen in the dark, and that, to keep things interesting, there should be *more*.

The problem is, of course, that suggestion is often more powerful than what the writer has to deliver. The inherent limitation of the blood-and-vomit aesthetic is that once you have shown everything, *there is nothing more to show*. If the point of the story is *shock*, the shocks can only keep escalating so far until we reach the level of a *Friday the 13th* movie and the result is either nauseating or just plain silly.

Yes, imagination is the key. The story has to remain magical. That means, when the author does pull aside the covers and show us the Horror or the Wonder, he had better deliver the goods, hopefully goods we have never seen before.

And our faithful correspondent **Greg Koster** is back again:

. . . issue 295. My favorite five are 1: "A Doll's Tale" 2: "Cloonaturk" 3: "The Disapproval of Jeremy Cleave" 4: "Love Song from the Stars," 5: "King Yvorian's Wager." The rest of the pack is way back in the dust.

I regret to say that this issue, to me anyway, is the weakest one you've put out. The lady critic who edits the bug-crusher would be justified in her complaint by Weird Tales®.

The two top tales are very funny rather than scary. The rest seemed competently done, but were pale. They were missing some literary vitamin that would make them memorable. This was particularly true of Mr. Lumley's tales. If you ever get a chance, compare "No Sharks in the Med" with "The Sun, the Sea, and the Silent Scream" (also by Brian Lumley) in the March 1988 issue of The Magazine of Fantasy and Science Fiction. *"No Sharks" is a carbon copy of his earlier tale, and a pretty pale one. You got the short end of this deal.*

However, I agree with you that Weird Tales® *is a magazine of merit. Without trying to define what "scariness" is, I will say that* Weird Tales® *has always made me feel that the money spent on a subscription is well spent.*

Question: Are the "Weirdisms" true, or just the product of an editor's imagination?

Vincent Di Fate is a talented artist, but his magic did not come through in this issue. Once again, I can't tell you why, but I am reduced to scratching my head and muttering, "Sorry chaps, this ain't it." About the only defect I can point out is that the illustrations usually did not seem to be of the most dramatic parts of the story; "The Demon Cat" is the best example of this.

In regards special issues: You have tried grouping an author's stories together, spreading them throughout the issue. I am in favor of the former approach — a group of tales seems more like a special issue somehow. I think it is the punch of a group that makes the difference. To be sure, weak stories will show up more prominently this way, but then, you don't buy weak stories, right? May I also request that you return to printing a checklist, not necessarily complete, of the featured author's works? The one of Tanith Lee was fine. I mention this because issue 296 features David Schow, which makes me scratch my head and mutter "David who?"

Gosh, we thought you knew. But there are so many books, so many authors, that if a writer is less famous than King or Asimov, there is going to be a substantial portion of the readership which hasn't heard of him or her. By now, of course, we hope you have read the Schow issue and been introduced to a "new" writer you will want to follow in the future. David is the author of *The Kill Riff* and a story collection, *Red*

9

Light (both Tor Books). The title story in the collection won the World Fantasy Award in 1987. It was originally published in *Twilight Zone,* to which he was a regular contributor, along with *TZ's* companion magazine, *Night Cry,* where he exercised his penchant for titles. We particularly remember "Blood Rape of the Lust Ghouls." He also writes for TV and movies.

To answer your other question: yes, the topics of "Weirdisms" are quite real. An acquaintance *saw* a hand of glory in an occult shop's back room. And Tibetan corpse-wrestling is described in Alexandra David-Neel's *Magic and Mystery in Tibet.* Tibetans, at least, believe in such things.

The Most Popular Story

We need your votes, readers. For issue 296, what votes we received covered a very wide spread, so that no fewer than seven stories got at least one first-place vote. In order to make some sense out of this, we shifted from just counting first-place votes to a point system: first place equals three points, second place two, third place one. By this reckoning, the result is even between Darrell Schweitzer's "King Yvorian's Wager" and Mervyn Wall's "Cloonaturk." By a straight first-place count, the winner would be Schweitzer, but Wall got more votes (second and third) overall. We declare it a tie.

We are particularly gratified that the Mervyn Wall story was popular. He is, in the opinion of some of us, the best living fantasy writer in the world. His two Irish fantasies, *The Unfortunate Fursey* (1946) and *The Return of Fursey* (1947) are simply wonderful, tragi-comedies in the manner of (and fully as good as) T.H. White. Look for an omnibus, *The Complete Fursey* (Dublin: Wolfhound Press, 1985) in Irish import shops. For all he is known to critics (see especially E.F. Bleiler's *Supernatural Fiction Writers*) he seems unknown to the general fantasy readership, simply because his books have never been reprinted as category paperbacks. It needs doing.   ▽

COMING IN OUR FALL 1990 ISSUE !

OUR SPECIAL CHET WILLIAMSON *TRIBUTE*

~ featuring ~

3 Mind-Boggling *New* Stories by the Best-Selling Author of *Dreamthorpe* and *Ash Wednesday !*

~ plus ~

THE FANTASTIC ARTWORK OF *BOB WALTERS !*

And coming up in future issues . . .

Robert Bloch	Jonathan Carroll
Hugh B. Cave	Nina Kiriki Hoffman
Joe Lansdale	Morgan Llywelyn
Brian Lumley	A. R. Morlan
Darrell Schweitzer	Nancy Springer
Keith Taylor	Ian Watson
Gahan Wilson	*. . . & many, many more!*

THE DEN

by John Gregory Betancourt

Win a zillion dollars!

One topic of interest among SF writers lately is the new Turner Tomorrow Award, which is being sponsored by Ted Turner (of Turner Broadcasting — CNN, WTBS, TNT, etc. etc. etc.). For the best entrant depicting a practical, positive solution to a world problem (presumably ecological), a prize of half a million dollars is offered. There will also be four runners-up, who will receive fifty thousand dollars.

First prize is more than a hundred times what most novelists ever receive for a book. But is it a good thing?

I think so. Not because dozens or hundreds of Great SF Novels will be generated; I have my doubts about how many professional science-fiction writers will even enter the contest. What with bills to pay and mouths to feed, most writers will stick with their steady contracts . . . this book has to be finished, and has to be done completely on spec, and that would be hard for the writer just scraping by. Doubtless some talented newcomer will win. Rather, I think it's a good idea because, in publishing, people listen to money. Cynical, yes, but certainly true. Think about it: whenever you hear about some SF/fantasy/horror book through non-SF media, isn't it because of money in some way — Stephen King getting $40 million for four books, or Dean Koontz signing a huge contract with Berkley, or something of the sort?

What Turner's award will do is focus (for a brief time) public attention on his award. Every writer I know is talking about it.

With the largest prize ever offered in science fiction, how can the Turner Tomorrow Award be ignored? It overshadows the Writers of the Future contest in every way.

If you're interested or want more information, you can write for complete rules and an entry form. Address: The Turner Tomorrow Awards, One CNN Center, Box 105366, Atlanta GA 30329. Deadline for entry is November 20, 1990.

Grumbles from the Grave, by Robert A. Heinlein
Del Rey Books, 281 pp., $19.95 (hc)

Grumbles is a curious book for the millions who grew up reading Robert A. Heinlein's work. Heinlein kept himself a very private person throughout his life, and few people in the field knew him, or knew much about him (as compared to, say, Isaac Asimov or Arthur C. Clarke). *Grumbles from the Grave* is to some extent a correction of that, since it provides glimpses of his life, thoughts, and opinions, mainly through correspondence with his literary agent, Lurton Blassingame.

Perhaps the most surprising revelation is Heinlein's relationship with his editor at Scribner's, Alice Dalgliesh. Rather than being an easy-to-work-with professional, Dalgliesh appears (from Heinlein's point of view, anyway) to have been meddlesome (she often insisted on rewrites, weakening stories), sexually repressed (she saw Freudian symbolism all over *Red Planet* — and of course moved to suppress it), and generally snobbish (she refused to use Hubert Rogers for covers on Heinlein's books because his work had appeared in *Astounding* — and the cover she sent Heinlein as proof illustrated one of Heinlein's pseudonymous stories).

Many of Heinlein's books were savaged. Excerpts from *Red Planet* and *Podkayne of Mars* appear in the appendices to bear out Heinlein's opinions. What's most surprising is that, after becoming a cult author and best-seller, Heinlein didn't insist on having all his books reissued as he wanted them. Which leads us to . . .

The Puppet Masters, by Robert A. Heinlein (expanded edition)
Del Rey Books, $4.95, 340pp., (pb)

The first two un-expurgated Heinlein novels have appeared: *The Puppet Masters,* and *Red Planet.*

The Puppet Masters is Heinlein's cold-war novel — a vast allegory on socialism. This time the communists are sluglike creatures which come from spaceships, attach themselves to humans, and take over minds and wills. Puppet masters indeed!

I'd read and enjoyed the book as a teenager, and as I read, I kept looking for differences. A few scenes seemed to go on longer than I remembered. And everything seemed less tense and *in*tense. And this version is far more sexist. But other than that — the same story.

Unless you're dying to reread it, you might as well stick with your old edition on this one.

Necroscope III: The Source, by Brian Lumley
TOR Books, 505 pp., $4.95

The back cover of *The Source* says, "Concluding a powerful trilogy of terror!" — but we know better. Lumley's made no secret of his intentions to make the Necroscope books into a five-volume series.

I'm pleased to say the middle installment is fully up to snuff. After finishing each of the last two books, I've thought, *But where can he go from here?* And he's always managed to surprise me.

The Source takes us away from our human Earth, to the parallel world which spawned the vamphyri. Travel to and from the vampires' Earth is result of a "gray hole" which a team of Soviet scientists unwittingly created (and now can't get rid of) when they attempted use of a new Star-Wars-like defense system. Unfortunately it's a one-way trip through the gray hole — you can either enter the vamphyri's world from ours and not get back, or enter ours from the vamphyri's world. And several quite unusual vampire-creatures have already come through. . . .

Of course the various British and American intelligence agencies want to know what's going on; the Soviets don't want them to find out; and again Harry Keogh, necroscope and former head of ESPionage for the British, gets pulled in.

But this isn't quite the same Harry we remember from *Necroscope II: Vamphyri!* — he's older, burned out, and still searching (without success) for wife and son, who disappeared at the end of the second book. But perhaps the gray hole will be the solution to his problems, too.

Lumley is still blending horror, fantasy, and science fiction. The returning characters are still like old friends. And new villains and heroes are still well drawn. It's a strong installment in the series. If you aren't already following it, read the first two books before *The Source* — Lumley ties up a number of loose threads.

I'm eagerly awaiting #4. Though what he's going to do *this* time is beyond me.

Consider Phlebas, by Iain M. Banks
Macmillan, $18.95, 471 pp.

This was my second stab at reading Banks's work. My first was his novel *Walking on Glass,* which I found dull to the point of impenetrability. That would have been enough to put me off his work for good, but I decided to try again because of the heaps of praise he'd gotten for his first novel (horror), *The Wasp Factory,* and his first science-fiction novel, *Consider Phlebas.*

I'm glad I gave him a second chance. *Consider Phlebas* is one of the best space operas I've ever read.

In a heavily populated universe, where star travel is cheap and easy, two forces are at war: the Idirans, giant aliens who want to subdue and civilize the rest of the universe as part of a religious mission; and the Culture, a loose amalgamation of humans and machines which is probably the largest federation in the universe. Our titular hero is Horza, a Changer — someone who has been genetically altered so he can shift to look like any human he wants to. Horza has thrown in with the Idirans due to ideological reasons; he sees the Culture as a stagnant dead-end and wants the humans' blissful existence in partnership with machines ended. In many ways he is prejudiced against machine intelligence.

Horza is an ideal spy. He is assigned the task of recovering a spaceship's computer brain from a dead planet, but gets sidetracked by the war and has to make his own way there in the company of a mercenary band. There are battles (small and stellar), memorably weird characters like Fwi-Song the cannibal priest and Balveda, Horza's counterpart in the Culture. And there are exotic machines, strange worlds, odd aliens . . . everything you could possibly want wrapped in a story of galaxy-shaking scope. Recommended.

Of note . . . :

Tales of the Cthulhu Mythos, by H.P. Lovecraft & Divers Hands
Arkham House, 529pp., $23.95

This is surely *the* definitive Cthulhu Mythos volume, with 22 stories by H.P. Lovecraft (2), Clark Ashton Smith (2), Frank Belknap Long (2), August Derleth (2), Robert Bloch (3), and one each from Robert E. Howard, Henry Kuttner, Fritz Leiber, Lumley, Ramsey Campbell, Colin Wilson, Joanna Russ, Karl Edward Wagner, Philip Jose Farmer, Stephen King, and Richard A. Lupoff. Whether you like your Unspeakable Things squamous or rugose, don't miss it.

Masques III, edited by J.N. Williamson

St. Martin's Press, 316 pp., $17.95

Some series seem to wind down the older they get, and the *Masques* series is starting on that track, if the latest volume is any indication. It's not a bad book by any means; all the stories are good, publishable stuff. It's just lacking in high points. There is no single story — like Alan Rodgers' "The Boy Who Came Back from the Dead" or Robert McCammon's "Night Crawlers" from the first volume — which will grab you by the throat and shake you till you pay attention.

But if there are no peaks, there are no valleys, either: not a dud in the collection, not even among the stories by new writers Williamson has discovered or is developing, which is quite an achievement because my tastes are very demanding. For a glimpse at future big names in the field, check out the second section, "The New Horror," which features work by rising stars (mostly from the small press).

There is also work by Ray Bradbury, Ed Gorman, Rex Miller, William F. Nolan, Dan Simmons, Ray Russell, Graham Masterton, and quite a few more. Check it out.

Midnight Graffiti #4
Midnight Graffiti Publishing, $4.95.
(13101 Sudan Rd., Poway CA 92064)

Midnight Graffiti is a delightful fan-produced magazine more about the horror field than anything else. #4 is the special dinosaur issue — with stories by David Schow, Joe Lansdale, and R.V. Branham — minor stuff, but certainly diverting. Schow's tale is an homage to Bradbury's classic "The Sound of Thunder." The real meat of the issue is Theodore Sturgeon's last interview.

If you order by mail, add $2.50 for postage and be prepared for a wait; they're a bit slow sometimes.

▽

ATTENTION BOOK LOVERS !

If you like fine hardcover editions of books, you may be interested in *Weird Tales Library*. Several times a year, we put together a huge catalog of small press books available through *Weird Tales* and mail it out to subscribers. Currently we offer titles from W. Paul Ganley: Publisher, Scream Press, Mark V. Ziesing, Donald M. Grant, and Pulphouse, among others. To get a copy of our latest catalog, send a legal-sized S.A.S.E. to: *Weird Tales Library*, P.O. Box 13418, Philadelphia, PA 19101.

SNICKERDOODLES

by Nancy Springer

"Eat this, son," Blake's mother told him, handing him a snickerdoodle. "It will help you know what to do."

That was different. She usually said, "It'll make you feel better." She held the cookie out toward him, and he noted without particularly noticing how its dimpled circular surface was incised with the simple six-lobed design some of the old people called a hex sign. This was not unduly strange. Enola Bloodsworth always decorated her cookies with hearts or tulips or some sort of design. And they did indeed make people feel better. This was a known fact in Diligence, PA, and would have enabled her to make a living off the things if she had cared to sell them. But she preferred, in her cat-walks-by-herself way, to control them, giving them only to whom she chose.

Her son had been the recipient of many such therapeutic cookies. But after what he had been telling her, about all the trouble he had been having in high school, Blake Bloodsworth had been hoping for something more from her than a pastry panacea. He shook his head.

"I'm not hungry. Jocks been slamming you against lockers all day, you wouldn't be hungry either."

"Eat it," she insisted. "Since when do you have to be hungry to eat my cookies?"

"Yeah, and I'm getting fat. It's bad enough being a geek without being a fat geek."

He was in fact small and thin, as he had always been. She sat down at the ashwood kitchen table with him and gave him a hard look.

"Eat the cookie," she ordered.

Tired of fighting, he took the sweet hex-marked circle from her and ingested it. Good, as always. God, why wouldn't she sell them and make herself as rich as the things that came out of her oven? A peering middle-aged woman, ever housedressed, spending her days in the kitchen passionately baking, she did not eat much or have any visible source of income. She appeared to Blake to live on air, like one of those spidery tropical plants from Spencer's Mail Order Gifts.

He wanted someday to make something of himself. He was a good student, especially in logical subjects such as math and science. Maybe he could be an engineer or a scientist, get out of Diligence and out of poverty. His mother's take-it-as-it-comes attitude toward life irritated him. How could anyone so proud be so sloppy, so blurred at the edges, in the way she dressed, her thinking, her housekeeping . . . her kitchen, which might as well be her soul, disgusted him. Dutch-kid plaques on the walls, along with a heart-shaped wreath of plastic roses. More plastic roses perched atop the cupboards. He hated them, and he hated her kitchen even when it was clean, but (to add to his adolescent irritation) from where he sat he could see the mess her day's cookie-making had left in it: clouds of flour everywhere, Crisco and eggs sitting out on the counter along with her cookbook —

14

"Hey." Blake's mood suddenly changed. Eyes glittering, he got up and went to look at the book as if he had never seen it before, though in fact he had been seeing it all his life. An old volume, handwritten and bound in black leather, it had belonged, so his mother told him, to his great-grandmother. Maternal great-grandmother, of course; he had no paternal relations. Not only was he a geek, but a fatherless geek as well.

"Hey," Blake repeated. He was beginning to get an idea what to do about the jerks in school, one of the best ideas he had ever had; where had it come from? The recipe book looked plenty spooky enough for what he had in mind. On its black leather cover was embossed, of all things, the slant-eyed face of a cat. He flipped its pages. Between cobwebs of text (brown-inked in a fine, fine hand) he saw illustrations: stars, several weird kinds of crosses, hex designs of all sorts. Cookie decorations. But the buttheads didn't have to know that.

"Mom," he demanded, "can I take this to school?"

"What for?" she asked in her dry way, seeming as always to know what he was doing, what he was thinking, but asking the proper questions anyway, as if to uphold a formality. Holding up his end, he always lied.

"To show the teachers."

"You expect them to read it? It's in German, you know."

"Of course I know." In fact he hadn't given the inscrutable text much thought. "So I show it to the German teacher."

She smiled with that odd weary pride and tenderness only mothers seem able to achieve. And if she indeed saw through him as he suspected, her pride had to be not for what he had said but what he actually intended to do.

After supper Blake retreated to his attic, his dusty lair where his mother never came. Once he had turned adolescent she had seemed to understand instinctively his need for privacy and his own space, moving him up under the eaves and turning his former bedroom into her storage area.

She understood too much. It was as if she looked at him and read his mind.

Blake lay on his narrow studio couch of a bed and felt faintly uneasy despite his excited plans. It seemed odd to him that his mother had so readily given him permission to borrow the recipe book. She used it every day, or else kept it constantly by her like a lucky charm, and it had been written by her long-dead grandmother, for gosh sake. The grandmother she had been named after. Another Enola Bloodsworth. So it had to be precious to her.

His mother was up to something, Blake decided. And no telling what. Enola Bloodsworth's thoughts and plans were strictly her own. All of Diligence knew her, yet she had no close friends. In a town full of couples and families she stood like a blackthorn tree, in proud isolation. Backward, the name "Enola" spelled "Alone."

From what Blake had heard, his great-grandmother hadn't been married either. He wondered if that long-dead Enola had done as his mother had done, taking a man for purposes of insemination then discarding him. His mother was quite frank about his father: the man had been no more than a make-do in her life, she scarcely remembered his face, his name was of no importance. She was just as frank about her reason for having seduced her unlikely lover: she had wanted a child badly. *Too bad she got me,* Blake thought. Probably she had been hoping for a girl to carry on the rather eccentric Bloodsworth breeding tradition.

Never mind, Mom. Plenty of the guys in school keep telling me I'm the next best thing.

It was tough being small in Diligence, a steel-mill town where even the houses stood tall and square-shouldered like the cock-of-the-walk football-playing Irish and Slavic and Italian guys in their muscle shirts and gladiator footgear. Quite aside from the fact that the jocks sometimes used him as their medicine ball, Blake had a problem with girls. He liked them. There was a word that rhymed with hex, and it was often on his mind, but he hadn't had any. With all the hunks to choose from, girls laughed in his face when he approached.

His mother knew, of course, though he told her nothing. "Someday there is going to be a special girl for you, Blake," she had said to him one evening out of thin shadowy flour-clouded air. "You're small and dark, and that means you're smarter than the others. So let the gadabout girls choose the big dumb brutes for now. Someday there will be a beautiful girl who appreciates you the way I do."

And then she had pushed cookies at his face.

Damn her, she adored him as only a mother could. And he hated her devotion, because it only made him ache for a similar love from . . .

Lying on his chaste bed, Blake allowed himself daydreams: not of any girl he knew, because they all scorned him, but of an ideal lover he had never seen. Passionate. Exotic. Erotic. A few years older than he, maybe, taller than he, even, but only his lovemaking could satisfy her. Greek profile, with that wonderfully patrician straight or slightly bowed line from brow to nose. Masses of black hair, huge dark — no, green — no, *purple* eyes above fashion-model cheekbones. In his imagination he kissed those cheekbones and her full hot lips and her exquisite collarbone and so on down her lithe, throbbing body to her breasts. She had more than two. The ones that showed through her clothes were full and bobbing, like a cheerleader's breasts, but on the ribcage just below them were two more, smaller ones with supersensitive nipples that excited her to do unspeakable acts, and in all the world only he, Blake Bloodsworth the Master Lover, knew of them —

Jesus, Blake mocked himself, adjusting the position of his hands. *Stop now and maybe you won't go blind.*

Trying to leave the fantasy woman behind on the bedsheets, he got up and went to his high, narrow window. It was dusk. An orange September moon was rising. Just outside the glass, so near that he could see their ugly little faces, bats were swooping down from the eaves, as they did every nightfall. Things that flew in the dark, like the succubus he could still feel writhing in his brain stem.

Far below, on the stones of the alley, sat a sleek black cat with its aristocratic head tilted back, looking up toward him.

"Hey, Geek," Jason Trovato cheerfully greeted him the next morning outside the school. "How's your love life?"

"Talk to your dad lately?" someone else put in.

"Long distance?" another butthead, Dane Orwig, suggested. More had gathered, grinning. They never let him forget. As kids they had chased him down and rubbed his face in the dirt. Their tactics hadn't changed much since.

"I've had it, you guys," he told them, his voice coming up squeaky out of his narrow ribs. "Lay off. I'm not going to take your crap anymore."

He knew they loved it when he tried to act tough. As he had expected they would, they laughed and stepped closer. But this time instead of wincing he smiled. For once he felt strong in his secret way, because he had a plan.

"Look," he told them quietly, "I'll warn you once, because hex magic is nothing to mess with. I've got hex witch

17

blood, and now I've been anointed. Anytime I want I can put a curse on you."

He did not himself believe any of this. His plan was to scare them, nothing more. Most of them had been nurtured under an incense cloud of Catholic mysticism. The few Protestants among them had received their share of fiery Revelation under revival tents pitched in cow pastures. He hoped all of them would at least halfway believe him. Maybe they did. They were still laughing, true, but it sounded forced.

"Hey!" called a big freckled football hero named Patrick Sullivan. "How'd you manage that? Does the coven meet in your ma's garage, or what?"

"Yeah, geek!" Jason Trovato sounded genuinely eager. "Tell us the details."

"You stop calling me geek and you can come watch."

"Sure, geek."

"So they meet in your ma's garage," someone else put in conversationally, "and they have rites, like? What do they do, geek? Dance naked?"

No, dammit, their laughter was not forced. They were loving every minute of this.

"Human sacrifice," Dane Orwig suggested.

"Hey, geekie-poo!" Patrick Sullivan pushed forward to physically accost Blake. "Burn any virgins lately?"

God burn them all, they knew quite well he was a virgin himself. Coldly furious, Blake threw off the hand clutching his arm. "Shut up. All of you. I mean it."

Of course they would not shut up. At this point they should start throwing him around. But Blake truly did not feel afraid, and something hard and glinting and more than a little sinister had gathered in his black eyes, because Enola Bloodsworth's black textbook rode in his jacket pocket. He pulled it out and held it up with its face toward them, like a hellfire preacher shaking the Bible. Slantwise the cat stared at

them from its cover.

"I can give you acne like you wouldn't believe, Sullivan," Blake challenged. "Hell, why stop at acne? I can give you AIDS. How would you like that, if I gave you AIDS?"

Because he wished it were true (though he knew it was not true) his voice deepened, intense. He knew they would not hit him now, because of the power in his voice. As in fact they did not. They stood wide-eyed, their grins pasted on their faces, and he opened the black book so that they could see the pages, the spiderwebby handwriting gone brown with age, the weird horned moons and pentacles and pyramids and hex circles and embracing snakes. They stepped back, then glanced at each other and seemed to find a second wind of truculence.

"How you gonna give him AIDS, geek?" Dane Orwig jeered. "Slit your wrists and drip on him?"

Blake told him, "For the last time. Don't call me geek."

"Geek, whatcha gonna do about it? Call up your faggot lover, the one with the red tail?"

"You're so nice, Orwig, I'll give you a choice." Blake began to flip through the pages of his grimoire. "Root canal work," he read, or pretended to read. "Sexual impotence. Drug-induced hallucinations. What do you say? Which would you prefer I cursed you with?"

Orwig stared at him.

Raising the black book, Blake smiled like a skull and began at random to read, phonetically intoning the weird foreign words. The recipes or whatever they were sounded wonderfully impressive when read aloud in a sonorous voice.

"Hey!" Dane Orwig flinched back. "You Goddamn geek, what the Hell are you trying to prove?"

Blake showed his teeth and read. Even if it was only the ingredients for snickerdoodles, still there was something potent in the feel of the gibberish coming up blood temp from his lungs, his gut, and rushing out of his mouth. He wished the hotshots would hit him, because he had a feeling they could not stop him even if they did.

But they did not. "We're gonna be late," somebody nervously suggested, and the group backed off and moved down the sidewalk, collectively sauntering so as to save face.

It was victory, glorious heady victory, but Blake had his pride. He did not yell *yahoo!* Instead, eyes darkly sparkling, he stood still and finished reading his curse, for effect.

By what must have been either incredible good luck or because of nerves, Dane went home sick at noon. And Blake's enemies watched him sideward and let him alone pretty much all the rest of that day.

"I had phone calls from the school today," his mother informed him over supper. "I understand you were drawing satanic symbols in your notebook during English class."

Good old Mrs. Xander, founder and adviser of the Bible club. He knew he could count on her to spread the word. She was so paranoid, she believed the Procter & Gamble symbol was satanic.

"So what did you say?" Blake asked. It was impossible for him to tell what his mother was thinking. She had spoken in the same level way as ever.

"I told her it was good for children to draw satanic symbols."

"Good going, *Mom!*"

"She is not pleased with me."

"I bet she's not."

"And then I had a call from your principal," Enola Bloodsworth said. "It seems you had been heard to claim you have hex witch blood."

"And?"

"I told him it was quite true."

Blake had lived long enough to feel some puzzled apprehension; things were going too well. Nevertheless, he smiled widely and asked her, "You mind if I take your book to school again tomorrow?"

"No, I don't mind. Have some gingersnaps."

He took several, to thank and please her. All of the dark spicy cookies were marked with hex signs: star hexes, swirl hexes, compass hexes. Come to think of it, this was odd, that she should have started decorating with hex signs. Blake had seen his mother spend hours inscribing the distelfink, the luck bird, by hand on the cookies she gave to acquaintances, but he had never known her to use these other hexes before.

He ate the things. They burned in his mouth and throat, as gingersnaps will. He noticed that his mother ate several too.

The black cat sat under his window again that night, and was still there in the morning, and though it welcomed no familiarities it walked to school with him, stalking at his side like a comrade to combat.

That day things stopped going well.

First thing, during homeroom period, Blake was called to the principal's office, where the latter, Mr. Lipschitz, awaited him with compressed lips. Mr. Lipschitz was a big man, an ex-Marine whose excess weight had not affected his confidence in himself. Even the jocks were a little afraid of him.

"Blake Bloodsworth. You stand there and tell me exactly what you have done to Dane Orwig."

To his chagrin, Blake could do no better than to squeak, "Nothing!"

"Listen, you punk." Mr. Lipschitz moved closer. "I've known the Orwig family for a long time." The look Mr. Lipschitz was giving Blake quite clearly expressed the principal's opinion of Blake's lack of such a family. "They are solid people, not the sort to get upset about nothing. So when I get a phone call from them in the middle of the night and they say you did something to Dane, I believe them."

"What am I supposed to have done? What's the matter with him?"

"You tell me, Bloodsworth!"

Blake wondered briefly if he had actually done something to Dane besides worry him. No, that was nonsense. He did not believe in magic, as a future scientist he could not believe such rot, he had to be logical. One of two things must have happened: Dane had worried himself sick, or Dane was smarter than Blake had thought, smart enough to outfox him. Because the Orwigs were indeed not the sort to get excited, he decided on the latter. Dane had to be a better actor than anyone knew.

"Is he saying he has AIDS, or what?"

School administrators in steel towns are not often heavily committed to modern educational ethics. Therefore it was nothing new when Mr. Lipschitz barreled out from behind his desk and started to slap Blake around. Some of the hotshots were almost used to this. But not being built sturdily to stand up to this sort of treatment, Blake began to whimper.

"I didn't do anything to him! It was just a joke!"

"Don't sound like no joke to me, putting a curse on a person!" Mr. Lipschitz tended to forget his grammar when impassioned.

Blake yelped, "If you knew, why'd you ask?" and Mr. Lipschitz hit him again.

"Where's the black book?" Mr. Lipschitz bellowed, mauling him. "Where is the devilish thing? Anything you bring onto school property I got a right to confiscate!"

Blake felt the dark stirrings of anger, and with it, some courage. No way was this rhinoceros going to get hold of his mother's book. Blake had stashed it above the suspended ceiling in the boys' restroom on his way to the office, and

no amount of abuse was going to make him say where it was.

"You answer what I asked you, boy!" Lipschitz smacked him on the ear. Blake said nothing, did not cry out, but with sudden angry strength pulled himself away from the man and glared at him with smoldering eyes. Lipschitz went pale and stepped back, staggering, fumbling at air with his hands. The big man seemed to be suffering some sort of shock. His fat heart bothering him, maybe, from overexertion. Blake could feel no sympathy for him.

"Evil eye," Lipschitz whispered. "Don't you evil-eye me, Bloodsworth. Get out of here. Stay out. Get away from me!"

Blake stared a moment longer, then left the office without getting his hall pass initialed. Now he was an outlaw, not a geek. Being an outlaw felt better, and he decided to keep going. He retrieved his mother's cookbook from its hiding place first thing, afraid that if Lipschitz searched he would find it. Then for the same reason he left the school building and walked home, shaky but defiant.

At the front entry, the black cat appeared out of the shrubbery and walked by his side.

Enola Bloodsworth seemed unsurprised to see Blake home from school in the middle of the day, laying her heirloom cookbook on her kitchen counter.

"I don't feel well," he told her.

She did not even blink at the lie. "You're suspended," she told him agreeably, "or possibly expelled. Your principal just called me."

The bastard was okay then. Damn. Blake had hoped Lipschitz would continue with his heart attack and be out of action awhile.

Enola added, "He says you're a dangerous young psychopath."

"I'm sorry."

"I'm not. I told him in a very literal

way to go to Hell."

Blake sat down at the ashwood table. "Mom," he admitted, "I don't understand you."

"Never mind." She picked up the black book and sat down beside him with the air of a woman enjoying herself. "Show me what you read to the Orwig boy."

Because of the mystic sigils inked on most pages it was not hard to find the passage. Blake remembered: it was the one headed by three inverted crosses and a symbol that reminded him of drawings he had seen on men's room walls. His mother read the section he pointed out in thoughtful silence. "Interesting," she remarked. "You seem to have given him syphilis."

The air had suddenly turned rarefied. Blake's mouth came open and pumped.

"Secondary stage," his mother added. "Rash, lesions, swelling joints, that sort of thing. It may be years before he goes insane."

"Bu— bu— but —"

"But what, Son? Isn't hurting him what you wanted?"

It certainly was. "But I didn't expect it to work," Blake managed.

"Of course it worked. You told him yourself, you have hex-witch blood."

Blake jettisoned all thoughts of ever being a scientist, because when he looked into her eyes suddenly it all made sense, he believed her utterly and felt at peace. Her eyes were golden yellow, the exact color of her rich buttery snickerdoodles. In the black circles of the irises he seemed to see hex signs turning.

"They may cure him," she said regretfully, "if they can figure out what's wrong with him. They have penicillin these days."

"They didn't when you started?"

"They didn't when the line started. But that's all right, we get stronger generation by generation. Look what you have done without even knowing

what you were doing." She smiled at him with a mother's pride and something more, something approaching deification. "I should teach you to bake."

The feeling of unreasoning peace left him, replaced by a catfooted fear. Of what? Of her? But how could she ever hurt him except by loving him too much?

"Mother," he told her, "I do not want to spend my life baking cookies, and I do not want to spend my life alone."

"Of course not, dear."

Walking to the corner store, Blake trailed rumor like a villain's cloak: he could hex with a glance, he wandered the night as a black cat spying on people's dreams, he performed salacious acts with animals. In his garage he had set up a black altar under a black pentacle hex and an inverted cross. There he killed stray dogs and mutilated them and drank their blood. Strange howling noises were heard in the sky above his house at night. Some of the schoolchildren swore they had seen on him the beginnings of a poison-tipped tail. Blake Bloodsworth was a hex witch and a priest of Satan, and wasn't it a shame for that nice mother of his who baked such divine cookies, she must be heartbroken. The boy's unknown father must be the devil himself.

Within a few days every God-fearing woman in Diligence had called her minister. The men of God counseled caution and discretion and not believing everything one heard. Then as early as their busy schedules would allow they met (those of them who practiced ecumenism and were on speaking terms) over morning coffee at the Diligence Café in order to discuss paganism, Satanism and the possibilities of exorcism. None of them disputed these isms, but they could not agree on a rite. It was each preacher for himself.

Within a few days Enola Bloodsworth (who belonged to no church) had received phone calls from every priest and pastor in town. In a voice flavored with honeyed venom she told Blake, "I've lived here for forty years and I never knew they cared."

"So what did you tell them?"

"I invited them over for cookies."

Blake eyed her warily. "Mother, what are you up to?"

"Well, if they think you are a hex witch, it seems to me we ought not to disappoint them."

"Mother," he said, using asperity to mask his less manly feelings, "am I going to have to leave town?"

"Why, perhaps eventually, dear. Don't you want to?"

In fact, he did. If there was going to be a life for him, he knew, it was going to be outside Diligence. A life, and someone to love him and teach him the mysteries of the word that rhymed with hex. To some extent, then, she understood him. Cared what he wanted, even. His fear of her eased.

"Yes," he said in a different tone.

"Then stop worrying. Just let me arrange things, dear. We're going to have a nice time with these people. You'll see." Humming, she stood at the kitchen counter and sifted flour white as voodoo capons and angel wings.

Her sanguine attitude was what puzzled Blake and made him feel so ambivalent about her. She should have showed some anxiety about the trouble he was in, if only because he was missing so much school, yet she seemed to feel none. Instead, she smiled at him across the kitchen table with those bright tawny eyes. Ever since he had hexed Dane Orwig she had been going through her flour-clouded days in some sort of unaccountable excitement, anticipation, exaltation, beatification.

But he had long since given up trying to understand her. It was enough that she was on his side. "What kind of cookies you baking today?" he asked idly.

"Pinwheels."

*   *   *

Enola Bloodsworth did not own a car, but used her garage for storage. A lawnmower sat foremost, two rakes hung above it on nails, discarded furniture and a chipped plaster flamingo were pushed against the walls. Most of the floor space she kept clear so she could get to what she wanted. It was all quite innocuous, as the ministers could see when she took them in there that evening.

"Sit down," she invited. She had swept the place and set up lawn chairs, so the ambience was not unpleasant by Diligence standards. "We're going to have our refreshments here. It's too crowded in the house." No wonder, since she had invited all of them at once. She scuttled out, leaving them with Blake.

He stood with their glances crawling over him like black ants. Mr. Lipschitz had come too (despite the nervous prostration he blamed on Blake's having ill-wished him), and Mrs. Xander, and a few of the other teachers, as well as the mayor and the chief of borough police. There were not enough chairs for everyone. Blake stood near a cardtable holding a borrowed coffee urn in the cleared space near the back wall. The others crowded near the door, and he did not dare to look directly at any of them in case his mother really was trying to get things back to normal.

Was she? With that going-to-heaven glitter in her eye?

"Here we are!" She came back in carrying a huge tray of pinwheels. "Please," Enola invited, offering the chocolate-and-vanilla cookies. "Please, everyone, have some coffee and something to eat."

No one could resist Enola Bloodsworth's cookies. Even the chronic dieters took at least one. Blake had about six himself. At least they were not hex circles. The thought caused him both relief and disappointment. Nothing extraordinary was going to happen after

SNICKERDOODLES

all —

A black cat appeared at the open garage door.

Dusk was darkening the sky, and a few stars had appeared, chips of broken glass left on a shadowy inverted floor. Enola Bloodsworth did not turn on the lights in the dim garage. Yet none of the guests had left. They took second helpings, seeming charmed by the occasion or by her courtesy.

The cat paused regally, surveying the scene, then with the dignity of a death angel walked in. Enola Bloodsworth looked down into its yellow eyes and smiled.

"Hello, Grandmother," she said.

Blake looked at the pinwheel cookie in the palm of his hand, and it started to turn.

And he saw now. Of course. It was a hex sign after all, of the most potent kind, not just incised but ingrained, hex to the core, why had he not seen it so before? They all were. Swirl hexes, symbols of transformation.

He looked at the cat, at the soul-deep black slits in its golden eyes.

Grandmother?

Its eyes were hex signs that spun before him, yellow and black, then changing, all the many colors of magic circling, circling in kaleidoscope symmetry. Cat eyes had taken over his world, they were big as sky, older and more powerful than stars and stripes, and they saw through him, they imbued him with hex magic and the power of his own aspirations —

Was he in fact a hex witch? Or was he the victim of his mother's lifelong plan?

He looked at her and saw instead the Grecian girl of his dreams.

All was changed. Where the coffee urn had squatted on its cardtable stood instead a black altar with a barn-hex top on which a black book lay open. Over it hung an inverted cross made of bleached bones and decorated in the most appalling bad taste, with blood-red plastic roses. The whole place was dotted with them, like a cheap Chinese restaurant: the furniture, the besoms that hung instead of rakes on the walls, the walls themselves, now rough-hewn stone instead of white plaster. A collar of the fake flowers bobbed on the neck of a white goat which stood bleating near the altar. Mr. Lipschitz wore one in his lapel and leered at Mrs. Xander, who had a wreath of the hideous things on her head. In fact all the guests were flower-bedecked and already in an orgiastic mood. They had gathered, after all, for a most special celebration of the black mass: a witches' wedding.

The bride wore a black lace mantilla and a blood-red satin dress and carried a heart-shaped bouquet of red plastic roses in her right hand. Her left hand she held out to Blake. She looked at him. She smiled.

He knew he should have run. Yet, Christ, the invitation in that smile was . . .

She was the girl he had created in his daydreams, exactly, in every detail: those full lips, those high cheekbones, that nubile torso with — he blushed, thinking of those extra, secret breasts. Knowing someone had watched his dreams like a peep show. Yet wanting to be lucky enough to find out: were the supernumeraries there, included in the package? Was she really his dream lover in every detail?

Or in every detail but her huge dark eyes. . . . He had settled on purple, but her eyes were any color and all colors. They took him in and spun him around. They were hex eyes.

Am I changed? he wondered. *Have I grown taller? Will I come out of this a man?* Glancing down, he saw that he also was dressed all in slim-fitting red, in a scarlet tuxedo and black cummerbund, with a plastic rose at his heart. All right, so his mother had wanted to decorate with the tawdry things. It was her party. He no longer minded.

The black cat leaped to the hex hub atop the altar, sat by the open book. Everything stopped whirling. Time stood still.

Will tomorrow come? If it does, will I be here or somewhere else?

The cat at the altar said in a soft, trenchant voice, "Blake Bloodsworth, approach your bride."

He should run. He should run. Maybe Diligence and a world of commonplace troubles waited outside.

Yet she was so beautiful. And he knew she cared about him in her way. And he knew he loved her. He had always loved and feared her, as long as he had been alive.

Her left hand still reached toward him. He took the necessary step, took her hand in his. It felt warm and lithe against his fingers, his palm.

The cat said, "Enola conceives and bears a son. The son marries and begets Enola. One becomes two so that two can become one again. Generation by gen-eration I grow stronger, I who walk alone."

One becomes two so that . . .

"Step to the altar, you who are two."

Blake obeyed her command, but looked at his bride. Her smile told him that tonight he would lie with her and learn all her mysteries.

What it did not tell him, he had the brains to know: afterward, in the morning light, he would look into her eyes and see truth and maybe not like it. Though he would have preferred green or purple, already he foresaw what color her eyes would be, come daybreak: from under the masses of her black hair they would shine out at him, all too familiar. The hex-yellow color of snick-erdoodles.

But in the night he would not have to see. For as long as it lasted he would think only of the night.

There had to be a way to make night last forever. And he was small and dark and smart; maybe before dawn he could come up with it.　　　　　　∇

STALLION

A crest curved symmetrically
　　With mane lying heavily
Like snow upon a willow tree
　　With mane lying heavily
Around his calla-lily ears,
　　Around his violet eyes.

He is the stallion of a dream.
　　He is not what he seems.

— **Nancy Springer**

WEIRD TALES TALKS WITH NANCY SPRINGER

by Darrell Schweitzer

Weird Tales: Your work has taken several radical shifts of late, both in approach and subject matter. One fan described it rather indelicately as "Nancy Springer is sure letting it all hang out." How do you account for this?

Springer: A couple of things. I just plain got tired of the high fantasy. I felt as if the constant writing in a semi-archaic style was turning my brain to mush. I really just wanted to use all those modern words. There are a lot of neat modern words in the English language that I wasn't getting a chance to use. Of course it goes a lot further than that. About four years ago my husband got out of the Lutheran ministry. I never realized while he was in it how much that constrained me, but it must have had some effect because since then things have been quite different in my writing. At the time he got out of the ministry we moved — this is a very good idea because you don't want to remain in the same place where you have served as a pastor — and the town that we *had* been living in was such a wonderfully bizarre and peculiar place that it has imprinted itself on my writing ever since.

WT: The obvious effects are that you're writing more explicitly about sex and you're using certain words you didn't previously — the ones the FCC won't let you say on the air — and also that you're writing more about childhood and growing up, possibly from your perspective as a mother. How

much of that — aside from modern words — could you have put into your previous fantasies, if more subtly?

Springer: The theme of coming of age, I think, has always been in my fiction. My writing, ever since Book One, has been a growth process for me, a kind of therapy for me, working out all the excess baggage left over since my 1950s childhood. It's just that now I am more conscious of it than I used to be, and I bring it out more openly, less symbolically. So I figured, "Oh, my writing is about coming of age. I might as well do that." I've been writing children's books, writing through my own childhood that way, and, yes, having children around the house does help. I eventually hope to write mainstream novels about adults, maybe even middle-aged adults like myself. You know, given time I might actually grow up. We live in hope.

WT: Some of your readers, jokingly or otherwise, might be disappointed if you grew up.

Springer: I think Ursula Le Guin said it best. An adult is not a child who died. An adult is a child who lived. So, the child will always be with us, but may now be better able to cope.

WT: The other obvious change in your work is that you are using much more modern — and largely untouched — material in such books as *The Hex Witch of Seldom*, rather than legendary magic from three thousand years ago. Contemporary magic, if nothing else.

Why did you feel constrained from handling such material earlier?

Springer: I don't think I felt constrained. I think it's more a matter that I swore I wasn't going to write fantasy anymore. I really just got tired of it. I was writing too many books too fast, I guess, of the high fantasy type. So what I thought I wanted to write at that time was mainstream, and writing contemporary fantasy was a compromise. I have financial responsibilities. It was something I felt I could market, which would be a step toward mainstream. But, darned if I haven't started enjoying the stuff. I think I'll go on doing it for quite a while.

WT: Were you reacting to the widely-perceived ossification of the fantasy category, by which fantasy novels — no, excuse me, fantasy *trilogies* — are seen as being fully as much a stereotyped product as, say, nurse novels?

Springer: I might have been, but I think it was more on a personal level, that I myself got tired of writing of them. But, yes, I think there might have also been a kind of ego thing there, that literary writers look down on fantasy writers, *ergo* I am going to show the world that I am a literary writer too, *ergo* I am going to write something else. I think I've gotten over that now.

WT: There's also the much more nasty bit of snobbishness one sometimes encounters, to the effect that generic fantasy trilogies are written by women who can't do anything else (e.g., science fiction).

Springer: Oh, gross me out . . . bleh . . . ick. I've never run into too much of that to my face. One is conscious of course of all sorts of things behind one's back, and it's not paranoia if it's true. But I've tried to get over reacting to other people in terms of what I'm going to do with my life and my writing and figure out what it is that I actually do well and actually enjoy; and by Jove I've discovered that I actually am a fantasy writer.

WT: So what about the mainstream novels you once planned?

Springer: I have a mainstream novel sitting at home in rough draft. I will go through it again and see what comes. But I will cheerfully continue to write fantasy as well. I don't think I'll ever get away from it.

WT: Ultimately we're all just writers, and the rest is marketing.

Springer: Really. I never thought of myself as a "fantasy" writer when I was starting out. I thought I was writing the American Novel. I was very surprised to discover that I was a category writer. Then I became a category writer because that was the professional thing to do, with marketing, and knowing about editors, and slanting things toward a market. It was all very heady. It made me feel very important for a while. Now I've gotten beyond that again and simply realized that writing what one does best or what you have in you to write is more important.

WT: When you went to research *The Hex Witch of Seldom* and such material, how did you do the research? Were you able to talk to real hex witches, or did you get all your information out of books?

Springer: Over the years I have met several people who have been *pow-wowed*, healed, including my own father-in-law, who was pow-wowed as a child by hex witches. I have since fantasized the hex magic. Your typical hex witch is nothing more than an Appalachian faith-healer: laying on of hands, mumble a few prayers, recommend chicken wings buried under the eaves to draw off the warts, that sort of thing. So my hex witches are not true to life as far as what hex magic is actually like.

WT: Do you find yourself tempted to say, "Oh what an ignorant superstition," when encountering something like this? Inasmuch as it is a religion rather than an attempted science, one has to respect it, for all you and I know that burying chicken wings is not going to cure warts. So, how do you deal with this problem?

Springer: As long as they do no harm — I think they do some good along the way — sure. What's the problem? I have the cynical "Oh what a superstitious lot" streak in me too, but I recall that as a girl I had about eighteen warts on my hand. This was when I was in high school. I was wretched, and my mother and my father kept telling me, "Go put milkweed juice on those, and they'll go away." I would never do it. I'd say, "Oh, that's dumb. That's an old wives' tale." The summer before I went to college I finally couldn't take it any longer and I snuck out back and put milkweed juice on my warts. *Blamed* if the blasted things didn't go away within a week. So there's always that possibility that there is something beyond scientific knowledge.

WT: If milkweed juice works for warts, that's not beyond scientific knowledge at all. The plant must have some beneficial property. Possibly no scientist has described it. But if you were told to bury chicken wings, that would have been a different matter.

Springer: If it works . . . [Laughs.] I don't know. I probably would have found ways to rationalize it.

WT: We have this problem with the influx of New Agers, that people are devoting their whole lives to things which are demonstrably untrue. Those of us who know this is untrue — astrology is a good example, or psychic surgery, which is even worse because it can kill you — are in a peculiar position. We know the Earth is not flat. What do you do when you meet a flat-Earther?

Springer: I myself think, well, let's talk to this person politely and go someplace else as soon as possible. I have myself always made a firm distinction between fantasy and reality. I write

about bizarre, supernatural occurrences. I do not necessarily believe in them. I don't usually believe in them. And I have difficulty with people who don't seem to be able to make the same distinction between fiction and reality. For instance, people might write me letters and say "How do I get to live forever like your characters?" Or, "How do I get to visit the countries you write about?" We don't answer this kind of mail. . . . But it's like Horatio says to Hamlet — there is this corner of my mind which recognized that there are things we don't understand which might still be true. It's a deeply hidden corner and it's not part of my daily functioning, but it is there.

WT: It seems to me that skepticism is not merely desirable but *essential* for the fantasy writer because otherwise you will begin to make writing and plotting decisions on a doctrinaire rather than artistic basis. If you have your own ideas about how magic works in the "real" world and your story requires otherwise, you're going to run into trouble. This is why most occultists do not write good supernatural fiction.

Springer: I agree with you. It bothers me deeply when a writer gets so buried in their fictional world that they start to let it impinge on their real life, as in, for example, forming societies of people who actually believe in the fantasy, or forming their own religions or believer-groups or establishing colonies, or whatever they do. Several examples come to mind but I don't want to name names.

WT: If a writer were in fact a scoundrel, it would be very easy to say that all the stuff in your novels is true, then start a religion — please send money.

Springer: [Laughs.] It's been done.

WT: Are you getting any strange mail for *The Hex Witch of Seldom*? People who say, "That all happened to me . . ."

Springer: Not for *The Hex Witch*, no.

It's almost a young-adult book, and it's just been accepted cheerfully as a nice sort of fun book to read. Lord knows what sort of mail I'll get for *Apocalypse*. *Apocalypse* is a very different sort of book. It's almost horror. It's a very angry, yet a very loving book, and it's very multi-leveled, by far the biggest thing I've ever written, both in terms of impact and in terms of number of characters and plot complexity, that sort of thing. I expect some misunderstanding from the part of the world where it is set. (It's set in western Pennsylvania, and the Four Horsewomen of the Apocalypse begin the end of the world there.) Most fantasies save the world. This one purports to destroy it. I won't tell you whether it succeeds.

WT: So, if not *Hex Witch*, what did generate the strange mail?

Springer: It came more from the earlier books. I got a letter from a guy in Leavenworth prison who wanted to know how to live forever. As a matter of fact he wanted me to donate a hundred thousand dollars to his society for the furtherance of research into eternal life so he wouldn't have to die shortly after he finished his sentence. Then, I think every writer has had this experience at some time or another: you run into someone who genuinely understands your work. They're discussing your book with you in depth, and you're lapping it up and saying, "Yes, yes, you understand," and all the sudden they say something and you realize they are cold-out crazy. Like, really wild in the eyes. I ran into one at a convention once who said he had been using my poetry in his rites to invoke the Mother Goddess. Then he followed me into my poetry reading and chanted along with me. He made me so freaked that, I think, if the door had slammed I probably would have fainted.

WT: This is one of those cases where it becomes difficult to respect the believer. You came to the conclusion the person was crazy. You didn't say, "Well, maybe there is something in this."

Springer: He had *the look,* as the Roxette song says.

WT: So we need a working crap-detector in everyday life.

Springer: You have to go with your instincts on some things. There have been times at conventions when I have met people whom I immediately and greatly liked for no discernible reason, and times when I met people whom I immediately and passionately disliked for no discernible reason. Then I later discovered that the first impressions were correct in most cases. So saying this person was crazy was a subjective judgment, but I've learned to go on the basis of that.

WT: Have you ever met a real, live practicing hex witch?

Springer: Not knowingly. I've just met a lot of people who said, "We used to have one in the neighborhood," or, "That house there. That's where the hex witch lives." I would have fictionalized said encounter anyhow. The hex witch in my book is based on my husband's grandmother. She was not a hex witch herself, but in other regards the characterization was pretty much based on her.

WT: I suppose the most famous example of hex witchcraft is the famous hex murder case of the 1920s.

Springer: Yes. That took place about six miles from where I presently live, and rendered that entire area — York County — very, very sensitive about its belief in hex magic. To this day there are people who really would prefer not to discuss it. My next-door neighbor, now in her late seventies, was a schoolteacher. When she went away to college to become a schoolteacher she was teased and called "Dumb Dutch" because she came from that area where people believed in hex magic.

WT: Could you explain for our readers what the whole incident was about?

Springer: Certainly. There was a youngish man whose name I have forgotten who was obviously very gifted. He could stop rabid dogs in their tracks by saying, "Down, hound, put your nose to the ground," or words to that effect. He could pow-wow all the usual ailments, take the fire out of burns, that sort of thing. Everything was going all right for him. He had a nice young wife, and so forth. Then everything started going badly for him. He lost his job. He lost his health. He lost his wife. And he lost his gift. Eventually he realized he had been hexed, and he spent the next ten years or so wandering around trying to figure out who had hexed him. He finally went to the river witch, who lived in Marietta, across on the Lancaster side, and she told him it was a chap named Nelson Rehmeyer of Rehmeyer's Hollow. The way to take off the hex was to go to Nelson Rehmeyer, get his pow-wow book, and a lock of his hair, I think it was. He and a couple of friends went there, but bungled the whole thing and ended up killing Rehmeyer. They bludgeoned him to death and they made a botched job of trying to burn the body, and then they went off leaving their personal traces everywhere. But the really sensational aspect of it was not that somebody murdered somebody else — that's fairly commonplace — but the hex-magic motivation.

WT: Presumably this didn't shake the belief of any of the faithful.

Springer: What it did was bring in news media from all over the country. Everybody converged on York County to see about this ever-so-exotic murder. I don't think it shook anyone's belief, no, but it made hex magic go underground. It used to be quite open. There would be shingles out in front of the houses — Pow-wow Doctor, or whatever. It was on pretty much the same basis as chiropractors are today, an alternative to the other kinds of medicines. Now you sneak off to the pow-wow doctor rather than just walk in.

WT: We may have had a few witchcraft murders in the United States recently. Certainly there was a human-sacrifice cult along the Mexican border recently. I can't help but feel that the Twenties were a more skeptical period, when people *could* be embarrassed by this sort of thing. If it happened today, no one would blink.

Springer: We've got a Satanic cult operating in Glen Rock right now — that's a small town in western York County — which is a matter of grave concern to the local Parent-Teacher Organization, but it certainly hasn't attracted any reporters from New York.

WT: The more straightforward aspect of the problem is not black magic, but simply that people who are in love with the idea of evil and engage in sadistic pastimes aren't the kind of folks you want your kids to associate with.

Springer: There have been a couple of teenage suicides which were blamed on it, and there have been mutilated animals. Rightly or wrongly blamed, I have no idea. It's hard to tell how much is hysteria and how much is actual fact.

WT: If after all this you were to go back and write an imaginary-kingdom fantasy, how do you think it would be different from the sort of book you did originally?

Springer: It would probably have modern, 20th-century people talking the way people really talk and acting with all the usual modern neuroses and phobias and whatnot. I'm not sure other than that. It would probably incorporate some sort of contemporary mythology. We build our own mythologies. We have baseball mythologies. We have rock-music mythologies, motorcycle-gang mythologies, street-gang mythologies. I would probably be more interested in using one of those than going back to some sort of ancient gods and goddesses. Modern gods. We have those

29

too.

WT: Do you find New Age beliefs at all useful in creating fantasy?

Springer: No. Not really. I am aware they are out there. They don't particularly interest me. I'm at the point now where I want most of what is in my fantasy to come out of my personal experiences and/or my own head. That way I can be sure it's original.

WT: I suspect most fantasy writers have very little use for New Agers or professional occultists, largely because we have better imaginations. We can make it up better than they can.

Springer: And why take someone else's rehash when you can mix up something fresh?

WT: And only the believers would be upset at your seeming "inaccuracy."

Springer: Please, don't anybody try to believe in what I write.

WT: Have you ever had anyone write to you and say, "It's interesting that you write about magic, but you've got it *wrong*. It really works like *this?*"

Springer: Yes, but that amuses me more than irritates me. It's like the vampire panel I was on today. Someone said, "Vampires are like this." "No, the more recent versions say they're like that." Such-and-such a writer says this about them and such-and-such says that. Of course it's *all* perfectly true because it's an evolving mythology. The good mythologies are alive and continue to grow and change. It's sort of like the folklore process. Everyone has a voice in it. But for one person to say

"This is the right way" to do magic or whatever is as ridiculous as to set up a dogma like that of an established religion. It makes no sense to me.

WT: It's also fun to make up folklore, where you take up genuine, traditional elements and you add some of your own, as if they were real folklore elements, including spurious verses of folk songs, which you quote.

Springer: [Laughs.] Darrell, you are a slimy person. . . . No, actually when I was writing the high fantasy I felt rather guilty sometimes about borrowing the mythological names. I felt as if I were leading future generations of readers astray, that they might never discover how glorious the original, say, Celtic myths, were, that they'd think that what I had written about a character with a silver hand was gospel; whereas this was adapted from something else entirely. So I am really quite glad to get away from that.

WT: What can we expect from you beyond *Apocalypse?*

Springer: I'm finishing the rough draft of something called *Volos the Unholy*, which deals with angelology — the mythology of angels, which is very complex, and with rock music, which has its own gods and its own mythology.

WT: Any idea when it'll appear?

Springer: Really, no. I'll probably finish it by the end of next year, but when it will be coming out and from whom I don't know at this point.

WT: Thank you, Nancy Springer.   ▽

We're raising our subscription price . . . !

Postage and paper costs are spiraling, and we've been forced to increase both our cover price and subscription rates with this issue. However, to be fair to all our old, established readers, we're giving you one last chance to subscribe (or extend your subscription) at the old rates. Turn to the inside back cover for details.

IMPROBABLE BESTIARY: THE POOKAH

A bold Irish spook, a weird beast is the Pookah,
The mischievous imp of indefinite shape.
And if, by some fluke, a pestiferous Pookah
Should latch on to *you* there's no chance of escape.
The Pookah resembles a hound or a hare,
An ox or a fox or a boar or a bear.
The prank-loving Pookah seeks fun; nothing more.
So never insult him, or else . . . he'll get *sore!*
And any palooka who tries to rebuke a
Pestiferous Pookah gets trouble galore!

Though Celtic by nature, and Irish by birth,
The Pookah's been sighted all over the Earth.
Reliable sources have spotted the Pookah
In Upper Zambezi and downtown Paducah.
A huge hairy Pookah, for reasons quite strange,
Invaded the U.S. Marines' target range.
"Kill that Pookah!" the general screeched to his aides.
"Use pistols! Use rifles! Use rocket grenades!
Unleash the commandos, and fetch my bazooka!
Declare total war! But just *kill that damn Pookah!"*
A joint Army-Navy-Marine exercise
Fired howitzer shells and rained death from the skies.
But when the dust settled, and then came the dawn
"What's for breakfast?" the Pookah remarked with a yawn.

A soldier named Duke, a John Wayne type of hero,
Said "Let's blast the Pookah; we'll make him Ground Zero."
And thus was constructed, with grace and aplomb,
A ninety-five megaton hydrogen bomb.
The bomber crew dropped its unstoppable load
On the spot where the Pookah relaxed in the road.
And then came a flash; the whole neighborhood glowed
While the Pookah-bomb's atoms began to *explode!*

And when it was over . . . there, in his peruke (A
small wig that he wore) — yes, and smoking a hookah,
And daintily sipping a glass of *Sambouca*
While strumming a uke . . . ah, you've guessed it: *The Pookah!*
And thus was established what none can deny:
You can't nuke a Pookah, so don't even try.

— F. Gwynplaine MacIntyre

THE DEER LAKE SIGHTINGS

by Patricia Anthony

The people on the north side of the lake had given him good information, but on the south side, closest to where the sightings had occurred, the families were so reticent as to be rude. By the time he'd reached the fifth house, where a woman was scrubbing her porch, his feet were tired and his temper worn.

As he started up the drive a liver hound rounded the side of the house. Harry stopped dead and stared suspiciously at it. "Shit," he said under his breath, holding his camera and tape recorder a little closer to his chest in case he had to run.

But it was the dog that fled, backing away with a hesitant growl at first and then taking to its heels with a yelp as if Harry had really flung the rock he'd considered throwing.

Harry took a long breath and let it out before he continued his trudge up the hill. At the bottom of the porch steps he stopped and pushed his glasses back up on the bridge of his nose with an irritated gesture. It was a hot day and the skin of his face was oily, his armpits damp.

"I'm Harold Sterns with Mutual UFO Network," he said, trying to conjure some warmth into his voice, "and I've been told that some of your neighbors have seen strange lights."

The woman didn't look up from her cleaning. She was on her hands and knees, a position which looked oddly natural for her; and her face was stamped with the seal of the mountains, an old-before-its-time sort of look.

Doggedly, Harry continued. "Your neighbors on the other side of the lake say that nearly every night for the past six months they've seen a flash just after dark that lights up half the sky. They've also sighted what they call 'little dancing balls' over here near where you live. You ever see anything like that?"

The metal bucket made a teeth-gritting sound across the concrete as she pulled it closer. With dull concentration, she plunged the bristle brush in the bucket to rinse away its coating of pink scum and began scrubbing the floor again. The air was prickly with the stench of ammonia.

"He comes ever night," she said without looking up from her work, "and stands just where you're standing."

Harry felt an icicle of fear dislodge from the top of his spine and slide its way downwards. The woman's brush made a shus-sha-shus-sha rhythm against the raw cement. "He?" Harry asked.

"Stands just where you's standing now. Then when we walk out, he comes up on the porch. Never comes in the house. At least he never come in the house." She paused in her scrubbing and sat up on her knees. Wisps of grey hair had come undone from her bun and they hung around her face like spider webbing.

Harry licked his lips. Surreptitiously he flicked on the tape recorder and noticed his hand was shaking with excitement. "Who comes to your house?"

She gave him a flat, country look and went back to her scrubbing. "Him. The

32

man."

"What does he look like?" Harry asked. He mounted the porch slowly, so as not to alarm her.

"Tall as you. Plaid shirt. Jeans."

Harry's face worked itself into a puzzled frown. "Is he human?"

The brush paused. The pause was so brief, so sudden, that it seemed that time itself had stopped. Then she picked up her scrubbing rhythm again. "Don't know."

"What does he say?"

"Nothing."

"He just stands on the porch?"

"Uh huh."

"And he never says anything to you."

"Wish he would," she hissed angrily. "Wish the bastard would say something."

"Uh huh. And then you come out on the porch to meet him."

"Don't have no choice."

The brush made a hollow **thunk** as it was tossed into the bucket. Taking up the handle, she walked into the house.

After a brief hesitation Harry followed her. The parlor was faded, the hooked rug worn. The floors smelled of oil, but there was another smell under that: the lye soap scent of clean poverty.

The linoleum in the kitchen had once been green. He could see glimpses of color in the corners. The traffic areas, though, had been bleached to an off-white. "What do you mean you don't have any choice?"

She poured the foamy pink water down the drain and filled up the bucket with clear from a tarnished tap. "He don't give us no choice is what I mean. Sometimes he comes at dinner and we get up from the table and walk outside." She had to raise her voice to be heard over the thrumming of the water.

"Like you're drawn or something?"

"Just like we don't have no damned choice about it. Just like we don't have no say in it at all."

34

"Tell me something, Mrs. . . ."

"Foote."

"Mrs. Foote. Do you remember anything after you get to the porch?" His voice was staccato with anxious energy. Harry had utterly forgotten how tired his feet were, how his back ached from his walk. "Do you find that after he's gone you've lost time? Like maybe you've been watching one program on TV and after he's gone another totally different show is on? Maybe it might seem like he was only there a few minutes, but you find out later a couple of hours have gone by."

She turned off the tap and looked at him. Her eyes were a dirty brown and her eyelashes were grey as her hair. He guessed her age in an indiscriminate area between a hard forty and a gently-worn sixty. "I remember," she told him.

"Remember what?"

"I remember what happens when we gets to the porch."

She pushed past him and walked outside where she splashed the clear water over the cement. Through the screen door he watched as she took up a broom that had been matted by time and use into a permanent comma. She began to sweep the suds away. In the middle of the porch was a stubborn, dark sienna stain.

"He cuts my heart out," she said.

"Excuse me?"

"He cuts out my damned heart."

The ancient broom moved methodically over the porch. Her arms were thick and strong; and when she swept the water she swept it out in a high arc across the yard. The motion of the broom was angry, as if she were imagining murdering someone.

The dog had come back and was whining under the stairs. Harry pushed at the screen door. It opened with a pained squeal. Careful of where she had swept, he stepped outside with her.

He considered turning off his tape recorder. "What are you talking about?"

"You ever been raped?" she asked suddenly.

Harry cast around for an appropriate answer, but found none. He shrugged and shook his head.

"That's what it's like. Being raped." There was an uncatalogable expression on her face.

Suddenly he understood the look. He hadn't recognized it at first because he wasn't expecting it. Mrs. Foote was watching him like a lost young kid might look for help from a policeman. Quickly he dropped his eyes. "I'd like to go over your statement again," he said.

Mrs. Foote dismissed him with a disappointed, cynical sniff. "You think you're so smart. How many times I gotta tell you?"

"You want me to believe that a man comes to the door, you come out, and he literally cuts out your heart while you're standing there, and you *let* him?" Harry couldn't help the tone that had crept into his voice. "Come on, Mrs. Foote. Really. If he cuts out your heart why aren't you dead?"

"Don't know," she said wistfully and without the abrasiveness he'd been prepared for. "Jimmy Lee killed hisself. Don't know why I don't take the shotgun to myself, except for the boy." She jerked her head to the right. Harry looked over to see a gangly teenager emerging from the barn. "Don't seem fair to the boy."

"Jimmy Lee?"

"Husband," she said. There were no more suds on the porch but she set to sweeping again, anyway.

"Mrs. Foote . . ." he sighed. Turning towards her, he saw she had halted in her sweeping to open her blouse. Embarrassment nearly made him leap down the steps to the ground. *Talk about rape,* he thought to himself. *She must be kidding.*

The neat, pink line stopped him in mid-flight. It ran from just below her collar and disappeared someplace past the still-fastened fourth button.

"He takes his finger," she said, "just so."

She stepped up to him and ran her own finger down the front of his shirt, etching a trail of cold through Harry's sternum.

"And I open right up, dress, bones, and all. Then he takes out my heart and holds it in his hand like he's giving me some sort of gift. He looks at me while he's doing it, looks right into my eyes. And I can see my heart move up and down like a mouse twitching in his palm."

She was standing very close to him, closer than he would want anyone he didn't know well to stand.

"I hate him," she said. "He cured my angina, but I hate him. It's like he comes back 'cause he wants me to know what he done for me. I don't give a shit. Wish I was back the way I was, even with the breathing hard to walk across the room, even with the waking up in the night with the pain in my chest. He hurts me," she told him. "He hurts me so bad. Seem like if it was a miracle, it wouldn't hurt so much, don't you think? Seem like if it was a real miracle he wouldn't have to come back all the time."

She stepped away. He looked down. The sienna stain was right between his feet.

A few yards away from the porch steps the boy stopped and made a hooting sound like a night bird. Harry flinched and glanced the boy's way. The boy's blond hair was plastered over his forehead with sweat. His eyes were the same dull, muddy brown as his mother's. His expression was frightened.

"It's all right," Mrs. Foote told her son. "He ain't here to hurt nothing. Just asking questions is all."

The boy made a 'whuh-whuh' noise that sounded like it might have been a question, but the woman ignored him.

The dog crept out from the shade of the steps to stand with the boy.

"Donnie was deaf," Mrs. Foote said as she turned to Harry, " 'til the man cured him. He hears now, he understands what I'm saying, but he still won't talk." She held out her hand to her son. "You want to come up and show him what that man done to your ears? You want to come up on the porch now, Donnie?"

The boy backed away three paces and then swiveled and sprinted back to the barn, the dog at his heels.

Mrs. Foote's blouse still gaped open. Harry's gaze was drawn to that line. It ran between the crepy mounds of her breasts, too straight, too neat, to be an incision.

She took the broom, placed it against the side of the house and then walked down to the yard, Harry tagging after. In the back was a clothesline with its burden of mended cotton. On the fronts of all the dresses were faded blotches of brownish red. There were dark auburn stains on the shoulders of the wash-stiff shirts.

"He holds onto my heart and looks into my eyes and I keep thinking that one night he'll squeeze. Donnie screams when he cuts into his ears. I don't when he cuts me, 'cause I don't want to upset the boy any more than need be. No need to make it any worse than it is."

"Who do you think the man is? I mean do you see him well enough? Do you remember him clearly?"

Her voice changed to a harsh, spitting whisper. "I'm afraid . . . sometimes I think . . . what if it's Jesus? I mean, he don't look much like those pictures they got in Sunday School, but what if it's Jesus all the same? Who else can heal like that?"

"The other people . . ." Harry said before his voice died. He had to clear his throat to ask the rest. "Your neighbors. Have they had experiences like this?"

She tossed a stiff, torn towel into her clothes basket and straightened to look at him. "Janie Mitchell killed herself three months ago. With her it was just the dyspepsia. The man took out her stomach just the same. Dutton Friendly put a gun in his mouth just last week. He used to have the arthritis in his back. I don't know. Some people can take it more than others, but you get tired of it, hear? You get real tired."

Mrs. Foote looked tired, tired in a way Harry knew he could never understand. Mrs. Foote was worn old by her very survival: the wood-stove cooking; the farming; the burden of the nightly miracles.

"And your husband?"

"It was his eyes," Mrs. Foote told him in a strained voice. Her face knotted up into an expression of pitying repulsion. "Oh, sweet Jesus," she said in a whimper, "Jimmy Lee just couldn't stand what that man did to his eyes."

Harry swallowed hard and pushed his glasses back in place. To Mrs. Foote's back the sun was crouching down fast behind a stand of trees.

After a moment she got her face back in control. She tried to smile, but shouldn't have. "Stay on a bit. I'm about to set out dinner."

The air was cooling down, but it was suddenly hard for Harry to breathe. "Maybe I'd better go."

"Sit a spell," she said. "Please. I'll fix you some tea and hominy cake and greens."

"I think . . ." He took a step backwards.

"It's hard being alone with Jimmy Lee gone. I don't mean . . ." she seemed embarrassed for a moment. A seemingly impossible blush spread across her sun-wrinkled cheeks. "I don't mean that, exactly. But you're different. From the city. Maybe he wouldn't come tonight if you was here. It's scary all alone."

He backed away another step. "I'm

pretty tired and everything."

"If you don't stay, you'll tell somebody? The government'll come out and tell the man to go away?"

"Yes. I could send somebody out," he agreed, knowing he'd never have the courage to talk about Mrs. Foote's visitor. Being a UFO researcher had held him up to all the close-minded ridicule he could stand. He had a sudden mental image of an army of Catholic priests, maybe a Bishop or two, standing around a plaid-shirted, jeaned Jesus, telling him to put the heart back in Mrs. Foote's chest. He tried to end the image by Jesus disappearing, but all his mind would picture was the sullen, angry look on the large-eyed face and the gout of blood as he squeezed his hand into a fist.

She shot him a knowing glance as if she had seen inside him to the dark nest where his cowardice lay. "Mind that you do," she said curtly. Then she gave up on her brief attempt at courage and started to cry silently. "It don't matter any more if he tells us why he's doing it. I'm way past that, now. Just want him to stop. Please. You got learning and all. Just make him stop."

Harry turned his back on her and started down the hill fast. The dog had come out of the barn and when it saw him it turned and ran again. *Yard dogs don't run,* Harry thought. *Holy Mother of God. I've never seen a yard dog run.*

He hit the dirt road at a brisk trot, his camera bouncing against his chest. Down by the lake night pooled among the trees. Bull frogs thumped in the reeds.

After a few yards Harry slowed reluctantly to a fast, purposeful walk. His lungs hurt; the backs of his legs were on fire. For the first time in five years he wanted a cigarette badly.

Ahead of him he could see lights blink on in the nearest house, turning the squares of the windows yellow. His flight became a limping, sore walk. Remembering his tape recorder, he glanced down to turn it off.

A strobe light went off in his face.

Flinching, he looked up. The light came again, turning a twenty-degree arc of the sky into noon. Above his head small orange spheres were dancing a waltz in the purpling, starlit sky.

"Damn!" he said. Raising his camera quickly, he started snapping pictures. Behind him a big dog howled a single, bass note of terror.

He saw the plaid-shirted blur through the lens first and slowly lowered his camera. The man was standing in the middle of the now-bright road, his arms down at his sides, a cryptic, gentle smile on his face.

"Please," Harry whispered.

The man walked towards him. Without wanting to, without having willed his legs to move, Harry found himself stepping forward to greet him. When they were inches apart, the distance of a lover to his beloved, the man put his hands up and tenderly slipped off Harry's glasses. Staring directly into Harry's eyes, he folded the glasses and put them into Harry's shirt pocket.

"No. Please." Harry was crying now, his cheeks and mouth twisted. He tried to move, but, like all the nightmares of his childhood, he couldn't.

Harry couldn't move his head, but his mouth was still under his control. There was no one around to see, and no one who needed him to act brave, so like Donnie, he started to scream.

The man seemed oblivious to Harry's weeping, his pleas. There was a piercingly sweet smile on his face, one that was sad but at the same time intensely, hurtfully loving. He put his fingers up, up, up towards Harry's eyes as if all in the world he wanted was to wipe the tears away. ▽

20

by Nancy Springer

There's a big lilac bush growing by Mrs. Life's porch, and I used to hide in the hollow under the green leaves next to the cinderblock to play that I was Pony Queen Of The Universe or just to get away from the neighborhood awhile. But I don't go there anymore, because I'm going to die, and what I heard there is what made me understand how that's going to happen.

Not that old Mrs. Life was not a nice lady. She sat on her porch all day every day from April to October and spoke to me like I was a friend every time I passed. "Veronica" she called me, because she said "Ronni" was a boy's name. It was pretty much the only way she didn't approve of me. Most people that old don't seem to like kids much, but Mrs. Life would invite me up on her porch to sit by her and talk to her and see what she was doing. Sometimes it was crocheting an afghan, and she would say to me, "I've put in a hundred and ten hours on this one so far." She would say, "I've crocheted sixty-six afghans since 1983." And she would show me her notebook. She had a little lined spiral-bound notebook like they sell in drugstores, and she had marked in it everything she had crocheted since she learned how to crochet, and how many ounces of yarn each thing took, and how much the yarn cost, and how many hours it took her to make it, and who she gave it to when she was done.

Or sometimes she was reading a book, one of those real fat paperbacks about the Civil War or something, and she would say to me, "I'm on page six hundred and forty-seven." She would say, "I read twenty-two books last year." And she had a notebook for keeping track of that, too. She had been a schoolteacher way back when my mom and dad were in school, so maybe that was why she had those notebooks and kept track of everything in very very tidy thin handwriting. Her handwriting made me shiver like having a fishhook caught in me.

She lived right in the middle of town, next to the church, across from the tavern. From up on her porch a person could see practically the whole town, because Pleasantville isn't very big. You could see all the important places, anyway: the Post Office, and the schoolyard, and the drugstore, and the house next to the tavern that my folks called the cathouse, though I never could figure out why. They don't have any cats over there that I know of. Sometimes I hung around in the alley behind the cathouse watching the windows and stuff, because I like cats, kittens especially. There's different girls and ladies who live there, and I never saw any cats but I did see interesting things happening, things to give me ideas what it might be like when I was a woman. I guess that's why I kept going back.

Anyway, everybody in Pleasantville went past Mrs. Life's porch to get to those places, and they all knew her, and most of them had had her as a teacher in school. And they all liked her, or at least seemed to. They all stopped to talk with her or at least said hi. So I knew she must be a nice lady.

Sometimes I didn't want to talk with her, though. Sometimes I just didn't want to be bothered with anybody, I didn't feel like part of my family at all, I wondered if maybe I was adopted or something, and that was when I would hide under the lilac bush beside her porch and play that I was Chinese Jumprope Master Of The Galaxy, and that was how it happened that I heard her arguing with Mr. Quickel.

It was pretty early in spring yet, and the blossoms were still on the lilac, and it smelled sweeter than a Church Ladies' Auxiliary under there, so I stayed longer than usual. I almost fell asleep. At least I think that was the day it was. It makes sense that it was, because lilac time is when people start mowing their lawns, and she was arguing with Mr. Quickel about what he was going to charge her to do hers again this year.

"Thirty dollars a week," he said. "Now you know that includes everything." She had a big lawn with lots of shrubs and things in it that had to be kept after.

"Why thirty? Last year you charged me fifteen."

"No, last year I charged you twenty-five. But the cost of everything has gone up, gasoline for the mower —"

"Last year you charged me fifteen."

Mr. Quickel was one of those people who had had Mrs. Life in school, and now he was a schoolteacher himself. My big brother, Greg, had him for Health and wrestling in middle school, and after going to a few wrestling matches I kind of got a crush on Coach Quickel because he was really good-looking for an old guy. Besides which he went to our church and everybody liked him. He mowed grass in the summertime because, my mom said, the school board didn't pay him enough. My mom said it was a disgrace to see a schoolteacher moonlighting. I had heard Greg and a couple of his friends talking about mooning a tour bus one night, and I

wondered if it meant the same thing.

Mrs. Life said, "The cost of gas hasn't gone up that much. You want to charge me double what you did last year?"

"Now I know you're getting up there, Mrs. Life." Mr. Quickel tried to make a joke of it and put on a sort of teacher tone, like to a kid who was being dense. "You think back, you'll remember I charged you twenty-five last year. Not that I blame you for forgetting. The years do have a way of piling up, don't they? You must be pushing eighty. Are you getting a little short-minded, maybe?"

"Nicholas Quickel." Mrs. Life's voice instead of yelling went low and cold, and I knew Mr. Quickel had made a mistake. A bad one. He knew it too, because he said, "I didn't mean anything, Mrs. Life." I also noticed that even though he had gray hair himself Mr. Quickel still called her Mrs. Life instead of Savilla the way some of the really old people did. "I just thought . . . my tax records show . . . never mind. Look, I guess I can still do your lawn for twenty-five. . . ."

Mrs. Life said, "I will get someone else," and I heard him walk away.

He should have known better than to think Mrs. Life was short-minded, the way she kept track of everything. I guess if she put a nickel in a Salvation Army kettle she went home and marked it down. All year long she kept track of her grocery coupons in a little notebook and every December 31 she knew how much she had saved. My mom said coupons and afghans and books and stuff weren't the only things she kept track of. Every time my big sister, Regina, was out on a date, Mom said, old Mrs. Life was watching to see how late she came in. I guess she counted how many times Regina kissed each boy. She stood back to watch, but Mom could see her shadow on the window.

That same night she argued with Mr. Quickel, Mrs. Life called and got my brother Greg to mow her lawn for ten dollars a week, and the first time he did it he made me come along and help rake, because I told him after he hung up the phone that he could have got fifteen. Mrs. Life watched him hard at first to make sure he mowed in nice neat lines, but after a while she went back to sit on her porch. Another old lady, Mrs. Simmermeyer, came by and stopped to talk, and I was raking the side yard so I heard them. They started with the preacher (they didn't like that he wore gray slacks instead of black) and practically went through the town person by person.

"I was just thinking last night about somebody I haven't thought of in years," Mrs. Life said after a while.

"Oh?" The other lady was happy to hear this. "Who might that be?"

"The Klunk boy. You remember little Charlie Klunk? What ever became of him?"

"Didn't you *hear?*" Mrs. Simmermeyer was in heaven. "He came home on early discharge from the Service, remember, and then he moved to California. And the Klunks all said he had married a nice girl and had two nice youngsters. But then along about 1973 — I think it was '73 — maybe it was '72 —"

Mrs. Life would've known whether it was '73 or '72. She knew what year people were born or graduated or married or died. Anyway, I knew she knew what year Charlie Klunk did what he did because I had heard her tell this same whole story to somebody else the summer before. But here she was sitting and listening to Mrs. Simmermeyer tell it and not even correcting her.

Mrs. Simmermeyer got back on track. "Anyway, he went and joined one of them Gay Liberation clubs. Came out of the closet. Here he was light in his loafers all along and none of us knew it."

"I knew it," Mrs. Life said, real calm.

"I could tell he was a sissy. I had him in school, remember? And I could always tell which boys to watch. But what's he doing now?"

"He lives with his *sweetie.* You know, his *boyfriend.* They run a *flower shop* together." Mrs. Simmermeyer laughed, but Mrs. Life just sort of nodded.

"He and Nicholas Quickel were in the same class, weren't they? And didn't they used to run around together a lot?"

"Did they? I don't remember."

"Well, I had them both in class, and it seems to me they were *very close.*"

I turned around and raked the other way so I could watch. There they sat with their heads together, their saggy old bosoms almost touching, and Mrs. Simmermeyer's baggy old eyes had opened wide. But Mrs. Life just said as if it was the weather she was talking about, "Nick Quickel was over here yesterday evening, was what made me think of Charlie Klunk. I wonder if they still keep in touch."

"Nicky Quickel. Isn't he the wrestling coach now?"

"Yes. Junior High. Last I heard."

They talked some more, and then Mrs. Simmermeyer went off about her business. Mrs. Life sat rocking on her porch in her wicker rocker, and after I had raked as much as I could for a while I went up and sat with her. I was kind of hoping she would have some sort of chore for me, because Greg wasn't giving me anything for raking grass except just letting me live. Sometimes Mrs. Life sent me across to the Post Office with a letter or across to the drugstore to buy her a magazine, and even if it was just a dinky little errand she always paid me at least a quarter. Like I said, she was a real nice lady.

But she didn't send me on any errand that day. We just watched the cars and stuff go by. When a tour bus went by Mrs. Life said, "That's the sixth one today."

The reason the tour buses go by is

that we sit along the river halfway between the Indian Rock Carvings upstream and the Indian Echoes Cavern downstream. And right outside town is the Indian Maiden's Leap. There's this high cliff above the river, and some Indian girl whose loverboy got axed was supposed to have killed herself by jumping off it. The thing they don't tell the tourists is that people still kill themselves by jumping off there. Our town is supposed to have the highest suicide rate practically in the whole country, and nobody could figure out why. It was in the paper last year, and my mom and dad talked about it for a week, how so many people in Pleasantville killed themselves when it was supposed to be a nice place to live, no drugs, old-fashioned values, all that. Of course not all the people who killed themselves took the Leap. Some of them took pills or shot themselves or whatever. My one girlfriend's grandpap killed himself with a hunting rifle last winter and he blew his head apart so good nobody could go in the room afterward. They had to pay a cleaning service eight hundred dollars to get rid of the mess, all the little bits of ear and nose and eyeballs and stuff. You would think he could have at least done it outside the house.

"Those tour buses smell terrible, don't they?" Mrs. Life said to me.

I went back to raking, and more people stopped and talked with Mrs. Life, and maybe she said something to them about how Charlie Klunk and Nicky Quickel used to be real close, but I don't know. It's not like I listened to everything she said to everybody. I mean, as much as I could I did, because I learned a lot that way, about different people and about what it's like to be grown up. But that day I sort of felt like I'd already heard enough.

About a week later Mr. Quickel came by one evening. We were all sitting out on the lawn, out in the dusk watching the lightning bugs, and he came and sat with us. He and Mom and Dad were kind of friends back even before Greg started wrestling for him, because of church. After a while Dad gave me a dollar and sent me across the street to the drugstore to get myself a candy bar, because I guess he could tell Mr. Quickel had something on his mind he didn't want to talk about in front of me. So after I came back with my Snickers I went up to my room. But my windows were open and I still heard them down below. Something about rumors all over town.

"You can't fight gossip," my Mom was saying. "Pay any attention to it and it just makes it worse. All you can do is ignore it."

"Talk about getting screwed from behind," Mr. Quickel said like he was trying hard to make a joke, and they all laughed a little.

By the time school was out even us kids had heard some things. Mr. Quickel was gay. Everybody said it, so it had to be true. People whose boys had had Mr. Quickel as a coach were worried. I noticed my parents took Greg off one evening and asked him some questions. Everybody knew gay people shouldn't be trusted around children.

"But he has a wife. Grown children," a woman said to Mrs. Life over the porch railing. I was under the lilac bush, playing Princess of California. I had been spending a lot of time under there lately. The real world had started to seem more and more like someplace to get away from.

"Now, I've never said that Nick Quickel is a homosexual," said Mrs. Life to her friend. "But I will say this, I have read that a fair number of men who are homosexuals can appear normal."

The woman was a school board member who had had Mrs. Life as a teacher once and wanted her advice. It seemed the school board had been getting let-

41

ters from people who had heard things about Mr. Quickel. "But nobody seems to have any proof," the woman said. "What if it's all just a bunch of hooey? The man's life is half ruined already. If we start a formal investigation —"

Mrs. Life said, "It seems to me as a teacher and a concerned citizen that we can't take chances with our children, no matter who gets hurt. People know when they go into teaching that there are certain professional standards they have to uphold."

"Then you think he'll understand we have to do what we have to do."

"I've known Nick Quickel for years, and I still think you have to do it whether he understands or not."

That was the year Greg had the paper route. About midafternoon every day a green van would come and a man would thunk bundles of the *Pleasant Day* on the sidewalk in front of our house. Greg usually got me to help him because I knew what he'd do to me if I didn't. We'd turn our fingers red tearing open the plastic straps because we were too lazy to go inside and find the scissors. After that we'd sit and rubber-band the papers all at once. The newsprint blackened our hands and smelled sickening, the way almost anything smells sickening if there is too much of it. Then we would load the papers in the bags and deliver them. Those bags were so heavy they hauled our shoulders down. Dragging a cross couldn't have been much worse. And the newsprint got on the bags and our clothes and our faces. It seemed to spread and stain everything, like sin.

Mrs. Life was always on her porch waiting for her newspaper. If we were even a few minutes late she would be starting to fuss. "I've taken the *Pleasant Day* for sixty-two years," she would say. "Never missed once and I don't want to start now." But one day early that summer Greg and I were a good ten minutes later than usual yet she didn't say an-

ything, just grabbed the paper from us and got the rubber band off it with her crooked old hands. I saw her scan the headlines then smile, and I started to feel like I wanted to hide in green lilac shadow, because I knew what she was looking at. Greg and I had both seen it when we were getting the papers ready. It was what had made us late. Front-page news: "Pleasantville Teacher Suspect." The school board had hired a psychiatrist and a private detective to give them a report on Mr. Quickel.

I waited until we were around the corner from Mrs. Life's place, trudging along under our loads, before I asked Greg, "He never did anything to you, did he?"

"Course not. The whole thing makes me sick."

"Me, too."

"Get used to it, Ronni. That's the way the world is. Sick."

Which was what I was trying to do: get used to it. See how it was run, how things were done. Watch the people who knew, to follow their lead. Learn the rules. Now it's too late I can see what I wish I'd done. But then I couldn't get a handle on what was going wrong. I hadn't seen anybody do anything bad. Hadn't even heard anybody tell any lies. Just had a feeling things weren't fair, that was all. Just a bad feeling.

Couple days or it might have been a week after the newspaper article, me and my mom were walking to somebody's yard sale when Mrs. Life called hello to us and beckoned Mom over to her porch.

"Have you noticed Nicholas Quickel hasn't been to church for three weeks now?" she said. She went to the same church as we did, the one right by her house. Everybody who wanted to count in that town went to that church. "Marjorie has been coming but he hasn't." His wife, Mrs. Life meant. "I wonder if they're having problems."

My mother said, "Um." Just barely

polite.

"I'm concerned for them," Mrs. Life said, her voice turning chilly. "I think we ought to pray for them."

"I think we ought to let them alone," Mom said. She told Mrs. Life we had to get going. After we were down the street a ways she started to mutter, "Concerned. Huh. Concerned just like a fox when there's a chicken in trouble."

A few days later I heard Mrs. Simmermeyer telling the lady behind the counter at the Post Office how Mr. Quickel and his wife were having bad problems, and no wonder, what with his being a queer and all.

Mr. Quickel came to our kitchen screen door one night while we were eating supper and let himself in. Dad told him to sit down and have something to eat with us, but he didn't. He just started to talk kind of wild. Didn't even seem to care that Greg and Gina and I were sitting there hearing every word.

"It's like a nightmare," he said. "It just keeps getting worse and worse. Now they're spying on Marge and me. They're saying she's going to leave me. How the Hell do they know she's going to leave me?"

"They're just guessing," Mom said.

"They're right. Thirty years, and she's going to leave me. She can't take disgrace. Neither can I. I can't take any of this. I'm going to lose my job. You know I'm going to lose my job. Pretty soon they'll start saying I'm going to lose my job, and they'll be right, I'll lose my job —"

"Nick, calm down," Dad said. He got up and went to stand beside him, started to touch him on the shoulder and then sort of stopped his hand and took it away again. "They haven't made a decision yet," Dad said.

Like he hadn't heard any of this Mr. Quickel kept on going. "I'll lose my job, and then they'll start talking about criminal charges, and whadaya know!

They'll be right about that, too. Somebody will bring criminal charges. See the headlines written on the wall?" He pointed at our kitchen wall as if he was really seeing something. " 'Former Teacher Indicted for Sex Crimes.' And then they'll start saying —"

"Nick!" my mother yelled at him. "Stop."

My father was still standing up, and he sort of shoved Mr. Quickel toward his chair, and Mr. Quickel sat down. But he didn't stop talking. His voice got quieter, but what he was saying got worse.

He said, "The Hell of it is, there's just a ghost of truth behind it all. That's what makes it so hard."

"What are you talking about?" My father sounded scared, but Mr. Quickel didn't even look at him. It was like he was talking in a dream.

He said, "Must have been thirty-five, forty years ago. There was this kid named Charlie Klunk. We got to be friends, and he and I did a few dirty things. Just fooling around. Testing out our chemistry sets. But then I went away to college and I put all that behind me. I knew I wanted to be a teacher, see. . . ."

He looked up at Greg and my dad and saw the look on their faces.

"It was back when I was a stupid kid," he begged them. "You know what they say about teenage boys, they're just hormones with feet. I'm not gay. Not once I grew up, anyway."

He looked at Dad and Greg some more and then he stood up to go. "Never mind," he said. "I know I'm a goner. Might as well kill myself and have it done with."

"Nick, no. Don't talk that way," my mother said.

He looked at her like she was throwing him a lifeline but it was way too short. "How the Hell did they know to hit me where I live?" he asked her. Then he went out into the dusk and we

43

didn't see him again.

The next day I was lying under my lilac bush, just lying there, not even playing anything, and I heard Mrs. Life say to somebody, "There goes Nick Quickel into the drugstore again. See, he's going back to the pharmacy counter to have a prescription filled. That's the third time this week. I wonder what can be the matter."

It was the old man who picked up tin cans around town she was talking to. I heard him say, "Why, what do you think it might be?"

"I'm sure I couldn't say. But don't you think he's awfully thin for a man his age?"

Mr. Quickel was a coach, for heavensake. I knew he jogged and everything to keep in shape.

"And pale?"

What with the Hell she had been putting him through, no wonder.

"Here he comes out again. Do you see all those red spots on his arm? Of course they might just be bug bites. . . ."

How could she see anything on his arm from across the street? She had to be making it up.

"You think he has that there disease queers get?" The tin can man had caught on pretty fast for a guy his age.

"I wouldn't want to go so far as to say that."

Only took a few days, though, before most of Pleasantville knew for a fact that Mr. Quickel had AIDS. Even the people who were still speaking to him before were afraid to go near him now.

I had started staying under the lilac bush and listening to Mrs. Life on purpose. Teachers in school were always telling kids to think for themselves, but this was the first time that a schoolteacher had ever really taught me to do it. I was starting to see evil when I looked in her face, and I was starting to hate her. But I wasn't used to going against adults or thinking that I knew better than them. I wasn't used to having my own ideas about things. It was a strange feeling, and I spent a lot of time under my bush sort of wrestling with it.

I heard Mrs. Life say, "I don't like to speak ill of anyone, but just the same, if I was a parent I wouldn't want my child to have him as a schoolteacher."

I heard her say, "Would you want to use the same restroom or water fountain as him?"

I heard her say, "Even putting aside all the rest of it, suppose he should cut himself and his blood got on some poor little girl?" I knew what I ought to do, but I just couldn't. I wasn't old enough or big enough or strong enough to speak out against her. I had plenty of anger, but I couldn't find any courage.

Mr. Quickel killed himself the day after his wife went to Arizona to stay with her mother for a while. He did it by cutting his wrists, and he stayed in the bathroom so there wouldn't be too much mess. He left a private note for his wife and kids and a public one for the rest of us. All it said was, "I never hurt anyone."

My dad is a Volunteer Fireman and answered the call when the school board's private detective found him that evening. Dad came home looking pretty grim and told the rest of us what had happened, and Mom said to him, "It's partly your fault."

"What was I supposed to do?"

"He came to you for help and you turned your back. How do you think that made him feel?"

He yelled, "What is it with you and Nick Quickel, anyway?"

She yelled back, "What's that supposed to mean?"

I left them fighting and walked into our front room and looked across at Mrs. Life's porch. She was out there, all right.

And one of the other firemen was leaning on her railing. I guessed I knew what they were talking about.

Then he left and she got up off her wicker rocker and went inside.

I must have been about half crazy. The whole thing made me so sad and mad and sick I could have puked. I walked out of my house and straight across to hers and barged right in her front door without even thinking. I still don't know what I meant to say to her.

And there she was at her dining room table with her old tortoise-shell fountain pen, writing in one of those little notebooks of hers that she kept track of everything in. She finished writing and closed it, and I saw it was just like all the rest, spiral-bound, with lined paper, except that it had a black cover. "So I'm short-minded, am I?" she said to it. "Short-minded, indeed."

Then she looked up and saw me there. But her face didn't change. It was still the same as ever.

"Witch," I said to her. I wanted to scream it, but it came out a whisper. "You dirty witch."

In a very quiet, very cold voice she told me, "Veronica Hoffman, you watch your mouth."

I was so nuts I didn't stop. "How many people you got in there?" I squeaked at her. "Go ahead, tell me. How many suicides have you done?"

"Nineteen so far," she said.

"Wonderful. One more and you'll be up to twenty."

"That's right." She stood up, and suddenly I was very scared. "Get out of my house."

I ran like a rabbit, and if there was a way I could have kept running clear out of this town I would have done it. But there's nothing I can do. Mom and Dad are quarreling. There's nobody I can talk to, nobody who can help me. And already Mrs. Simmermeyer is starting to talk about how little Veronica Hoffman spends so much time at the cathouse, what can a girl her age want at that place?

I know who number twenty in Mrs. Life's little black book is going to be.

∇

AULD LENG SIGNS

Young Akeley, final scion of his line,
Brought back from Arkham shards of Lengish glass:
Pale clouded souvenirs without design
Through which (if one stared long) strange shadows passed.
No knowledge had he of the Hyades,
Celaeno, Yith, or Yuggoth on the Rim;
Yet trial & error showed him all of these,
Until his ignorance caught up with him.

Toward midnight at the closing of the year,
His worried friends broke down his study door.
They found glass fragments splintered on the floor,
A severed tentacle, *one reddish smear,*
& knew (as they ran shrieking from the spot)
That auld acquaintance might best be forgot.

— **Ann K. Schwader**

THE PRONOUNCED EFFECT

by John Brunner

Never in all her nineteen years had Lies Andrassy wished so devoutly her father could be with her. She had been tense and edgy throughout the 200-mile bus ride which had brought her here; now, in the huge hall of the hotel where banners welcomed the annual convention of the Linguistics Society, she was positively trembling. She had only seldom been among such a large group of people before — there must have been at least a thousand, milling around or waiting patiently in line — and the sheer pressure of their presence was upsetting.

Worst of all was the fact that she didn't know a single soul, and nobody knew her.

However, she was determined to put a bold face on it. She had checked into her room easily enough, and then come down to collect her conference documents. Tables had been set up with signs above them: **PRE-REGISTERED A — K; PRE-REGISTERED L — Z; OFFICIALS AND PARTICIPANTS; NON-REGISTERED** . . . She had duly joined the line at the first table, but it was moving dreadfully slowly, and she had far more time than she wanted to look about her and envy those who had friends to talk to.

One man in particular, of early middle age, with a big red beard and a booming laugh, was holding forth to half a dozen seeming admirers just far enough away for her not to catch what was being said, but everybody in the group was obviously vastly entertained by his witty conversation. Well, maybe by the time the weekend was over she too might be chatting happily with new acquaintances. But Monday seemed like an awfully long way away from Friday, and in her heart of hearts she could not be optimistic. She was acutely aware how confident, how poised, most of the women were who strode briskly across the hallway, and how out of keeping her own "safe" tailored suit was compared with the up-to-the-minute styles most of them wore. People who wanted to be polite to her called her "cuddly," or at worst "plump," but in fact she was fat; and, worse yet, she had had to wear glasses since she was six. It looked, in short, as though nature had marked her out for the same kind of dull academic career her father had endured.

Not, of course, that he had ever admitted to finding it dull; indeed, he more often talked of it as though it were some kind of grand contest, in which there were skirmishes and duels and outright battles. But how on earth could anyone get excited about whether or not a certain word in a dead language was pronounced *this* way rather than *that* way?

On the bus she had read and re-read the paper of her father's which she was scheduled to present tomorrow in his place, until she had practically memorised it. She muttered a phrase from it which was supposed to be some kind of grand curse, calling up a veritable devil, as she went on staring at the man with the red beard.

"Oh, excuse me!" a light voice said at

46

her side. "Did I bump into you?"

She returned to the here and now with a start, and realised that the line she was in had moved without her noticing, so there was now six feet between her and the person ahead. Hastily she closed the gap, at the same time glancing — glancing *up* — at the man who had addressed her. He was very tall and quite indecently handsome: a shock of fair hair, neatly brushed, incongruously dark eyes above well-modelled cheekbones, a light summer jacket, open shirt, silk choker . . .

He had been among the early arrivals; he already carried his file of conference documents, and pinned to his lapel was a badge identifying him as

**J.R. DeVILLE, Ph.D.,
MISKATONIC U.**

Not a college Lies had ever heard of — but then, she hadn't heard of half the places represented this weekend. There would be almost two thousand teachers and students of linguistics and etymology assembled by tonight. And how bare her own name-badge would seem among all these doctors and professors, without a single qualification!

But that was irrelevant. What mattered was that he still thought her under-the-breath exclamation had been due to his bumping into her, and he had apologised needlessly. She summoned a smile.

"That's all right, Doctor! You didn't do anything."

"I'm glad," he said, and flashed sparkling white teeth as he made to turn away.

Before she could stop herself, she had caught his sleeve.

"Excuse me!" she heard herself saying. "But do you know who that man is over there, with the red beard?"

"Hmm?" Dr DeVille checked and looked around. "Oh, that's Professor Simon Tadcaster. One of the — ah — more conspicuous delegates, as you might say. . . . Is something wrong?"

48

For on hearing the name Lies had turned pale and started to sway, furious because she could not control the impulse.

"I'm — I'm all right," she forced out.

"You don't look all right," he contradicted, taking her arm. "Let me help you to a chair."

"No, no — really!" She straightened and released herself from his grip. "I don't want to lose my place in line, do I? And I really am all right, I promise. It's just . . ."

She felt obliged to explain. "I simply didn't realise that was Professor Tadcaster. He's — he's my father's greatest enemy."

It sounded ridiculous, put like that. But what else could one call a person who set out systematically to mock and ridicule the life's work of a professional colleague?

Dr DeVille raised his eyebrows. "Really? Your father being —?"

"Well . . . Well, Professor Julius Andrassy. I don't suppose you ever heard of him."

"Heard of Andrassy?" DeVille countered with a trace of sarcasm. "Of course I have! He's giving a paper tomorrow on the way the pronunciation of Latin and Hebrew was affected by local dialects in Central Europe, and I certainly don't intend to miss it! It sounds fascinating!"

"Oh, you *do* know about him! I thought . . ." Lies licked her lips. "But he's not giving the paper. He's too ill to come, so I've got to do it instead, and I don't more than half-understand it. . . . And it's all that Professor Tadcaster's fault, I'm sure!"

"Well, I must admit," DeVille said after a slight hesitation, "he has been a bit scathing in the professional journals about your father's theories, and I suppose most of the people who turn up will be there in the hope of watching a grand set-to between them. . . . But never mind that for the moment. You said you're actually going to present the paper?"

"Yes, I promised I would."

"Then you're in the wrong line," DeVille said briskly, and taking her arm urged her over to the table for officials and participants, where there was for the moment no line at all; the girl on duty was leaning back in her chair and covering a yawn.

"But — !" Lies began.

He ignored her. "Do you have Professor Andrassy's documents there?" he was saying. "He can't come but Miss Andrassy here is his daughter and will be making the presentation in his place. You'd better let her have the professor's file, and make out a participant's badge for — ah . . . ?"

"Lies Andrassy, *L-I-E-S*."

The girl smiled and scribbled a note on a scrap of paper which she passed to a young man behind her seated at a large electric typewriter with an Orator all-capitals face. In a moment the badge, red-bordered to indicate her status as an official participant, was slipped into its transparent cover, and DeVille pinned it to the front of her jacket with quick, deft fingers.

"Thank you!" he said to the girl as she handed over the file of documents, and continued, taking Lies's arm, "I really am most interested to meet you! If you're not doing anything, come and have a drink."

"I — uh — I don't drink, I'm afraid," Lies said selfconsciously.

"Nonsense. My doctorate may not be in medicine, but I know enough to assure you that a glass of sweet wine would be medicinal to someone in your condition. This way!"

Such was his self-assurance, Lies felt herself helplessly swept along.

Moments later they were seated at a secluded table in a dimly-lit bar. With a snap of his fingers DeVille summoned a waiter and ordered sherry, one sweet, one very dry. Offering a cigar, which

she refused — a little surprised that he should offer such a thing to a girl — and receiving her permission to light one for himself, he went on, "Now explain what you meant when you said your father's illness is due to Tadcaster!"

"It's true!" Under the table, Lies clenched her hands on the file of conference documents, into which she had slipped her copy of the paper she must deliver tomorrow. She was afraid to let it out of her sight, even in a locked hotel room. "He's being hounded! Absolutely *hounded!* And he hasn't done anything to deserve it. . . . Have you ever met my father, Dr DeVille?"

"No, I never had the privilege. And, by the way, nobody ever calls me Doctor except people I don't like. My name is Jacques."

"Are you — are you French?"

"Not by birth, if that's what you mean. Go on. You were telling me about your father."

"Well, he's a marvellous person, and lots of people think he's brilliant, including me, but he's — I don't know how to put it!"

"Unworldly?" Jacques suggested.

She seized on the word gratefully. "Yes, there's a lot of that in it, but something else, too. You might say single-minded. You might even say *obsessive.*"

There: it was out. And to a perfect stranger. Something which before she had scarcely dared admit to herself.

The waiter delivered their drinks; to cover her moment of alarm, she sipped the wine Jacques had chosen for her, and found it not only delicious, but warming. What a stroke of luck it had been to meet somebody like this, who simply by talking to her was bringing back a little of the confidence she had feigned to her father but never really felt.

"I think I see what you mean," Jacques was saying as he raised his own glass. "Cheers, by the way, and lots of luck

49

tomorrow morning. . . . Yes, I've had something of that impression from the papers of his that I've read, especially the one on anomalous vowel-shifts among initiates of the alchemical tradition in Prague and Ratisbon."

Lies stared at him in genuine amazement. "You've read as much of my father's work as I have myself!" she exclaimed. "That was — oh — about the second paper he published after he learned English, wasn't it?"

"And very well he learned it, too. Amazingly well. Or do you help with the final text?"

She felt herself blushing. "Well, of course after Mother died *someone* had to . . . So for the last five years, yes, it's been me."

"Congratulations on your editing job, then. But fill me in a little more on his background. I know he was born in Hungary, and left in 1956, and then he came to the States and found this post at Foulwater, a place which practically nobody wants to work at because of its name, only the trust under which the college was endowed prevents it being changed — isn't that right?"

"Yes," Lies confirmed. "Apparently our founder had a macabre sense of humour, which is why ninety per cent of the faculty are of foreign origin; the name doesn't bother them. The students, on the other hand . . . But we've always had enough, and sometimes after what they thought of as a bad start they've gone on to great things, because some of the teaching is superb. At least, so I've always understood."

"Your father has been happy at Foulwater?"

"Oh, yes! Most of the time. I mean he met and married Mother there, and except for a year or so after her death, he's always been content to carry on with his work. He's one of the old school of European scholars, basically; he loves learning in the abstract, and I suppose that's why people might call him — as

I said — obsessive." It was easier to utter the word the second time.

"And you think Tadcaster has been hounding him. How?"

"I don't think, I know!" Lies flared, and took another sip of her wine. "It's one thing to disagree with a colleague's argument, or reasoning. It's something else to mock his integrity, and — well — practically accuse him of forgery!"

"I take it," Jacques said thoughtfully, "you're referring to that unfortunate comment Tadcaster made during a discussion at last year's convention, when he said something to the effect that until he himself was able to subject the Foulwater texts to scientific analysis he would continue to doubt their authenticity?"

"He was much ruder than that, wasn't he?" Lies exclaimed. "When my father read the Proceedings, he was beside himself! He swore that even though he hates big gatherings like this he would attend this year's convention for the first time and show up Tadcaster for a scoundrel and a mountebank! But he's an ochlophobe, and the prospect of having actually to confront hundreds of people in a totally strange environment drove him into a decline. For months he's been shaking and trembling, and finally the stress brought on an ulcer, and right now he's in the hospital and hoping diet and tranquilizers will fix it without an operation. Which is why I'm here instead of him. Me, who don't really understand a fraction of what he wants to prove!"

"I see now why you got so upset in the lobby," Jacques said sympathetically. "And you have no real need to worry, you know. Many of the people who will attend the lecture tomorrow are definitely on your father's side, because Tadcaster is a man who makes enemies easily, and what's more he doesn't really have friends, only hangers-on and toadies. But of course his academic reputation is very high, and he works at one of the most famous universities in the world, and there was some substance in the charge he made that your father had never submitted the texts he's relying on to independent scrutiny."

"But he can't let them leave Foulwater!" Lies exclaimed heatedly. "The only thing he managed to bring with him when he left Hungary was this crate full of his prized collection of late-medieval and early-modern manuscripts and incunabula, and the only way he was able to secure a post at Foulwater before he spoke proper English was by donating them in perpetuity to the university library. That was more than a quarter of a century ago! Surely people who want to examine them for authenticity have had plenty of chances to go there and inspect them? Surely the people who inspected and valued them for insurance when he first arrived were satisfied about their genuineness?"

She looked beseechingly at Jacques for reassurance; there was a lurking terror in the far corners of her mind, to the effect that one day her beloved father's collection might turn out after all to be spurious. . . .

To her surprise and delight, he was nodding vigorously.

"Oh, yes! I can testify to that. The expert they called in was my old teacher at Miskatonic, Professor Brass, and he came back saying that we no longer had the finest collection of mystical and alchemical texts in the New World! He was made permanently jealous by what he saw! Not, of course, that some of the stuff wasn't duplicated by our own holdings, and anyhow we're more interested in the content of such texts than in their linguistic and etymological associations. So I don't suppose anyone from my place has studied them since, let alone anybody from the other and stuffier foundations which look down on Foulwater as the back of beyond."

Taking another sip of wine, Lies said, "I've always found that a very strange attitude. If it hadn't been for his fear of strangers, I'm sure my father would have gone anywhere to confirm or disprove his conclusions. All my life, I remember him reading every single publication that he could lay hands on, studying them down to the tiniest detail, making piles of notes . . . Oh, he's so *dedicated!*" She drained her glass and concluded, "And I have to stand in for him, and I'm terrified!"

"I don't see why," Jacques riposted, looking genuinely puzzled. "I mean, he's made out an excellent case for his views."

"But Professor Tadcaster —"

"I know, I know!" He signalled the waiter for another round of drinks; Lies made to decline, but thought better of it, for the sherry had definitely relaxed her.

"But," Jacques went on, "the main thrust of his objection is not so much that he thinks your father's texts are forged — excuse me, but you did use the term forgery, and I think that's pitching it too high. It's more that, if he's right, we shall have to think again about how the learned words from Latin, Greek, and Hebrew were pronounced in the days when they were the common means of communication among the academics and specialists of all Europe. Right?"

"Y-yes!"

"And this means that those words which then entered the common tongue, the vernacular, must have been pronounced differently from what we've assumed for more than a century, and we may even have to re-write that fundamental dogma of language study, Grimm's Law. We shall have to revise our view of the Great Vowel Shift, we shall have to reconsider everything we have been teaching for generations. In short, people like Professor Tadcaster will have to make an about-turn and start teaching that what they taught yesterday was wrong after all! Worse yet, they themselves will have to go back to studying instead of merely passing on what they learned in their youth as though it were Holy Writ! And *that* is why Tadcaster in particular is so fierce in claiming that we cannot base such a radical revision of our views on a bunch of mystical and alchemical books which at best may have affected a small in-group of initiates among whom it may well have been a mark of distinction to know how to *mispronounce* certain words. Unworthy or not, though, it is a rational objection."

A fresh glass of wine appeared before her. Lies drank deeply to cover the fact that her eyes had filled with tears. She had dared to think that this wonderful stranger, so tall, so friendly, so handsome, so well-spoken, might be on her side. Instead, he had just presented Tadcaster's case better than he might have done himself.

She muttered something and made to rise. Jacques caught her hand.

"Please! Don't go away. I do appreciate how you feel — I felt just the same myself one time when old Brass told me he had screwed up his engagements and I'd have to deliver a paper he'd written because he couldn't be in two places at once. Which quite destroyed my respect for him — I'd been firmly convinced for three years that he could!"

Against her will Lies found she was chuckling at the joke, and once again able to relax.

"Even so," she said after a pause, "I don't really know what I shall be talking about tomorrow. I mean, how can I possibly understand it in my bones the way my father does? I can't make myself believe that it *matters* how some particular word was pronounced five hundred years ago! I can see how it can be *interesting* to some people, but *important* . . . ?"

"Maybe in a way," Jacques said judiciously, "it's a shame your father didn't find his way to Miskatonic. I can assure you there are occasions when the correct pronunciation is very important indeed. Today, for instance."

Lies blinked at him. She registered peripherally that the bar by now was crowded with convention delegates, exchanging shouted greetings or engaged in heated debate; all that, however, was washing past this charmed circle enclosing her and Jacques. They might as well have been on a private island.

"Do you mean," she ventures, "that when one is talking about such a rarefied subject it's essential to get across in speech the same as what you'd put over in IPA?"

"If, back in the Middle Ages, someone had had the wit to invent a perfectly phonetic script, things might have been very different." Jacques gave a lazy smile, and sipped his very dry sherry before crushing out his cigar. A wisp of smoke rose from the ashtray.

"No," he went on, "what I meant was something else. Ah . . . Well, perhaps I could make my point clearer if you told me what exactly it is about this speech that's bothering you."

"I'm not sure I could explain —"

"Oh, come on! Try, at least! After all, I seem to be the only person here from the only other university in North America where they have the same sort of respect as your father for the *recherché* and the arcane. I promise you, I'm not one to dismiss a source merely because it relates to a subject like alchemy, or raising the devil, which has subsequently gone out of style. The important thing is that these people believed in what they were doing, and as the saying goes, faith can move mountains. It may take a long time — you may have to wait until that faith invents dynamite — but it does work. I have a suspicion that under Tadcaster's bombardment your father is losing faith in his own convictions. Am I right?"

She gave a little sad nod. The same had often occurred to her. Had he really believed in his assertions, he would not, surely, have abandoned her — ulcer or no ulcer!

She said at last, in a low and confidential tone, "There is one thing that I'm sure people are going to ask about, and I don't think I can answer. It's when he's analysing some macaronic verses, a sort of incantation in mixed-up Latin, Greek, and Magyar, and —"

"Have you got a transcript?" Jacques interrupted, leaning across the table.

"Oh, yes! I have photocopies of all the pages he cited!" Hastily she opened the file at her side, fumbling for the sheet in question.

Jacques studied it gravely. He said at length, "This isn't where you got what you were saying when I bumped into you."

"But you didn't actually —" Lies put her hand to her mouth. "I didn't know anyone had heard me!"

"I heard. And what's more I can testify that your pronunciation was impeccable, otherwise I wouldn't be here talking to you. But this must have been one of the passages that afforded a clue, right?"

"You *heard* what I said?" Lies mourned. "Oh, how awful! I didn't really mean to say it, I promise. I just felt so —"

He laid his hand soothingly on hers and pressed gently.

"Don't worry. Please! There probably aren't more than two people in this hotel — at this entire congress! — who'd know it for a diabolic invocation, and even if you were brought up to believe that swearing was a bad habit, like drinking, I can promise you that now and then there are exceptions. You're enjoying this sherry? I thought you would. I can feel how much more relaxed you are now. Your pulse has steadied and you aren't perspiring the way you were, and your attention is fully engaged in the important subject under discussion. One rescue operation under way."

There was something infinitely reassuring about his cool, almost surgical dissection of her condition. Lies felt a smile creep unbidden across her mouth.

"I guess you missed your vocation. You're one Hell of a therapist, aren't you?"

"If you said that twice I wouldn't accuse you of exaggerating. But let's get back to the main line of the argument. I take it that this must be one of the passages in leontine verse which, because its rhymes are from the middle of the line to the end, strike your father as supporting his claim that the broad *a* sound had already started to approach the broad *e* long before . . ."

At some stage during the next hour, in order to get a clearer sight of the papers she was spreading on the table, Jacques left his chair facing her and came to sit beside her on the padded bench he had gentlemanly urged her to accept on their arrival; she hadn't paid much attention at the time. The bar was now packed. There was a sort of humming in the air, an excited and exciting sound. It matched her mood. She was almost delirious. For here was this amazing stranger giving her the insight into what she must say tomorrow which even her beloved father had failed to communicate.

Well, of course, if the Romans themselves had pronounced such a word with a soft *w* sound, and yet in modern languages it had been replaced with a harsh *v*, and virtually no other word in any of the languages that survived exhibited a similar change, then somebody must have had a reason for meddling with it. And given that the scientific method was just being devised as a universal standard, it followed that —

And if this other word had an otherwise unaccountable broad *i*, and most similar words had a short one, and the surrounding consonants didn't match the standard pattern — and — and . . .

"I'm getting hungry," Jacques announced suddenly. "It's after seven. Let's go grab a table in the restaurant."

"Wait a moment!" Lies exclaimed. "I was just going to bring up another point here on page . . ."

And then the awful reality dawned on her. The budget allotted by Foulwater U. for this trip wouldn't stretch to eating in hotels or real restaurants; she was resigned to making do with MacDonald's or whatever the equivalent was in this strange city. She began to gather her papers.

"You've been very kind," she said. "But really I can't —"

"Can't accept my invitation to dinner? Oh, my dear Lies! I came here expecting the usually dreary round of back-slapping and in-fighting and general bitchiness, and here I am with somebody who actually cares about what we're all supposed to get worked up about, and you're telling me I can't go on talking to you over a meal? Honestly, that's ridiculous! You just come with me and bring the whole pile of paper and we can eat and talk at the same time. I think," he added meaningly, "we can lay a little trap for Professor Tadcaster . . . don't you?"

An hour earlier she had been imagining disaster during tomorrow morning's inevitable interrogation — disguised in the convention programme as "discussion," but nonetheless merciless if Professor Tadcaster were to be there. Now she was almost looking forward to it, for Jacques had shown her connections between one word and another, and cited other references from different sources — most of which she had never heard of — that did, taken together, tend to support her father's favourite theory. . . .

She mastered herself. She reminded

herself that merely accepting an invitation to dinner was a normal thing in the lives of most young women, even though at home in Foulwater there had been very few men who made the offer. She was in a big city, attending a major academic congress. She must pretend she was in Rome, and behave like the Romans. . . .

Up to a point.

Smiling, she said, "Very well, Jacques." It was the first time she had used his name. "If you *insist* . . ."

And there was a delicious meal, with white wine — she once again pleaded that she didn't drink, and was persuaded to take a glass, that became two, but not three, because he was tactful enough not to press it on her. Two were fine; they made her loquacious and even vociferous, as she picked up the threads of her father's argument and improvised a defence for them which yesterday she could never have guessed at. Jacques sat — on her right this time, at a little square table whose far corner afforded a place to lay out the sheets of paper they were not currently consulting — smiling and nodding approval, and now and then offering a hint or clue that led her to yet further comprehension.

She was astonished at what was happening to her. She did now at last have some conception of what so fascinated her father, and all these other people assembled for the convention, about the words which were the basic tool of human communication. Jacques, whoever he was, must be a great teacher! If only he had turned up soon enough to be of help to her father!

Or would that rigid and now elderly man have taken advice from someone twenty, thirty years his junior . . . ?

She realised suddenly she had no idea how old her companion might be. Sometimes he gave a mischievous grin which made him seem like a teenager; sometimes he spoke with a gravity that made him seem infinitely old, infinitely wise. . . . But did it matter? She was enjoying his company more than anybody else's she could recall, and occasionally he was making her laugh aloud, something she could not have believed when she got off the bus this afternoon, quailing at the prospect of her ordeal by Tadcaster.

She said as much, and Jacques cocked one eyebrow.

"Speak of the devil, as the saying goes . . . Here he comes now, with a bunch of his cronies, and I think he just caught sight of you."

Fear clutched Lies's heart. Jacques set his hand on hers, and warmth seemed to flow from it.

"Be polite," her murmured. "Just make him understand that he can't walk all over you tomorrow. And he can't. It's been arranged."

Nonetheless she was shaking inwardly as the red-bearded man advanced.

"Miss Andrassy?" he said in a voice as resonant as his big booming laugh. "I'm told your father is *unfortunately* indisposed, isn't that so? A shame! I had been looking forward to a debate with him in real time, instead of through the slow and fallible channels of the professional journals."

Lies sat tongue-tied, an artificial smile on her face. She would rather have replaced it by a scowl, but all her upbringing militated against it.

Having waited just long enough for her to answer if she chose, Tadcaster went on, "Well, I'm sure you'll do what you can tomorrow to defend his reputation. But I really think that someone who relies on weird alchemical texts as the basis for a so-called 'scientific' hypothesis owes more to his colleagues than a presentation by someone totally without qualifications in the field. With all respect, Miss Andrassy. But you don't yourself possess a degree of any

kind, I'm told — is that correct?"

A hot and horrible blush was spreading over Lies's round face; she could feel sweat starting to loosen the grip of her spectacles on her nose. She was afraid even to nod miserable confirmation of Tadcaster's charge, for if she did she could imagine having to rescue them from the table, or worse yet the floor.

"Well, it's very irregular," Tadcaster said, making to turn away. "But I suppose the organisers must have their reasons. I think, though, we should make certain such a thing doesn't happen twice."

Several nods greeted this remark from the party standing at his back, those whom Jacques had termed cronies.

Lies sat rock-still, wishing she were safely home in Foulwater . . . even if, back there, she was always the wallflower, always the gooseberry, always the unwanted third. Being humiliated in person was nothing compared to sitting here and feeling her father humiliated through herself. Didn't Jacques realise? Was he going to say nothing?

Just as she was prepared to believe she had been betrayed, he gave a little sleepy smile, turning toward Tadcaster.

"If you'll forgive my saying so, Professor, I think you may be in for a surprise. I've had the pleasure and privilege of a preview of Professor Andrassy's paper, and in my view the logic is unassailable."

"Have you now!" Tadcaster exclaimed. "And by what right did you enjoy the preprint of this paper, which has been denied to the rest of us?"

"Oh, come now, Professor," Jacques chided mildly. "You know as well as I that the provision of preprints is optional, and in fact most participants prefer not to destroy the spontaneity of discussion which follows a live presentation. As a matter of fact, I recall that you yourself have delivered eight

55

papers at conventions of this Society, and not one was circulated as a pre-print."

Tadcaster was taken aback, but only momentarily. He said, "I was complaining that a preprint had been made available to some people and not to everyone!"

"Oh, that's not the case. I've merely had the good luck to consult with Miss Andrassy, and coach her on a few points concerned with presentation of what I assure you is a most remarkable and insightful argument."

For a second Tadcaster seemed at a loss. Then he collected his wits and, bending close, carefully read Jacques's name-badge. Straightening, he said contemptuously, "Oh, you're from Miskatonic, are you? Never heard of it."

"Most people say the same," Jacques sighed. "Until . . ."

"Until what?" Tadcaster blinked uncertainly.

"Until," Jacques concluded briskly, and turned back to Lies. "Now, my dear, let's just run over that matter of the *u*-to-*w* shift again, and I think you should be able to cope with any questions anybody throws at you."

Visibly disturbed — to Lies's great delight — Tadcaster withdrew, while his cohorts pestered him with questions he was plainly in no mood to answer. His food grew cold on the table, and he kept casting anxious glances in Lies's and Jacques's direction.

Very shortly, however, she was so engrossed in Jacques's commentary on her father's paper that she was able completely to ignore him.

Eventually:
"Well, I'm damned! It's eleven o'clock!" Jacques exclaimed, consulting a watch which, like everything else about him, was slick and up-to-the-minute.

"Oh my goodness!" Lies said, paling. "And I promised father I'd get to bed early tonight, too, because — well, you

know they've put me on first thing tomorrow morning, at nine o'clock."

"In the dead slot," Jacques said, signalling a waiter and flourishing a pen to sign the check with. He amplified: "At a time when people who have spent the first evening partying neither wisely nor too well won't be around to pay attention! But never mind. You're assured of one thing. Tadcaster will be there."

He scribbled something generous ending with a percent sign on the form the waiter proffered, and rose, extending a hand to assist Lies. Not that she needed assistance, she assured herself. It was just that with so many bits of paper spread around . . .

"You have your key? You remember your room number?" he inquired, as he escorted her across the lobby — where late arrivals were still checking in — towards the elevators.

"Yes, of course," she said a trifle crossly. She might not be in the habit of staying in hotels like this, but forgetting her room number was . . .

Was a recurrent nightmare since the moment she realised she might have to come here alone. Was there no limit to this man's insight?

To damp that down, she produced her key with a flourish. Catching sight of its tag, just as an elevator arrived and shed its passengers, he exclaimed, "Why, 668! We're neighbours — I'm in 666!"

And ushered her into the empty elevator and hit the DOOR CLOSE button.

For a brief while they were silent and alone, enclosed by the warm and purring walls of the machine. Hundreds of improbable thoughts flashed through Lies's mind, creating an infinity of imagined futures . . . but in fact all that happened during the brief upward ride was that he gave her a broad grin, and she felt the muscles of her face responding to it.

They stepped out on a long deep-carpeted corridor, and — still in silence

— walked the twenty or thirty paces to her door, turning one corner on the way. And they had arrived.

He stood facing her, less than arm's reach distant, and smiled again.

"I'm very glad to have met you, Lies," he said after a brief hesitation. "You're underestimating yourself, you know. I can't remember when I last enjoyed talking to somebody so much."

The alarming thing was, he sounded as though he meant it. She felt another hateful blush redden her face, and hoped the late-night lighting was not bright enough for it to show.

"Thank you!" she forced out. "And —"

"Yes?" He glanced at her alertly.

"Just now you said one thing was sure about tomorrow morning. . ." Her voice faded on the final word. He went on looking at her with complete attention.

"Yes?" he repeated.

"Well — I mean . . . *You'll* be there, won't you?"

He threw his head back and laughed, taking her free hand in both of his.

"My dear Lies, I wouldn't miss it for the world! I think you're going to make mincemeat of Tadcaster, and I'm sure your father is going to be very proud of you. As a matter of fact, *I* shall feel proud of you, because it isn't often that someone takes a rise out of that puffed-up, self-important, egotistical stick-in-the-mud!"

"Are you sure?" she ventured timidly.

"Sure as I can be of anything!" he declared. He still had not let go of her hand. And went on after another brief pause, "I do like you, you know. Very much. May I kiss you good night?"

It wasn't the first time Lies had been asked that, but it was the first time — so at least it felt to her in that instant — that she had been asked by somebody who was genuinely asking *her,* instead of just the last girl left over at the end of a dance, or a party. Blushing more furiously than ever, she gave a timorous nod, not quite knowing what to do with *this* hand holding her key and *that* hand holding her file of papers.

Not that it seemed to make any odds. He embraced her with a mixture of confidence and delicacy, and with the tip of his tongue he stroked her lips apart. For the first time (was there no end to the first times he could create?) she found herself enjoying the taste of a man in her mouth — a little of his cigars, a little of something else, a trace perhaps of the wine from dinner, a little of something *him* . . .

She had no idea how long the kiss lasted. She only knew it was marvellous, delectable, fantastic, and made shivers go through her clear down to her heels. Only the sound of the elevator doors cycling made her break off, and that was with regret.

He drew back to arm's length, not letting go of her, and gazed into her eyes.

"Thank you!" he said in a faintly impressed tone. "You're delicious!"

No boy had ever said that to her, back home in Foulwater. She felt giddy. All she really wanted to do was start again, now it was plain that the people from the elevator had turned the other way; their cheerful voices could be heard receding. On the other hand, that wasn't the only elevator, and there were already sounds that suggested another group of people was about to stop off on this floor. . . .

An idea gripped her, which was at first horrifying, then somehow incredibly natural. She almost giggled.

This is me? Me, Lies Andrassy, having this kind of thought? I don't believe it! It's shocking!

But I like it!

The other people from the elevator had stopped to say goodnight to one another, which implied that some at least of them would be coming this way in a moment. She turned to her door, raising her key, feeling magnificently brazen.

"Won't you come in for a moment?" she said, copying the phrase from something she had heard or read.

And what would be his reaction?

Prompt, and flattering, and at the same time sympathetic — everything she had ever dreamed of in a man.

"I'd love to! But — but I'd hate to keep you up so late you didn't have all your wits about you in the morning! So only if you're absolutely certain . . . ?

Without the slightest fumble she had slotted the key into the lock and given it a brisk turn. By the light which leaked from the corridor she was able to put down it and her other burden as he followed her over the threshold.

Turning, she said, "I'm not going to sleep either way, am I? So I might as well choose the nicer."

The door clicked shut on darkness as she found herself thinking again: *This is me? This is really me?*

But nineteen years of instruction in decorous, lady-like behaviour were evaporating in the heat of their renewed kiss.

He was fantastic. He was incredible. He was everything she had ever not quite dared to dream of, even down to his oh-so-polite inquiry about the Pill and her momentarily panicky admission no, and his utterly matter-of-fact follow-up question on a subject she had never talked about to a man before, and his brief pause for calculation and the assured statement that if there were a safe time in her month it must therefore be exactly now, a statement which she accepted on trust more total than even what she would have accorded to her father. Whereafter he did amazing things to her body, and made her laugh and sob by turns, and ultimately melt into his arms, asleep.

Even that, however, didn't prevent her having nightmares in which she

58

was standing on the dais of a huge lecture-hall confronted by thousands of faceless people all of whom were simultaneously bombarding her with questions she didn't know the answer to. There were many such dreams, and the last brought her awake gasping, in the conviction that Jacques too had been a dream.

He wasn't. He was there at her side, and soothing and caressing her and uttering words of reassurance.

It wasn't going to stop. He enjoyed her again, and then showered with her, and looked over the wardrobe she had brought and overrode her choice of apparel, and advised her on makeup, and escorted her to breakfast in the hotel's coffee-shop with his arm round her as though he were genuinely flattered by her company . . . an idea which, little by little, she grew timorously to accept. Even this early, even in the large stark coffee-shop, there were women looking predatorily about them, and now and then their eyes lingered on Jacques, and then on her, and their faces registered surprise before they glanced away.

She said nothing as she drank her orange juice and coffee and swallowed some dry toast, but her heart was singing, and she was telling herself that whatever happened from now on she must *must* MUST remember that she could be a whole person in her own right, not just a shadow of the mother she now only vaguely remembered because her recollections had been overlaid by her father's non-stop comparisons, not just a surrogate for someone other . . . but herself.

Jacques was gazing into her eyes again, with a penetrating stare that seemed to transfix her very soul. And saying, "Was it by any chance your first time?"

Instantly she was embarrassed, seeking a flip phrase to cover the fact. Looking anywhere but at him, she said,

"Was it so obvious?"

"Oh, I didn't mean it that way!" He caught her hand and squeezed it hard. "I swear, I couldn't have guessed except — Well, except that you were so *delighted* with everything!"

And, not letting her speak, he leaned close and whispered confidentially, "If that's how well you can make out on a 'first time,' then Tadcaster is in for a rough ride, just as I predicted!"

Which brought back her nervousness in full spate, and she had to abandon the rest of her breakfast.

But even for that Jacques had a remedy. He said in a clinical tone, "You have stage fright. All the great actors always say that if they don't they turn in a lousy performance!"

Which cheered her up all over again and carried her through the ordeal of making her way to the lecture-hall where this, the first major event of the entire convention, was scheduled to take place. The place was only half full when the chairman, a polite grey-haired man with an absent-minded manner, led her on to the platform and introduced her to the young man who was going to display photostat pages from her father's books on an overhead projector.

But among those present were Tadcaster and his entourage, and at the sight of the red-bearded man Lies's heart sank. He looked as though he had a head like a bear's, and kept snapping at even the friendliest remarks.

It encouraged her only marginally when she saw Jacques take his place in the front row and signal her okay, making a ring of his thumb and forefinger. She almost blushed again. Somewhere in the course of checking up on her father's references she had run across the real meaning of that commonplace gesture.

And then it was too late to worry any more, for the chairman was saying,

"Much as we regret the absence of Professor Andrassy, I'm sure his daughter will prove an admirable stand-in . . ."

In a tone which made it plain that he didn't believe a word of what he was saying.

The lights went down, except for a shaded one over the lectern where she had disposed her text, and the first page she was supposed to invoke as authority was projected on the big screen hanging behind her.

The last image she carried into the near-darkness was of Jacques smiling at her, and it worked the miracle. She found herself able to believe that it *was* important to know how one particular word was pronounced by people long dead on another continent. The chains of inexorable reasoning which led from one conclusion to another seized her; now and then as a fresh document appeared, copied from one of those mouldering tomes her father was so proud of, she heard a hissing intake of breath from somewhere in the shadowy hall, and once or twice the chairman actually had to call for order as a buzz of excited conversation broke out.

At the very least, she realised, she wasn't going to disgrace her father.

But the discussion period loomed, and no matter how long and loud the applause which followed her presentation of the paper, it wasn't going to save her from being roasted.

The lights went up, and there was Professor Tadcaster first on his feet and speaking without benefit of microphone, yet audible to the farthest corners of the room.

"We have heard a most seductive argument, Mister Chairman! And I'm sure it is not in any sense the fault of the young lady who has so gallantly stepped into the breach due to her father's — ah — *indisposition* . . ."

He paused, and was rewarded with sycophantic chuckles.

"No fault of hers, as I say, that it is

59

too elegant, *too* neatly tailored to fit purported evidence which I'm certain none of us here ever had the chance to examine under strict scientific conditions! Indeed, had the conclusions been reached in advance and the evidence prepared to support them, there could scarcely have been a closer match!"

This time the chuckles were more like guffaws, and some people in the seats nearest nudged one another.

"Not, of course, that I'm for a moment suggesting that there has been any falsification! Far be it from me to impute such motives to someone who, as we all know, suffered terribly in his early days, and was only able to secure a post at an academic institution here in the free world thanks to the miraculous preservation of a corpus of otherwise unknown and inaccessible texts, dealing with *mysticism* and *alchemy* and *devil-raising!*"

Lies wanted to scream. This man was a past master of snide innuendo. He had said nothing outright libellous, yet every listener knew he was undermining her father's reputation — implying that he had been mentally deranged by his experiences, hinting that whether or not the texts he relied on were authentic, they could not be regarded as authoritative because of the questionable nature of their subject-matter. How could she rebut an attack on this abstract level?

Yet she must. She must find a way, or her father would be sneered at for the rest of his life, and even in the quiet purlieus of Foulwater his colleagues would reject him. . . .

Tadcaster hadn't finished. He was winding up to a peroration.

"It therefore seems to me, Mr Chairman, that we would be ill-advised to discard our traditional understanding of these pronunciation shifts on the mere say-so of someone who, leave us face it, was not even brought up to speak a member of the Indo-European

language family as his mother tongue!"

And there it was, nakedly out in the open: the ancient hatred of the believer in Aryan culture for anyone whose parentage stemmed from Finno-Ugrian, or any other stock. . . .

Of all the people who had worshipped Aryan culture, the Nazis had been the fiercest. Didn't this man know that?

Lies looked a wordless appeal at the chairman, but he was saying to his microphone, "I think we must all agree that Professor Tadcaster has a valid point, and we shall all be most interested to know whether Miss Andrassy has a counterargument. Miss Andrassy?" — turning to her.

She sat petrified, hunting in vain for a perfect retort, for several eternal seconds. And then — oh, miracle!

"Mr Chairman!" In a voice that was nothing like as loud and impressive as Tadcaster's yet contrived to carry as far. Jacques was on his feet, attracting the chairman's eye.

On the nod, he identified himself — "Dr Jacques DeVille, Miskatonic University" — and continued.

"I think I can set Professor Tadcaster's mind at rest quite easily. We are — are we not? — considering whether Professor Andrassy's view can be substantiated, or validated, or in a word proved."

"Oh, proof!" Tadcaster was heard to say.

"Very well, I accept the correction. Shall we settle for a balance of probabilities? I am convinced Professor Andrassy is right. I think that if the gentleman in charge of the projector will be so kind as to put back what I recall as the third of the pages we have seen on the screen . . . and if the lights could be lowered again . . ."

There was a pause, and buzz of hushed but excited comment. The tenor of it was a question: who was this person from some university no one recognised?

THE PRONOUNCED EFFECT

But soon enough the lights were lowered and the page requested was again thrown on the screen.

Jacques said, "Professor Tadcaster, you can read this passage?"

"Of course!" — crossly. "It's an invocation to raise a devil called Jacaroth!"

"Would you care to read aloud the first two lines? In your preferred pronunciation, that is."

"Oh . . . ! Oh, very well!" Tadcaster rose to his feet again, just as Lies caught on. Twisting around in her chair, she recognised the passage Jacques had selected as the very phrase she had uttered under her breath when he crossed her in the hotel lobby yesterday.

And Tadcaster was reading it aloud, in accordance with the precepts he believed in — nothing like the way she herself had pronounced it.

There was a pregnant pause. Eventually the chairman said, "Dr DeVille, was that the only point —?"

"No, no! Just the first point. Nothing happened, right?"

"Ah . . . Well, nothing that any of us noticed, I guess!"

"Exactly as I would have expected. Now, Professor Tadcaster, be so good as to repeat the passage in the pronunciation Professor Andrassy advocates. I seem to recall that a transcription in IPA is available —"

"Never mind!" Tadcaster hauled himself to his feet again. "I don't for the life of me see what merely reading it over in another version is supposed to prove, but — Oh well! Here goes!"

And he spoke the words.

Afterwards Lies remembered something like a giant lightning bolt which spanned half the hall and for the moment it lasted took on the shape of a claw, or talon. Later still, but mainly in her dreams, she remembered a warning on the page preceding the invocation Tadcaster had been persuaded to read aloud, to the effect that some sort of diagram must be inscribed on the floor around the person uttering the invocation — a five-pointed star, or something equally ridiculous — but all that immediately belonged to the past.

For there was no Tadcaster, not even a trace of him, except just possibly a smell in the air as of roasting meat, and the applause for her presentation was still going on, and she was rising and bowing shyly and . . .

And being complimented on how well she had made her father's case, and asked to send him best wishes for a speedy recovery, and interrogated about the corpus of material he based his theories on, and given the phone-numbers of the editors of journals where his next paper — or, come to that, hers — would be sure of publication, and so forth.

It lasted all day.

Not until, long after midnight, she wearily opened the door of her room and switched on the light, did she think again about the amazing Dr DeVille, or the wicked Professor Tadcaster.

Then she stood transfixed, realising suddenly that since the conclusion of this morning's lecture she had heard no mention of either. They might as well never have existed.

A sheet of paper propped against her bedside lamp caught her eye. She picked it up. For a moment it conveyed a clear and unambiguous message.

Yesterday you spoke the invocation, so I came, astonished to find you protected by a pentacle of virtues: love, duty, honesty, humility, and self-sacrifice. No one else has ever called on me without the vices of selfishness and greed.

So I looked around, and decided that neither you, nor your father, nor the academic community, deserved a Tadcaster.

When he called on me, I came again in my true form, and when I went, I took

61

him with me.

But in between I came with you, and much enjoyed it. Not all of us DeVilles are as nasty as you humans like to make out. I hope you learn, soon, to make out with one of your own kind. He'll be a lucky man. Just in case you don't, you will remember one special passage in your father's books, even though you're obliged like the rest to imagine that what actually happened didn't.

I don't think we shall meet again, though. You're too much your own woman to follow in your father's footsteps all your life. Lots of love (no, love is not forbidden us!).

— Jacques Roth DeVille a.k.a. Jacaroth

* * *

Then, between blink and blink, there was a dazzling flare and a tingling in her fingertips and a reek as of brimstone, and all she could think of was how she was going to tell her father that in future he would have to present his own papers at these conventions because she was far more interested in —

Well, something else. Tomorrow would be soon enough to work out what. Happily she undressed and tumbled into bed, and by the morning Tadcaster was no more than a nightmare and Jacques a pleasant dream she was determined to live up to. ▽

HAPPILY EVER

After Cinderella married the prince
    There were bills to be paid
    And the palace roof leaked
    And next came morning sickness.

After colic and teething the children grew tall
    But Cinderella grew short of breath
    And needed bifocals
    And radical bladder surgery.

Everyone knew hers was a life
    Of fairytale proportions,
    Yes early sufferings but then the magic wand
    And the ample and romantic reward,

Therefore no one understood or cared
    When after all she became afraid of death
    And began to wonder how and why
    She stopped having a ball.

— Nancy Springer

ROCK MY SOUL

by Nancy Springer

Her secret slogan was, "I don't get mad, I get even." With this motto in mind she sat pressing her bedroom phone's redial button with grim persistence until she had gone into a trance of spite and was startled when she actually got through.

"Dedication Hour, this is the Soul of Rock and Roll, hel-LO! Who are YOU?"

It was the first time she had done this. She took a heartbeat to answer. "Michelle."

"Michelle. Well HEL-lo Mike. Does anybody ever call you Mike?"

"No." She was sort of the class nerd, too inward, always thinking too much, even though she had traded in her glasses on contacts. Who would call her Mike?

"Mickey? Shelley?"

"No." Where did he get off making fun of her name? He didn't even use his own name on the air, just called himself the Soul.

"Just plain Michelle, huh?"

Plain was the word, all right. "Yes."

He gave up on getting a reaction out of her. "Well, what can I do for you, Michelle?"

"I want to make a hate dedication."

"A *hate* dedication!" He pounced. "Oh, my goodness! How come? What has somebody done to you, Michelle?"

"Well. . . ." Well, why not? Automatically she edited her speech to sound more like a typical teenager and less like the geek she was. "There's this guy, see, and we were supposed to go to the junior prom tomorrow night. And I've got the dress and everything . . . and

today in the middle of the cafeteria he *informs* me he's going with his old girlfriend instead."

"No kidding! Like, what a slimeball!"

"Yeah." For the moment she let it go that the Soul of Rock and Roll was an obnoxious deejay, his reaction felt so good to her. Though in fact she had not managed to convey to him a quarter of the story. The boy who had broken her heart was Robbie Diehl, a biker with a messed-up head and long bleached hair and a skull painted on the back of his denim jacket, the only cool guy who had ever liked her. She had thought she loved him. And what she had gone through to catch his eye, and get her father to let her date him, and make her mother buy her a prom dress he wouldn't laugh at, was a soap opera in itself.

"He is really horse boogers, you know that?" the Soul expanded, using to the fullest the limited vocabulary he was allowed on the air. "Like, this guy is cow snot, Michelle."

"Yeah," she fervidly agreed.

"He did a tap dance on you, Michelle! Nobody should treat you like that. Tell you what. I, the Soul of Rock and Roll, am going to take you to the prom myself."

"Sure." Her voice went flat again. Some people had the balls to make fun of anything.

"I'm serious! I want to take you to the prom. It's tomorrow night, right? I'll see you then, okay?"

She said sarcastically, "Right."

"There, that's settled. Now, what

song do you want to send out to this piece of crud?"

She loved to listen to rock music, but the demands of her parents concerning her schoolwork didn't leave her much time for it. No longer sure that she knew which were the cool songs, she said, "You choose."

"All riiiight! Michelle, I got a song here I been just waiting for a real wad of scum to dedicate it to. What's this guy's name?"

"Robbie."

"Okay, Michelle, your song's going out to Robbie right now."

She hung up and lay back on her bed, turned up her bedside clock-radio and listened. After a few lines of the song she started to smile. The lyrics made her feel much better.

> You're just a big ding-a-ling
> Can't keep your hands away
> from your thing
> Look at you. My oh my
> If you ain't the Lord Of The Fly.

That was Robbie all right. She hoped he was listening somewhere public, like the Sub Shop hangout where he used to take her. The Soul of Rock and Roll had done good.

A few lines into the next song, a sticky love ballad, the phone rang. Her parents always expected her to pick it up. Without enthusiasm Michelle did so.

"Hello?"

"Hello! Were you afraid it was going to be Robbie?"

It was the Soul. She recognized his brash young voice and wondered briefly how he had gotten her number when he did not know her last name. There must be some sort of tracing device at the studio, she decided. Tracing calls was not as big a deal as TV cop shows made it seem. Her parents had once ordered a trace to stop the nuisance phone calls she got from kids who didn't

64

like her in seventh grade.

She told the Soul, "I wouldn't care if it was Robbie. I hope he heard that song. It was perfect."

"Hey, I'm glad you liked it." His tone had changed completely. "Michelle, listen, I guess you think I'm kind of a prick, but that's just on the air. Really, I — I'm a thumbsucker, okay? I hug my teddy bear every night and cry myself to sleep. Listen, I'm a lonely guy. If you still want to go to the prom, and if you need an escort, I really would like to take you."

"Give me a break!"

"I mean it! Listen, it's not like you'd look stupid with me. I'm only a little bit older than you."

He had to hang up then and take the next dedication, then call her back. He had done this twice before she began to believe him.

"I don't know. . . . What do you look like?"

"What do you want me to look like?"

"Would you get real?"

"Hey, I'm the Soul. You'd be amazed how real I can get. Who's your favorite rock star?"

"Jon Bon Jovi."

"You got it."

"You kidding? If you come here with hair like Jon Bon Jovi's, my parents won't let me out the door."

"Hey, Jon's been talking about getting a haircut anyway. It'll be cool. Trust me. What time should I come?"

"I haven't said you should come at all!"

He said, "In time to take you out to dinner beforehand, right? That way if you really hate me. . . ."

He sounded hurt. She said, "Oh, for God's sake," and he knew he had won.

"I'll pick you up around six, then."

In the morning she told her parents that her best friend had arranged for a cousin to escort her, an obliging big-brother sort of boy, very nice. Though they did not say so, she could tell they felt relieved that she was going, not so much for her sake as for the sake of the money spent buying the prom gown, which might have gone to waste. Not to speak of the hassle spent buying the prom gown. Michelle's mother had wanted long, lacy and pink, with white gloves and little puff sleeves. Michelle had wanted short, strapless and black. The compromise, lipstick red with swoop hemline, pleased neither of them.

Standing in the harlot-scarlet thing on prom night at six, pretending to fuss with her hair, already feeling the sweat crawling in her naked armpits, Michelle felt certain not only that she was going to be stood up but also that she somehow deserved to be. Sweet sixteen and almost never; who could want such a dweeb? Though she herself knew what she wanted, exactly what she desired of this magical night. She wanted someone good-looking and male to avail himself of the terrific access provided by her low-cut gown and touch her virginal breasts. She wanted maybe even to stop being virginal. And with such sluttish thoughts she would be stood up, she deserved to be stood up —

A throaty rumble sounded in the driveway out front. Michelle hurried to her bedroom window, took a look and for a moment believed that fairy tales do come true: there in the warm late-day May sunshine sat an impeccably restored 1956 Thunderbird convertible, lily white. And getting out of it was a guy who looked like Jon Bon Jovi with Michael Damien hair.

Facing him in her living room a few minutes later, she began for the first time in her young life to understand the feeling of superstitious apprehension people get when things are too good to be true.

Her date did not look just like Jon Bon Jovi after all: he looked better. Electric-blue eyes in the shadow of his dark, dark hair. Face worth fainting over. And the mouth, that sensitive,

mobile, wide and full-lipped mouth — somehow every singer she had ever worshipped was in that mouth.

What the Hell did he want with her?

Yet there on her mother's sensible Sears carpet he stood, in a classic black tux — not a rental, that tux, it fit him too well, its fabric clung to the lines of his broad shoulders, its shining lapels were ever so slightly worn. It had to be his own, he wore it with an ease most guys gave only to jeans, and there he stood charming her parents with a well-bred young man's poise and manners, and smiling at her. Smiling at her. Just a little, as if to tell her he knew she knew what he was doing.

Who was he? What was he doing?

Once her mother had mistily pinned onto Michelle's red satin bodice the white corsage he had brought her, once under way in his purring T-bird, she asked him in a small voice, "What am I supposed to call you?" The name he had told her parents had been a joke only an adult would miss.

"Soul. What else?" He turned on his expensive, deep-voiced car stereo, and it played oldies, classic rock, stuff so good that she who listened to her radio all summer every summer should certainly have heard it before. But she had never heard it, any of it.

"I thought maybe you had another name."

"Hey, Mike, I got lots of names. Just call me Soul."

"Where are you from?"

"Everywhere."

He looked exotic enough for that to be true. Skin like tan satin. High cheekbones under those shadowed eyes.

"Soul, what are you doing this for, really?"

He looked at her, and his eyes made her think of both fire and ice. She knew her parents had been fooled, that he was not nice. The knowledge thrilled her; she felt as if she had straddled a beautiful, dangerous stallion. While

65

she was with him people would look at her in awe; his beauty augmented hers. In answer to her question he said only, "You are exquisite in red," and she knew she had a right to believe him.

"Want to cruise?" he asked her.

Of course she did. Just out of sight of her house she had removed her maribou capelet and the rhinestoned spaghetti straps her mother had insisted on. Of course she wanted to be seen, in that wind-splitting albino bird of a car, bare-shouldered, her hair blowing back. With him.

She had the satisfaction of seeing heads turn all along the town loop.

"Hey. Can I tell my friends you're the Soul of Rock and Roll?"

"You want to show me off? Radical affirmative, Mikeybabe. Where are the cool dudes and their dates going for dinner?"

Into the city.

His charm was not only for her parents. By the time they got in sight of the skyscrapers he had her giggling. He took her to a tony place, bribed the headwaiter with a fifty because they didn't have a reservation, walked behind her to the red-leather booth and slid in on the same side as her. From other booths some of her classmates gawked at her, or rather at the conjunction of her and him. Without directly looking she saw their heads, spiral-permed or bristling with mousse, come up. The moment could have been made better only if Robbie and his precious Apryl had been there.

No. She was better off not seeing Robbie yet.

Where was he?

Damn him, what did she care?

Soul ordered them wine with their dinner and got away with it. After the bobbing waiter had gone he turned to Michelle and said to her gravely, "Mike, before we go much farther there's something I want to get out of the way," and he leaned over and softly, expertly

kissed her. Startled, she stiffened but did not pull back, then surprised herself by laughing out loud. He settled back into his seat and grinned.

"There, isn't that better? Now we can enjoy the dance. We won't have to spend all evening wondering about later."

She felt weightless with delight and terror, as if she could walk through walls and see mysteries. "You hot dog," she said, though not at all harshly. "Who the Hell do you think you are?"

"I know who I am."

She said, "So do I." She said, "Just a backwoods kid, right? Born in a little place on a road with no name, right? A sharecropper's cabin, maybe a row house in a steel-mill town. Your mother died when you were little. You never got along with your father. Always a rebel, always a loner —"

His head jerked around, and his eyes hushed her, frightened her for a moment, not because they blazed blue as coal fires but because they looked so naked. He said, "How do you know all that?"

"I just know." Because she thought too much about things, especially about the things schoolteachers considered peripheral, such as the music she heard on her radio and the Soul of Rock and Roll. And since he had kissed her, she felt bold and challenged and entitled to fluster him a little if she could. As if a friendly devil sat on her shoulder and told her the words she said, "You always grew your hair too long, you fought everybody, you knocked your father down and ran away from home before you were through school. You had your first girl when you were twelve, your first drink before that. Probably drugs too."

Without looking at her he said, "Reefers. That's what we called grass back then. The hard junk came later."

"I guess you did every kind of sex and drugs before you were done. You were an outlaw." She spoke the last word not

ROCK MY SOUL

without admiration.

He said quietly to his hands on the candlelit table, "Don't forget the gambling."

"Right, okay, so you shot craps too."

He looked at her then with a wincing smile. "You don't know everything after all. The gambling was the best and the worst part. Not craps. I mean the kind I did onstage, with the guitar."

"Right, I forgot to mention the guitar. About the same time as you got the first girl you would have got the guitar and learned how to make it do everything but the dishes."

Straight to her he said, "Are you gonna listen to me, Michelle? Being onstage, singing to people, it was everything to me. It was my chance to be — accepted. I'd risk and risk for that. I'd put my heart on a platter, give my soul, spend everything I had on those faces in the dark beyond the spotlights if they'd just —"

His voice faltered. She reached over and touched his hand, finding it warm and very human, like his lips. "All right," she said softly. "I'm sorry. We don't have to talk about it anymore."

"Don't ever be sorry. Hey." He recovered quickly, giving her a madcap grin. "Don't mind me. It's like I told you, I'm still crying for my mama. Never gonna get all the way grown up like you."

She made a face at him. Their dinner came; he didn't eat much, but sat and played with the black lace gloves she had laid on the table. With hungry eyes he watched her swallow lobster. He urged her to order dessert. Smiled as she forked strawberry pie.

On the way out he handed her the car keys. "You drive."

"You're putting me on, right?"

"Don't you want to?"

"Drive the Bird? Does a jock want to spit?"

She turned the radio up high, floored the Thunderbird up the ramp and onto the expressway, broke the speed limit all the way to her home town and its country club.

"Here?" Soul, loafing in the passenger seat, straightened and looked around as she turned in at the gates, showing dismay when all her wild driving had caused him none.

"Sure. Where'd you think it would be?"

"At the school, in the gym."

"This is the eighties, Soul."

"Damn, you're right." He turned on his megawatt grin, dropped whatever bothered him in the shadows behind it, changed moods like changing costume between sets.

Blipping the accelerator, toying with the power at her daintily slippered toes, Michelle circled the country club grounds twice. Enjoying the car, showing off, drawing a crowd outside with the T-bird's roar — and terrified to pull up at the door. Robbie might be there.

Yet she wanted him to see her with her heartthrob of a date.

And there under the entry awning he stood, staring, with blond punk Apryl on his arm. Michelle saw him the moment she pulled up, feeling adrenaline surge turn her to neon in her red dress, waving like a movie star at everyone but him.

She greeted friends as Soul parked the car: "Hi, Tiffany. Hi, Denise. Hi, Nicole."

"Hi-Michelle-who-is-that-GUY!"

They squealed like pigs when they found out, then mobbed him and asked him for autographs on their gowns. With rakish deejay wit he refused, making his way through them to Michelle. He put his arm around her bare shoulders and walked her toward the music. Passing Robbie and his Ape, she gave them a killer smile.

Into a ballroom decorated with balloons and crepe paper in her school colors, red and white. "Some things don't change," Soul remarked. "Dance?"

67

he asked her.

"Of course." Though she had never been a confident dancer before.

He made her look good just because she was with him, as she had known he would. He moved like a tropical god, savage, exalted, instinctive. And it was live music, hip-thrusting arm-pumping heartbeat music, rock classics plus the throbbing big-city pulse of more recent tunes. And though strapless beauties were panting all around — and though in a general way Soul was aware of them, Michelle could tell he was — he looked mostly at her, and not like someone who was doing anybody a favor. His eyes had gone soft as blue candleflame.

"Which guy is Robbie?" he asked once, and she pointed out Robbie and Apryl dancing near the edge of the ballroom. He said, "He dumped you for *that*?" and made her smile. Across the dance floor Robbie's eyes had met hers, tense, unhappy. She tried not to glance at him again.

At the punchbowl between dances, once more she asked Soul, "Why are you doing this?"

"Drinking this awful stuff? I'm thirsty."

"Smartass, you know what I mean. The dinner. Letting me drive. Being here. Being so nice when I know it has to go against your nasty nature. All of it."

He hesitated, then said, "Can't you feel it, Mike?"

"Maybe. Feel what?"

"Magic in the night. Innocence. Young love. They're always in the air thick as honeysuckle perfume on prom night."

She danced with him more and had never felt so desirable. At some time she went to the restroom. In her stall was an ancient graffito, maybe from another prom night two decades before, scratched deep: "Jim Morrison will come again." She remembered that afterward because it seemed strange in retrospect how she had noticed it that

68

night, mulling over the inscription about Morrison the Lizard King before she went out to rejoin her strange rock angel of a date and watch the crowning of a prom king and queen.

Then the slow dancing started. Softly Soul gathered her in so that her head lay on his shoulder, so that she felt his warm breathing just like that of a real human being on hers. So that they danced heart to heart.

A dance later his hand had slipped down her snugly zippered back just to her coccyx, pressing a little. His hips tilted toward her. Her red satin belly felt what was happening under his tuxedo slacks, and she did not try to stop it. Against his hard black broadcloth shoulder her lips moved, smiling.

"Awright, break it up!"

Jerking upright, she thought at first it was one of the teachers, or a chaperone. But most of them turned a blind eye by this time of night. In fact it was someone far younger and angrier: Robbie, standing spraddle-legged with his thin fists balled to fight.

"Get the fuck off her!"

Soul stood half a head taller than him, outweighed him by maybe forty pounds of muscle. "Are you cutting in?" he asked with courtesy meant to scald.

"I'd like to cut your —"

"Robbie!" Michelle wanted to slap him for acting like an asshole in front of everyone. "What are you trying to prove?"

He ignored her, saying to Soul, "I guess we all know who thinks he's Lord of the Fly."

So he'd heard the song. Suddenly Michelle felt half sorry for him. But only half. Silencing Soul with a hand on his arm, she said, "Robbie, for God's sake get out of my face. You don't own me. Go back to Ape."

"Apryl got mad and went home an hour ago." Robbie was talking straight to her and only to her, all his anger gone, only worry and vehemence left.

"Michelle, c'mon, let me take you somewhere. Listen, you gotta blow this guy. He thinks he's big stuff. You know what he wants."

Soul gave a single snort of unperturbed laughter.

"Michelle, *please*." Robbie was begging her, he was pleading, and she could hardly believe it; entreaties were not his style. "I know you're smart. Think what you're doing. This guy'll hurt you and never even notice."

Though no longer angry, she told him, "You had your chance, Robbie. Butt out."

"Michelle —"

"Hey, Robbie." With two careless fingers Soul pulled a packet of white powder from his tux breast pocket. "You seem to be a nice kid." Just the slightest leer on *nice*. "Here, I'll make you a peace offering. This is for you to get lost with." He slipped it into Robbie's rented cummerbund, patted it. At the sight of the stuff Robbie's face had changed. He looked dazed, unfocused.

"I want you to remember I tried," he said to Michelle.

Suddenly she was furious at him again, this time because he was giving up. "Get out of my life, Robbie Diehl!"

She turned her back on him. Soul pulled her into his arms. "Lady in Red" was playing, and they were slow dancing, swaying to the music. The crowd on the floor was thinning as couples slipped away, and Michelle felt scared and daring and alive all over, thinking about what was next. She belonged to none of the cliques; she had not been invited to a party, a bonfire. She would be on her own. Out in the country somewhere, probably.

"Ready?" Soul asked her softly.

"Yes."

In the white rumbling Thunderbird she snuggled against him and thought about how he had kissed her already to get it out of the way. About how his lips had felt. About him. About who the

Hell in fact he was.

She said quietly into the silence, "You're all of them. Elvis and Buddy Holly and oh, I just don't know, all those guys who did sex and drugs and rockandroll and died young."

He said just as quietly, "Not Buddy Holly. He was different."

"But the others."

"Yes. Morrison and Hendrix and a hundred others who burned out fast." He kissed her hair. "Lay your head in my lap if you want to."

She did, curling her feet up on the seat, feeling the hard muscle of his thigh swell against her cheek as he worked the accelerator. The boning of her dress had begun to hurt her; she could hardly wait to take it off. She said into the darkness under the dashboard, "You're still rebels. You're supposed to be dead."

"Don't think so much." He turned into a dirt lane and slowed the T-bird, stopping in the shadow of a woods. She sat up, then when he came to her door got out to walk with him. He put his arm around her. Over the other he carried a blanket he had brought out of the trunk. Quite a Boy Scout. Prepared.

"Moonlight," he murmured as they came out of the woods into a luminous hilltop meadow.

"Has it been awhile?"

"Yes."

"It's hard for you to be real? When you're on the air you don't bother with the body?"

"Shhh." He hushed her by taking her elbow, turning her toward him and kissing her.

A different sort of kiss, this. Just as expert, but far more urgent. Like his dancing, it was potent, primal and utterly confident. With equal confidence his hands took charge of her shoulders, the arch of her back, the tilt of her breasts. And she wanted him. She wanted him. She wanted him never to stop, what girl would not want a dream

69

lover like Soul for her first time, and there would be no condom, no danger of anything — yet the part of her that never stopped thinking, thinking, saw everything about him in that ecstatic moment as a whole, a pattern, and she knew with panicked gunsight clarity that he had to stop.

"Soul." She pushed him to arm's length; her voice was a whisper, almost a sob. "No. Don't make me love you."

He obeyed her. In the moonlight she could see his beautiful face, shaken. His hands reached toward her head, did not quite touch it.

"Michelle." His voice, a breath like hers. "Shel." No one had ever called her that. "Who's making who love who?"

"Listen." She stepped back. "Just listen to me. I figured it out, why you came. Prince in a white car. Gave me gifts. Carried me away to fairyland." She was crying without noise, the tears shining on her face. "It's love you want, isn't it? You crave love like a junkie. Growing up the way you did, it made you compulsive, a gambler for love. Doesn't matter whose. Could be anyone's. Mine will do."

"Shel —"

"You know girls like me, the plain ones. You know what you can make me do."

"Shel, what are you thinking? I would never hurt you!"

"I know that!" She stamped her foot, anguished, wishing she could sing to him what she needed to say; words alone were such clumsy plodding things. "Soul, I know Robbie's wrong. Some people you might hurt. Not me. Don't you see? It's not me I'm trying to save. It's you."

He grew as still as the night.

"A few more kisses and I would love you, adore you, worship you — and isn't that what has always destroyed you?"

She had thought it out until she could almost see it happening: the superstar singing his heart out in his terrible

need, *love me, love me,* and the many lovers tearing at his clothes, his face, his hair, drunk and riotous on wine of his sacrifice, wanting to eat him like communion bread, swallow him whole. But he would go on singing, *love me, love me,* until finally in despair of ever loving him enough the lovers would cry *Crucify him, let him die.*

Soul turned half away, staring off into the west. After a while he said faintly, "It's not the love itself that finishes me. It's — the hunger."

"Can you separate them?"

"No. Desire in me, it's like a monster. Never gets enough. It's a fire that feeds on itself."

"Until there's nothing left."

"Yes." He turned to her with a stark look. "Why do you want to save me? I've never wanted to save myself."

She stood with the tears drying on her face. "Because you're beautiful," she said. "That's all." Hoping he would always be beautiful and knowing he would never be wise; he would never change, never grow, never learn. Knowing that for his own sake she must not let him touch her again.

"You're very different," he said softly, scanning her as if to memorize her. "You see through me. I've never met anyone like you."

"I almost blew it," she told him. "I think you'd better take me home right away."

He reached into a pocket, handed her something that jingled like money: his keys. "Take the Bird and go," he said. "I'm not as strong as you."

"You want me to just leave you out here?"

"I'll fade in a few hours. So will the T-bird. Better hurry. I want very much to kiss you." He kept his hands clenched at his sides.

She left, turning once to wave goodbye, looking back once more when she got to the white car. He stood on the hilltop in the moonlight, watching steadily after her.

Driving, she grew conscious that she was shivering, and covered her shoulders with the maribou wrap that had lain all night abandoned by his gearshift. Back home, she parked the car around the corner from her house but kept the keys, hiding them in her evening bag as she walked to the door. Her corsage, she noted, had wilted. All the lights were on, bright; her mother was waiting up for her.

"Where have you been? The prom ended two hours ago!"

"Just driving around and talking, Mom."

"You should have called. I've been worried sick you were with the wrong crowd. Did you hear about Robbie?"

Robbie?

"They had to take him to the hospital. He thought there were lizards crawling on him. Cut himself all over with a razor trying to get them off."

Robbie —

"Some kind of dope he took drove him screaming crazy."

Oh, Robbie.

"I didn't know Robbie took drugs. You are not to see him again, Michelle, do you hear me? I don't want you going near him anymore. I'm so glad you found a nice boy to take you to the prom tonight. Did you have a good time, dear?"

She pleaded weariness, went upstairs and got out of the red gown, leaving it on the floor. Then she lay on her bed but did not sleep. When dawn started to light her room she got up and picked up the gown so her mother would not yell at her, and emptied her fancy evening bag. The Thunderbird keys were not there. Sometime they had dissolved into air.

Before her parents were up she called the hospital. No, it would not be possible for her to see Robbie Diehl. She could send him a card care of the psychiatric ward. His condition was stable.

No, he was not expected to be released anytime soon.

She went back to bed, keeping her eyes closed when her mother opened her door to offer her breakfast. Since she had been up late her parents ate and went to church without her. She did not have to deal with them until Sunday dinner, when she told them as little as she could.

In early afternoon her phone started to ring. Tiffany, Denise, Nicole, all sounding shocked and pale. No one, least of all Michelle, wanted to talk much about the Soul of Rock and Roll; it was all Robbie, Robbie, Robbie who would never be the same. Midafternoon, dazed, Michelle found herself lifting the receiver yet once again and this time listening to Apryl sobbing.

"It's — all — my — fault."

"No, Apryl, not really." Michelle had little use for Apryl, but truth was truth. Apryl had not given a packet of white powder to Robbie.

"You don't know," blurted April between wet sounds. "I made him — take me to the prom. I told him I'd — I'd k-k-kill myself if he didn't —"

Robbie, you sap, why did you fall for it?

"— so he did. But you're the only one he — he cares about. You were — you were straightening him out, and then I had to come along and mess him up again. If I'd just let him alone none of this would have happened."

In a weird way that was true. If Robbie had taken her to the prom he would never have met the Soul of Rock and Roll.

Sundays were always long. So peaceful, quiet, smiling, virtue-imbued. This was the longest Sunday of all. Michelle avoided her parents, wore her oldest jeans for comfort.

That evening at nine sharp, as if an alarm had gone off, she shut herself in her room and turned on her radio.

"HEL-lo, lovers, this is the Dedication Hour, and the Soul of Rock and Roll is ready to hear you bare your hearts."

She would never in all her life forget that voice.

"And for once I'm going to bare mine." His tone changed, in that chameleon way he had, completely. "Tonight every love song I play is dedicated from me to Michelle."

She waited, listening, lying on her bed with one hand to her lips. Knowing he wanted her to call him. Knowing what would happen when she didn't.

He took all the usual syrupy requests — with something less than his usual mouthy flair, she noticed. He sounded subdued tonight. Muted, like an old guitar. She pictured him out there in the night somewhere, in a metal tower, suspended in a limbo between earth and sky. Bodiless in darkness.

"Michelle," he said into that darkness, "the last song tonight is all for you. If you're listening, Shel, or even if you're not, this is yours alone. Straight from the Soul."

> Lady you see right through me
> You get to me
> You undo me.
> Lady I've never felt so melted
> Never been so broken into
> As by you
> My Lady of Love.

Like "Lord of the Fly," it was not a song she had ever heard before. She had an idea where they both came from. If all those blaze-of-glory-gone-by rockers could get together enough juice to manipulate telephone wires and airwaves and generate themselves a wet-dream body, they could get together enough to make music. She imagined they had

one Hell of a band.

The song faded into ads. Her phone rang.

Knowing her parents were planted on the sofa and would not answer it, she let it ring four times, until the first yell sounded from downstairs, before she answered it.

"Hello?"

"Shel."

It was him, as she had known it would be, and it would take maybe one more hour together for her to fall in love with him. And not too many days after that for the finiteness of her love to destroy him by way of his infinite need. She said quietly, "Yes, I was listening."

"Shel, I mean every word of it. You've got me down on my knees. I've never — nobody's ever understood me before, nobody's ever played it straight with me the way you do. Please. I've got to see you again."

Had to see her again or he'd live. And living was growing. And he couldn't have that, could he?

He said into her silence, "Shel, I'm begging you."

In the shadows behind her eyes she heard Robbie screaming. She said, "All right. Yes."

"Milady. Thank you."

"Come tomorrow, Milord. Be Axl Rose, okay? In a new Corvette. Candy-apple red."

She would skip school in the wanton spring weather. As Robbie lay strait-jacketed and sedated in a darkened hospital room, somewhere out in the honeysuckled countryside she would take the Soul of Rock and Roll and unzip him utterly.

Before she went to bed Michelle painted her nails scarlet.   ∇

SWAN'S LAKE

by Susan Shwartz

Denied even the small luxury of a maudlin binge, the tutor Wolfgang had drunk himself sober while the sailors spent the night dragging the lake. Now, clouds scudded over the rising sun. It looked pale and impossibly remote. Wind rose and scattered great white feathers of spume onto the rocks. Tolling from the lake, bells echoed from castle to cliffs and down to the village. The lake's surface teemed with tiny boats on which tiny figures moved silently, heavily. They lowered the great seining nets, raised them, then lowered them again and again. Each time, their movements were more and more hopeless.

Finally, the boats came in to shore. The thirteen swans who floated there in a silent cortege parted, as if to escort the fishermen to the docks. Wolfgang was waiting at the landing, flushed but otherwise far, far too sober. Benno, who had been the Prince's closest friend, stumbled as he disembarked. The fishermen steadied him. Wolfgang wrapped his own marten-lined cloak about the younger man, who was trembling, and hugged him for a moment. Then, he pulled out the inevitable flask of brandy.

Benno tried a weak grin; Wolfgang's fondness for the grape was an old joke among . . . there were just two of them left now to mourn. Abruptly, both men looked at the flask and winced at the coat of arms stamped into the heavy silver. The flask was a new one, Prince Siegfried's last gift to his old tutor only

a day ago. It had been the anniversary of his birth — his twenty-first birthday and his last.

"We dragged the entire lake, Wolfgang," muttered Benno. "And do you know what we found? One odd white rock, shaped like an owl, some branches, and an odd boot or two. Sweet suffering Christ, how shall I tell the Queen her son is drowned?"

Wolfgang shut his eyes in grief, wishing that it were merely the pain of a hangover. Benno was just Prince Siegfried's age. He had tutored them both, birched the one and scolded the other when both were boys. They were the only sons he was likely to have, and he had entertained bright hopes for the men they might become.

Last night had been Prince Siegfried's twenty-first birthday. As always, the royal Birthday was celebrated with a ball. At this year's Ball, however, he had been formally invested as Heir. That was — or was supposed to be — his moment to choose a bride. At supper, with trumpets before and fireworks thereafter, the betrothal should have been announced.

Six lovely princesses, all young, all dancers, had been invited so that he might make his choice. They had been half in love with him already, had waited, hoping wistfully that he might hand one of them the bouquet that Queen Hedwig Elisabeth had laid in his hand. But the Prince had wanted no part of them. Even after Her Majesty had risen from the throne and rebuked him sharply, the Prince had drawn

73

apart.

God knows, it had not been that the Prince didn't know what his duty was. Wolfgang had spent hours dinning the customs and proprieties of the Birthday into the Prince's hard head, but the boy had not wanted to settle into life as Heir, husband, and — inexorably — father quite so quickly. He had wanted time to dance, to hunt, and to laugh. Had any of those six dreaming, dancing princesses wanted a friend, a brother, a dance partner, she might have twined him about her delicate fingers, but no, they had had to dream about *him* . . .

And then *they* had entered the room in a flash of splendor. The dark, glittering princess in her gown black as night and sewn with stars and her tall, avian father strode into the ballroom, accompanied by a retinue of magnificent strangers from the warm southern lands, outshining the somber Northern court. They looked more regal than even the Queen.

The man had gestured. The Princess had danced; and their retinue, from golden baskets, had flung apricots, dates, amber pears, and glowing Valencia oranges to an astonished court, greedy as children for that one evening. For all the good, though, that the court had had of them, they might as well have hurled poison.

The black-clad Princess had dazzled Prince Siegfried. He had needed no reminders of duty to declare his eternal love and homage. No sooner were the words out than her father extracted the Prince's solemn vow to wed his daughter. But it had all been a trick. Once the promise was out, they taunted Siegfried with a vision of a maid he had betrayed — he who had never willingly harmed man, woman, or child in all his life. Even then, the girl had tried to warn him. Her white hands fluttered like tired wings, but, intent on his betrothed, he did not see.

Finally he noticed — or was permitted to notice. When he saw the maid who had trusted him weeping in despair, he too despaired. Then those two regal sorcerers had laughed at him, scoffed at his pleas, and disappeared in a crack of thunder as sharp as heartbreak. The white flowers of what should have been a bridal bouquet lay on the parquet of the dance floor, petals bruised and scattered.

Wolfgang shook himself like an old dog. *Faithful hound, worn out in my Prince's service,* he thought. *I'd hoped to spend these last years at his fireside, with children tugging at my ears and heartstrings.*

He sighed and took Benno's arm. The surviving lad hadn't yet learned that what could not be cured *must* be endured; and God knows, there was no cure for this sorrow, short of the grave. Wolfgang could feel Benno's bone and muscle under the heavy cloth of his cloak. The man was young, taut, fit; yet Wolfgang knew that during the long climb up the clifflike rocky stair to the Castle, he was the stronger man.

"These same miserable rocks . . ." Benno muttered. Wolfgang tightened his grasp. This very dawn, the Prince had hurled himself from these very rocks, following the maid who refused to live loveless and enslaved.

"You dare not think of that, lad," he said.

Behind them came the tread of heavy fishermen's boots that all but drowned out their scandalized whispers and hisses to one another not to bother the gentry with the clack of their gossip. For all Wolfgang cared, they could go straight to Father Bertwald and let him deluge their little boats with holy water. There was no comfort for any of them either in faith or in reason right now, as Wolfgang knew.

Well, he had spent many pleasant, tipsy years as the mildest of Epicureans, preaching pleasure and joy — always in moderation, though; he would

KELLY FREAS 89

not be the first philosopher who turned Stoic in his old age.

"Lord Benno, Master Wolfgang!" a voice trained to halloo out over wind and rain hailed them. "Look over there!"

Young Jurgen knelt beside a boulder the size of a turret. He reached forward, raising by her slender wrists a girl who would have been lovely had she not been so terrified. Her hands bled from grubbing up pebbles to cast at the fishermen. Her lips were pulled back in a silent shriek. Her dark eyes were full of anguish, but no tears. Though a cloak trimmed with ashen feathers lay crumpled beneath her, she was clad only in her long hair. It too was the color of cold ashes on the hearth; but when the pale sun struck it, it gleamed.

Benno's head shot up. Angry recognition began to smolder in his amber eyes, and Wolfgang could follow his thoughts. Change that maid's hair from ashen to ebony, stitch a proud crimson smile on that pallid face, garb her in black satin and lace, not the pathetic grace of her own skin, and she would resemble the sorceress who had destroyed their Prince.

Wolfgang jabbed the younger man with his elbow. "Not now, fool!" he hissed. Not when they were both worn out and heartsore; they could imagine anything. But as Wolfgang gazed at Jurgen, the young fisherman who held his surprising new catch, he didn't think that he imagined how much the man resembled the last Prince. Both men had dark hair that flowed over tanned brows, brown eyes more apt to flash with friendship than with anger or scorn, and wide, generous mouths.

For that matter, both men resembled Prince Siegfried's father, who had always loved his people well . . . far too well, muttered Queen Hedwig Elisabeth, who had reasons of her own for that sour, pinched-lip look she too often wore.

Benno too stared at the sailor and the girl whom he struggled to enfold in the strange feathered cloak. So like the Prince and that dark Princess; and yet, where Siegfried had been all fire and dreams, this Jurgen was sober and kind. Where the dark Princess had been sure and brilliant and cruel, this maid was terrified past anguish. She flailed her arms in a feeble attempt to ward off the cloak's soft embrace.

"Little lostling, see, it's warm and fine. I can give you nothing else that is so fine," he coaxed.

"Stop trying to shoulder me aside," Benno hissed at his former tutor. "I swear, that girl is . . ."

As if sensing the rage in the grieving man, the girl flung herself onto the ground. Her white naked back turned in as graceful a line as the neck of a swan. Jurgen reached down and gathered her in to rest against his rough jacket. His weathered hands smoothed down her long, silver-gray hair, which tangled and clung to his fingers. He glanced up reproachfully at Benno.

"What's thy name, lostling?" he asked.

Her lips moved, but no sound came.

"A mute!" Benno exclaimed under his breath, his fingers moving in an old sign. "The other one could laugh, at least."

The girl's lips parted again. Jurgen bent closer to listen. He was half in love with the chit already, thought Wolfgang. Though he himself could hear nothing, Jurgen nodded. "Dillie," said Jurgen. "Is that your name?"

The maid shook her head.

Dillie? Too close by far to Odile, the name of the dark princess. Yet, Jurgen had not been to the ball, had not seen her . . . would not know. And how could Wolfgang be so sure?

"Shall I call you that till you tell me your true name?" Jurgen asked. "Yes? Here now, then, Dillie, just let me wrap this . . ." Again, the girl writhed away from the feathered cloak. Her back and bare legs were very white. Some of the fishermen crossed themselves or reached for charms. Others simply looked away.

Jurgen fumbled at his jacket, and Wolfgang winced at the thought of the coarse wool and leather against that white, white skin.

"Give him your cloak for her," he hissed at Benno. After all, it had belonged to him first. He would go colder this winter so that this foundling would be warm, but the Prince would have expected nothing less of him. (The Queen, however, would bite her lip at the tutor's extravagance.)

Slowly, Benno took off the cloak and offered it, though with little of his usual courtliness. With a nod of thanks, Jurgen accepted the garment and laid it tenderly over the girl's slender shoulders. Then he swung her up into his arms.

"My mother has lacked a daughter. And see, Dillie trusts me," he explained. "Besides, you will not need me up at the Castle."

That one had a head on his shoulders, Wolfgang thought. It would be savage cruelty for Queen Hedwig Elisabeth to have to face a man as like her only son as his brother.

A murmur arose from Jurgen's companions, and he glared at them. "Will it satisfy you if I fetch Father Bertwald and the Sacraments to her?" he asked them, his chin lifted defiantly. It could have been the Prince himself speaking. Wolfgang had been proud that His Highness had grown up without superstitions; he himself had never shared the local beliefs in woodwoses or shapechangers, creatures who shuddered away from the touch of cold iron or garlic (so fine in venison or a stew!) or who recoiled at the peal of church bells. These villagers and the fishermen gave more heed to herbs and berries, markings on old stones, than to the Creed.

Dillie's slender white feet dangled as Jurgen carried her down the track toward the village. She glanced out once, saw the white rock like an owl's skull in the center of the lake and hid her face in Jurgen's shoulder. Benno stirred at Wolfgang's side, ready to follow.

"The Queen needs us more," Wolfgang reminded her son's friend.

They climbed the last rough stairs, and still Wolfgang could hear Jurgen's voice. "Now then, no need for this fear. Who would hate a pretty thing like you?"

Many, feared the tutor. One of them walked at his side.

Above them pealed out the chapel bells: nine strokes of the passing bell for a man, followed by twenty-one more — one ring for each year of the Prince's life.

Night was her friend. At night, the hearthfire died into embers so comforting to her eyes after the glare of daylight. At night, her new friends, the old woman with the warm eyes and gentle hands, the young man who had carried her down from the rocks she feared, would fall asleep. Now they even left their door unlatched. Now they trusted her enough to believe that she would not wander up the cliffs or down to the shore.

She feared the cliffs, of course. As for the lake, the one time she had gone there, the water had been brackish . . . *like the sea,* a stranger's voice whispered in her mind. Dead fish littered the shore. She had heard Jurgen and the suspicious men who stared at her too much talking that over. She had eluded them and run to the water's edge, but the white swans had been there, and had left the ruined water to hiss at her and dart forward, stabbing at her bare feet with their strong bills, flapping their wings in her face until she recoiled and, amazingly, found herself caught up and cradled in Jurgen's arms.

But the swans had reminded her of what remained for her to do. For a week, she had waited, regaining her old friends' trust. Then, silently, she slipped from her pallet, flung the fur-trimmed cloak, gift of the young man with the angry eyes, about her, and let herself out the door. The hearthcat stirred at her going, then laid its head with its black and white mask back down and slept again, white paws twitching as it hunted in its dreams.

She ran to the cemetery. Already, she had been this way twice before: once when the man in black, whom they called Father Bertwald, splashed sweet water on her face and chanted strange words over her; a second time when more people than she ever dreamed could exist in one place crowded into the banner-hung chapel. The weight of grief would have made her faint if Jurgen had not taken her away. How they had muttered at that!

It was time, and past time, for her to act, and then to be free. No need, now, for her to have to enter the chapel again. What she sought lay outside, tenderly clustering by the old, leaning stones that the villagers tended with such care. Fragile blue asters, cold, perfect asphodels. Rue, yes, and fragrant rosemary. She broke them from their stalks, breathed upon them, and began to weave them into garlands. Though she realized that she had never done such work before in her life, her fingers were very nimble. Always before, she had had servants, maids . . . *had* she, indeed? Only that day, she had scrubbed the hearth; impossible to think that ladies waited on her as if they had been serving girls themselves; yet that was what the fragments of her memory assured her was true.

The moon soared high in the night sky, giving her light for her work, and she wove faster. As she worked, she moved her lips in silent song. The pain that had waked her in the night, that had forced her to creep onto the ledges below the castle to watch swans and

stones and sorrowful men, seemed to ease somewhat.

Night after night, urgent compulsion woke her. She stole to the graveyard to pray her silent prayers over her weaving: aster, asphodel, rosemary, and rue, each bound into a chaplet tied with three strands of her silvery hair. Silvery hair? She remembered rising once in the middle of the night, and catching sight of herself in well-polished brass. How odd: she had remembered her hair as being dark. It was always dark in the terrible nightmares that mention of a tainted lake, a Prince who had hurled himself into its depth, brought on. The grief of such events seemed to heal her somewhat too. Each chaplet eased her burden further. Now she found herself able to murmur, not just to move her lips.

"I knew you could speak. Try again, Dillie! Try to speak to me! Say my name!"

She started violently. Lilies scattered from her skirts over her feet. Before her stood Jurgen, her rescuer and her friend. His face was set and pale. Her lips formed his name, her shattered memories all but reminded her of charms and artifices, but no sound came from her.

"What is this rubbish?" he asked her, his voice as angry as the eyes of some of the villagers, yes, and even some of the castle-folk when they looked through her, or when they spoke of the ruin of their livings or of their dreams. "Is this witchery that you do here?" He held out a hand to her. Despite its strength, it shook.

She shrank back. Jurgen was so strong. In an instant, he could tear up the garlands that she had already woven; and already, it was nearly autumn. A week, two weeks more; and no flowers would bloom until spring. And by then, it would be too late. The white stone in the center of the lake, the one shaped like an owl — by spring, it would have poisoned the lake past all remedy.

By spring, then, the swans, too weak to fly south, would have frozen or starved, assuming that no bowman shot them first. The girl felt an urge to flee with the garlands that she had woven, but forced herself to remain crouched beside a leaning gravestone, watching Jurgen as he forced one callused hand out to touch a wreath.

She nodded and held it out to him while, with her free hand, she stroked his cheek. He laughed hoarsely and gathered her up into a bearlike hug. She rubbed her face against his rough garments.

"Maybe you swept up your footprints, Dillie, but this morning, the hem of your cloak was wet. So I watched you . . . and followed you here when you slipped out."

She had no words yet to plead with him, so she followed him with her eyes.

"You want me to let you finish whatever this is, don't you?" he asked, and she nodded vehemently.

"Can you tell me why it is so important to you? Do you not know what people might say if you are seen here?"

This is life, freedom, atonement! she thought, but had not the words to say so.

"You wish I could understand too? Dillie, this is dangerous. People might fear . . . some think you're half a woodsprite now. Can you promise . . . would you swear before Father Bertwald — that what you do holds no harm?"

She nodded. Then she felt Jurgen sigh. He leaned down and kissed her hair. "Then that's good enough for me. Just try not to be seen, love. If people saw you in the graveyard by night, I don't know how I could explain it."

As if sealing a bargain between them, he handed her back the chaplet. Solemnly, she took it and laid it in its hiding place with the other ten. Each was as fresh now as the one that she had most recently woven.

Now she realized that there were other ways than words to tell him what she did here. Hesitantly at first, fearful of her feet on the rough ground, she began to dance. Her toes ached at first with the unfamiliar, lovely motions; but as she danced, she gained strength and passion. Memory of dancing flowed back into her, dancing before another man with Jurgen's face. She smiled, but her smile lacked the craft of the last time she had thus danced.

About the only thing, Wolfgang thought, about being regarded as an old, scholarly sot was that people confided and gossiped when he went among them. The late King and Queen Hedwig Elisabeth had found his ability to charm stories from their subjects very helpful. Wolfgang himself saw it as a mixed blessing. Long before the folk at the castle heard, Wolfgang knew that the changeling down in the village wandered by night in the graveyard, where she picked flowers and sang spells over them. Worst yet, when the moon was high, rumor had it, she would dance amidst the tombstones.

Old men sleep little: the next moonrise found Wolfgang kneeling in the chapel where the Prince's banner (a swan, argent, on an azure field beneath a crescent moon) overhung his empty tomb. That they had never found Prince Siegfried's body was a familiar, even a homely grief by now.

Moonlight filtered through the delicate rose window, moonlight and something more: lightnings without rain or thunder. The night before, St. Elmo's fire had flickered on the castle turrets. Some called it a sign of the trouble that had befallen. Fire walked the roofs, and, in the lake, which had fed the people roundabout for as long as anyone or his grandsire could remember, the fish died because the water turned from fresh to salt. The fishermen had taken especially to avoiding one spot in the lake after a boat capsized by the great white rock that resembled a snow owl. Now there was mourning in the village, some hunger, and the promise of more privation in the cold season that approached. And the swans whom some called the village's luck were feeble.

Wolfgang read those signs like a primer. Perhaps they were indications of magic and perhaps not; he neither knew nor cared. They were, however, signs that soon the people would seek a scapegoat for their misfortunes. A lost girl who never spoke and who haunted tombs by night was perfect for such a role.

Nor was it only the commons who sought someone to blame. Wolfgang had seen Benno speaking with those strangers from the East Marches. One of them bore a heavy, black-letter volume. *Malleus Maleficarum,* the Hammer of Witches, was stamped on the worn leather binding. Wolfgang had glanced into that book once and seen only torture of the helpless, the deluded, and the simple. He saw a mute, frightened child strapped to one of the instruments in the crude, lurid woodcuts, her mouth open in a silent scream. How would she confess, even with a lie, if she could not speak?

And what of Jurgen, who loved her? He was strong enough to withstand torture for a long time, yet his only crime was to love a maid whom he had rescued. Wolfgang thought of the young man, so like the dead Prince, his fingers crushed, his spirit broken, and he was hard put not to cry out in grief.

Benno was too angry to judge wisely. But give him his due; there was reason to fear.

Shivering a little in the dank chapel, Wolfgang rose from creaking knees, and limped out through the small door in the chapel's carven narthex.

What he saw froze him in his place. Like children intent on the most innocent of games, Jurgen and the girl knelt in the shadow of a tombstone so old that the engraving on it wasn't honest Latin, but spiky, angular chisel blows and serpentine scrawls, much worn away by generations of the curious. The maid's eyes were fixed upon her lap, and Jurgen's eyes upon her with such an intensity of love and protectiveness that it hurt Wolfgang to watch. Just so Prince Siegfried had regarded Odette that night before the fatal dawn. Just so he had regarded the dark witch Odile before she had scorned him. Just so he had looked before he and Odette embraced for the last time, and he had followed her up the cliffs to hurl . . . Wolfgang would not think of that. It had taken an eternity for the two slender bodies to hit the water.

He glanced up at the quivering stars and fancied that he could hear a crystalline, sweet humming. After a time, he looked around. The stars were silent, but the humming continued. Gradually, he realized that it came from the lips of the girl who he had believed was mute.

"One more garland," Jurgen's voice came low. "And then what?"

The girl held out a chaplet adorned with pale, funereal flowers and what Wolfgang realized had to be her own hair. Jurgen took it and thrust it into hiding. The girl rose and began to dance, a series of steps about casting away, of greeting, of relief. At first, her motions were halting, but they gained speed and assurance as she circled the stones. For an instant, she stood poised as if listening to the music Wolfgang had thought that the stars were singing. Then she began an intricate, exultant series of flashing turns, her face spinning about, always turning toward Jurgen, spinning faster and faster with innocent, unselfconscious bliss . . . there was joy in that dance, and hope, and then the stirrings of some sad, benign power . . .

"Just as I told you," Benno's voice

SWAN'S LAKE

from the shadows broke the lovely spell. "Witch . . . and her warlock with her."

The girl broke out of her spins. Only her astonishing grace kept her from falling and harming herself. She staggered off-balance only for an instant, then rose to curtsy to Benno.

"Didn't I tell you that the village lay under a spell?" Benno demanded. "We'll have the good fathers here examine the witch and her lover. Take them!" He beckoned, and the black-robed strangers emerged from the shadows. Their eyes glistened in the light of the torches that they carried along with the heavy book in their arms, and they could not take their eyes from their prey.

If she had her voice back, the girl would have shrieked that she needed more time. Now they would seize her, those cold-eyed men in black, so unlike the gentle man who had laid hands on her brow, gazed into her eyes, and not recoiled from her. He had even blessed her, "Not for what thou art, but for what thou wouldst be." These men saw only what they wanted her to be — what she had been. Dark beauty. Witch. Fallen princess, not a creature of ashes, love, and hope.

Though the men of the village shrank from the task, they finally came forward to seize her. She spread her fingers wide, as if clutching at fragile stems to stay rooted where she was. When they pulled her away, the flowers came free in her hands. Frantically, she began to weave them into one last crown.

"What about her man?" came a voice behind her.

Poor Jurgen had done her only good. How much he looked like the Prince that she had betrayed while she was Odile. But he loved *her* as she was now. If he kept very still, very silent now, he just might have a chance to live.

Of course, he did not.

It might be justice that she be for-

bidden to accomplish her dream of expiation. It might be that the fear and the silence were not sufficient penance; perhaps she needed further punishment before she could earn forgiveness. But Jurgen was innocent. Odile turned in her captors' lax hold to look at the fisher. Then — and how she despised herself for her fear! — her glance slid over to the bushes in which she had hidden the chaplets.

"What does she stare at?"

"Look!" ordered one of the men in the stark black robes.

Using a long stick, a reluctant fisherman drew the chaplets from their hiding place and flung them to lie at Jurgen's feet.

"In my country," the man opened the thick book, "there is a simple test for witches. Fling the witch into the water. It is the natural property of bodies to sink. Should she float, however, she is no woman but a witch . . ."

"What if she sinks?" The old man, the red-nosed one called Master Wolfgang, asked that contemptuously.

"Then she dies in a state of grace. Trust heaven to know its own. Unless, of course, you yourself dive in to save her. But I do not think that would be wise."

Wolfgang stared at Benno and his witchfinders. How Prince Siegfried would have mourned to see hate transforming his friend. Benno would never permit this girl to be fished out before she drowned. Natural properties be damned, Wolfgang snorted to himself. Hadn't these fools ever seen a swimmer? Certainly, they smelled as if bathing were something unknown to them. The live body's natural property was to float — unless you had to count anyone who was able to float as a witch. In that case, the witchfinders would simply have to condemn the village, the castle, and their own ignorant selves. Best not even give them the glimmerings of such

81

an idea.

Wolfgang gestured at Jurgen to stay down. Probably the girl was doomed, but there was still a chance that Jurgen could be gotten off. Then the fisherman looked at her as she stood between her tall, reluctant guards — his old friends — and she tore away from them, twining the flowers she still clutched into a chaplet like those on the ground.

The stranger-priests shouted in outrage and holy horror. "Even now she works her spells. To the rocks with her!" They dragged her hands down to her sides and pushed her up the steep rock stairs, past the point at which Jurgen had found her, lost his heart, and maybe his soul along with it, all in the same moment, until they reached the peak from which Siegfried and his beloved had cast themselves. Wolfgang swallowed hard and looked away. He was glad to see that Benno looked sick.

You've got second thoughts now, have ye, lad?

From this height, the village looked very small, and the lake seemed leaden, except for the white owl-shape of the rock in its center. Now it resembled the skull of some bird of prey. By the shore floated the swans, their graceful necks bowed, their feathers dingy, and their movements sluggish, as if they were sickened by the water in which they lived. As the fishermen dragged the girl to the cliff's edge, the swans raised their heads to look at her. One opened its bill as if it might sing for the first and last time.

The girl shrank back, but her guards forced her to the brim as the blackrobes muttered their prayers of exorcism.

Wolfgang muttered a child's prayer, which was all he could remember at the moment. He reached for his flask, but found it empty. Then he heard shouts, rapid footsteps pounding up behind him. He felt a hard hand shove him aside — to think that he, at his age, would be set sprawling thus! Jurgen

82

raced up to where Odile stood pinned. His arms were full of garlands: aster and asphodel, rosemary and rue.

Men tried to stop him or trip or hold him, but he dodged them all. *My poor lad,* Wolfgang thought. *You have doomed yourself. Just like the Prince.*

What looked like half of the men of the fishing fleet bore down upon Jurgen, and Benno drew his sword. But Jurgen rushed to the cliff's brink and tossed the garlands into the water. Then he took the girl into his arms.

"At last we will be together," he said, and laid his cheek against her ashen hair as it whipped about them like the banner of some forlorn but starlit hope. People were reluctant to compel them, Wolfgang saw, and he had a brief, bleak hope that they might yet be spared.

"Get a boat pole up here and *push* them off!" shouted one man, and that hope quickly died.

Jurgen tightened his arms about the girl and moved between her and the mob. She gazed out of the water, where the flower crowns, twelve of them and one, floated untouched by the salt that slowly was killing all else within the lake.

Slowly, painfully, the swans came toward them. Odile raised her eyes. The night *those others* had died, a storm had risen. How she remembered the lightning and the wind. The wind! A tiny breeze blew, then strengthened, tossing her hair about her hot face. In toward the thirteen swans drifted the garlands. Each swan extended her neck, then plunged it delicately beneath a garland to emerge crowned with asphodels and aster, rosemary and rue . . . and a lock of silver hair.

The hands that pinioned Odile's arms went limp. She flung herself forward to kneel over the cliff, her arms outstretched. Tears burned down her face, and she fought to breathe. As the crowned swans turned in toward the land, moving more surely, more swiftly with every yard, she drew breath in a great sob.

"Odile," Jurgen tested the name, which had been that of the dark princess. "Is that truly your name?"

She had her hands over her face now, and tears dripped into them. Now he would know for certain, and now he would turn from her. She had all but cost him his life . . . and she might yet do that too. But he was kneeling at her side, was forcing her hands away so he could gaze into her eyes.

Now her tears dropped down her fingers and splashed into the lake far, far below.

"You can weep now," he marveled. "Odile — is that truly the name I should call you?"

"Give me another!" she cried. "Call me love!"

She buried her face against him. Now that the constraint that had locked her voice was gone, her tears came easily and brought healing with them. Where they dropped into the lake, light danced on the water. Blue ripples, the color of icemelt, spread out until the lake gleamed with healthful splendor. The owl-shaped rock began to crumble. The ripples caught it up, and it fell in on itself, and was gone.

As the sun rose, its light turned the long, flowing strands of Odile's hair to silver and shed glory on the crowns worn by the thirteen swans. It even cast a healing light on the faded gilt letter of the priests' book in the instant that they turned to go. But the lovers, lost in one another, did not see them leave, nor did they notice the transformation of the lake.

Not until gasps of wonder broke their wonderment in one another did they notice the thirteen maids who set bare foot on shore and walked toward the village. Each wore a long white shift through which her flesh glowed like spring roses. And on her long, gleaming hair, each wore a crown of flowers and herbs that cast a rare, lasting fragrance.

The swan-maids walked to the church where Father Bertwald stood waiting. Hand in hand, Jurgen and Odile followed them. And the bells rang out to celebrate their wedding.

∇

MOVING?

Don't forget to take *WT* with you! Send your old address (don't forget the zip code) and your new one. We'll make sure you receive copies without delay.

Not a subscriber yet? Easily remedied! Turn to the inside back cover for more information. Remember, the best way to support a magazine is directly ~ through a subscription.

THE LOST ART OF TWILIGHT

by Thomas Ligotti

I have painted it, tried to at least. Oiled it, watercolored it, smeared it upon a mirror which I positioned to rekindle the glow of the real thing. And always in the abstract. Never actual sinking suns in spring, autumn, winter skies; never a sepia light descending over the trite horizon of a lake, not even the particular lake I like to view from the great terrace of my great house. But these *Twilights* of mine were not merely all abstraction, which is simply a way to keep out the riff-raff of the real world. Other painterly abstractionists may claim that nothing is represented in their canvases, and probably nothing is: a streak of iodine red is just a streak of iodine red, a patch of flat black equals a patch of flat black. But pure color, pure light, pure lines and their rhythms, pure form in general all mean much more than that. The others have only *seen* their dramas of shape and shade; I — and it is impossible to insist on this too strenuously — I have *been* there. And my twilight abstractions did in fact represent some reality, somewhere, sometime: a zone formed by palaces of soft and sullen color hovering beside seas of scintillating pattern and beneath rhythmic skies; a zone in which the visitor himself is transformed into a formal essence, a luminous presence, free of substance — a citizen of the abstract. And a zone (I cannot sufficiently amplify my despair on this point, so I will not try) that I will never know again.

Only a few weeks ago I was sitting out on the terrace of my massive old mansion, watching the early autumn sun droop into the above-mentioned lake, talking to Aunt T. Her heels clomped with a pleasing hollowness on the flagstones of the terrace. Silver-haired, she was attired in a gray suit, a big bow flopping up to her lower chins. In her left hand was a long envelope, neatly caesarianed, and in her right hand the letter it had contained, folded in sections like a triptych.

"They want to see you," she said, gesturing with the letter. "They want to come here."

"I don't believe it," I said and skeptically turned in my chair to watch the sunlight stretching in long cathedral-like aisles across the upper and lower levels of the lawn.

"If you would only read the letter," she insisted.

"It's in French, no? Can't read."

"Now that's not true, to judge by those books you're always stacking in the library."

"Those happen to be art books. I just look at the pictures."

"You like pictures, André?" she asked in her best matronly ironic tone. "I have a picture for you. Here it is: they *are* going to be allowed to come here and stay with us as long as they like. There's a family of them, two children and the letter also mentions an unmarried sister. They're traveling all the way from Aix-en-Provence to visit America, and while on their trip they want to see their only living blood relation here. Do you understand this picture? They know who you are and, more

to the point, where you are."

"I'm surprised they would want to, since they're the ones —"

"No, they're not. They're from your *father's* side of the family. The Duvals," she explained. "They do know all about you but say [Aunt T. here consulted the letter for a moment] "that they are *sans préjugés.*"

"The generosity of such creatures freezes my blood. Phenomenal scum. Twenty years ago these people do what they did to my mother, and now they have the gall, the *gall,* to say they aren't prejudiced against *me.*"

Aunt T. gave me a warning hrumph to silence myself, for just then the one I called Rops walked out onto the terrace bearing a tray with a slender glass set upon it. I dubbed him Rops because he, as much as his artistic namesake, never failed to give me the charnel house creeps.

He cadavered over to Aunt T. and served her her afternoon cocktail.

"Thank you," she said, taking the glass of cloudy stuff.

"Anything for you, sir?" he asked, now holding the tray over his chest like a silver shield.

"Ever see me have a drink, Rops," I asked back. "Ever see me —"

"André, behave. That'll be all, thank you."

Rops left our sight in a few bony strides. "You can continue your rant now," said Aunt T. graciously.

"I'm through. You know how I feel," I replied and then looked away toward the lake, drinking in the dim mood of the twilight in the absence of normal refreshment.

"Yes, I do know how you feel, and you've always been wrong. You've always had these romantic ideas of how you and your mother, rest her soul, have been the victims of some monstrous injustice. But nothing is the way you like to think it is. They were not backward peasants who, we should say,

saved your mother. They were wealthy, sophisticated members of her own family. And they were not superstitious, because what they believed about your mother was the truth."

"True or not," I argued, "they believed the unbelievable — they acted on it — and that I call superstition. What reason could they possibly —"

"What *reason?* I have to say that at the time you were in no position to judge reasons, considering that we knew you only as a slight swelling inside your mother's body. But I was actually there. I saw the 'new friends' she had made, that 'aristocracy of blood,' as she called it, in contrast to her own people's hardearned wealth. But I don't judge her, I never have. After all, she had just lost her husband — your father was a good man and it's a shame you never knew him — and then to be carrying his child, the child of a dead man . . . She was frightened, confused, and she ran back to her family and her homeland. Who can blame her if she started acting irresponsibly? But it's a shame what happened, especially for your sake."

"You are indeed a comfort . . . *Auntie,*" I said with now regrettable sarcasm.

"Well, you have my sympathy whether you want it or not. I think I've proven that over the years."

"Indeed you have," I agreed, and somewhat sincerely.

Aunt T. poured the last of her drink down her throat and a little drop she wasn't aware of dripped from the corner of her mouth, shining in the crepuscular radiance like a pearl.

"When your mother didn't come home one evening — I should say *morning* — everyone knew what had happened, but no one said anything. Contrary to your ideas about their superstitiousness, they actually could not bring themselves to believe the truth for some time."

"It was good of all of you to let me go

on developing for a while, even as you were deciding how to best hunt my mother down."

"I will ignore that remark."

"I'm sure you will."

"We did not *hunt* her down, as you well know. That's another of your persecution fantasies. She came to us, now didn't she? Scratching at the windows in the night —"

"You can skip this part, I already —"

"— swelling full as the fullest moon. And that was strange, because you would actually have been considered a dangerously premature birth according to normal schedules; but when we followed your mother back to the mausoleum of the local church, where she lay during the daylight hours, she was carrying the full weight of her pregnancy. The priest was shocked to find what he had living, so to speak, in his own backyard. It was actually he, and not so much any of your mother's family, who thought we should not allow you to be brought into the world. And it was his hand that ultimately released your mother from the life of her new friends, and immediately afterward she began to deliver, right in the coffin in which she lay. The blood was terrible. If we did —"

"It's not necessary to —"

"— *hunt* down your mother, you should be thankful that I was among that party. I had to get you out of the country that very night, back to America. I —"

At that point she could see that I was no longer listening, was gazing with a distracted intensity on the pleasanter anecdotes of the setting sun. When she stopped talking and joined in the view, I said:

"Thank you, Aunt T., for that little bedtime story. I never tire of hearing it."

"I'm sorry, André, but I wanted to remind you of the truth."

"What can I say? I realize I owe you my life, such as it is."

"That's not what I mean. I mean the truth of what your mother became and what you now are."

"I am nothing. Completely harmless."

"That's why we must let the Duvals come and stay with us. To show them the world has nothing to fear from you, because that's what I believe they're actually coming to see. That's the message they'll carry back to your family in France."

"You really think that's why they're coming."

"I do. They could make quite a bit of trouble for you, for us."

I rose from my chair as the shadows of the failing twilight deepened. I went and stood next to Aunt T. against the stone balustrade of the terrace, and whispered:

"Then let them come."

I am an offspring of the dead. I am descended from the deceased. I am the progeny of phantoms. My ancestors are the illustrious multitudes of the defunct, grand and innumerable. My lineage is longer than time. My name is written with embalming fluid in the book of death. A noble name is mine.

In the immediate family, the first to meet his maker was my own maker: he rests in the tomb of the unknown father. But while the man did manage to sire me, he breathed his last breath in this world before I drew my first. He was felled by a single stroke, his first and last. In those final moments, so I'm told, his erratic and subtle brainwaves made strange designs across the big green eye of an EEG monitor. The same doctor who told my mother that her husband was no longer among the living also informed her, on the very same day, that she was pregnant. Nor was this the only poignant coincidence in the lives of my parents. Both of them belonged to wealthy families from Aix-en-Provence in southern France. However, their first meeting took place not in the old country but in the new, at the American university they each happened to be attending. And so two neighbors crossed a cold ocean to come together in a mandatory science course. When they compared notes on their common backgrounds, they knew it was destiny at work. They fell in love with each other and with their new homeland. The couple later moved into a rich and prestigious suburb (which I will decline to mention by name or state, since I still reside there and, for reasons that will eventually become apparent, must do so discreetly). For years the couple lived in contentment, and then my immediate male forbear died just in time for fatherhood, becoming the appropriate parent for his son-to-be.

Offspring of the dead.

But surely, one might protest, I was born of a living mother; surely upon arrival in this world I turned and gazed into a pair of glossy maternal eyes. Not so, as I think is evident from my earlier conversation with dear Aunt T. Widowed and pregnant, my mother had fled back to Aix, to the comfort of family estates and secluded living. But more on this in a moment. Meanwhile I can no longer suppress the urge to say a few things about my ancestral hometown.

Aix-en-Provence, where I was born but never lived, has many personal, though necessarily second-hand, associations for me. However, it is not just a connection between Aix and my own life that maintains such a powerful grip on my imagination and memory, a lifelong fascination which actually has more to do with a few unrelated facts in the history of the region. Two pieces of historical data, to be exact. Separate centuries, indeed epochs, play host to these data, and they likewise exist in

entirely different realms of mood, worlds apart in implication. Nevertheless, from a certain point of view they can impress one as inseparable opposites. The first datum is as follows: In the seventeenth century there occurred the spiritual possession by divers demons of the nuns belonging to the Ursuline convent at Aix. And excommunication was soon in coming for the tragic sisters, who had been seduced into assorted blasphemies by the likes of Grésil, Sonnillon, and Vérin. De Plancy's *Dictionnaire infernal* respectively characterizes these demons, in the words of an unknown translator, as "the one who glistens horribly like a rainbow of insects; the one who quivers in a horrible manner; and the one who moves with a particular creeping motion." There also exist engravings of these kinetically and chromatically weird beings, unfortunately static and in black and white. Can you believe it? What people are these — so stupid and profound — that they could devote themselves to such nonsense? Who can fathom the science of superstition? (For, as an evil poet once scribbled, superstition is the reservoir of all truths.) This, then, is one side of my imaginary Aix. The other side, and the second historical datum I offer, is simply the birth in 1839 of Aix's most prominent citizen: Cézanne. His figure haunts the Aix of my brain, wandering about the beautiful countryside in search of his pretty pictures.

Together these aspects fuse into a single image, as grotesque and coherent as a pantheon of gargoyles amid the splendor of a medieval church.

Such was the world to which my mother reëmigrated some decades ago, this Notre Dame world of horror and beauty. It's no wonder that she was seduced into the society of those beautiful strangers, who promised her an escape from the world of mortality where shock and suffering had taken over, driving her into exile. I understood from Aunt

THE LOST ART OF TWILIGHT

T. that it all began at a summer party on the estate grounds of Ambroise and Paulette Valraux. The Enchanted Wood, as this place was known to the *haut monde* in the vicinity. The evening of the party was as perfectly temperate as the atmosphere of dreams, which one never notices to be either sultry or frigid. Lanterns were hung high up in the lindens, guide-lights leading to a heard-about heaven. A band played.

It was a mixed crowd at the party. And as usual there were present a few persons whom nobody seemed to know, exotic strangers whose elegance was their invitation. Aunt T. did not pay much attention to them at the time, and her account is rather sketchy. One of them danced with my mother, having no trouble coaxing the widow out of social retirement. Another with labyrinthine eyes whispered to her by the trees. Alliances were formed that night, promises made. Afterward my mother began going out on her own to rendezvous after sundown. Then she stopped coming home. Thérèse — nurse, confidante, and personal maid whom my mother had brought back with her from America — was hurt and confused by the cold snubs she had lately received from her mistress. My mother's family was elaborately reticent about the meaning of her recent behavior. ("And in her condition, *mon Dieu!*") Nobody knew what measures to take. Then some of the servants reported seeing a pale, pregnant woman lurking outside the house after dark.

Finally a priest was taken into the family's confidence. He suggested a course of action which no one questioned, not even Thérèse. They lay in wait for my mother, righteous soul-hunters. They followed her drifting form as it returned to the mausoleum when daybreak was imminent. They removed the great stone lid of the sarcophagus and found her inside. *"Diabolique,"* someone exclaimed. There was some question about how many times and in what places she should be impaled. In the end they pinned her heart with a single spike to the velvet bed on which she lay. But what to do about the child? What would it be like? A holy soldier of the living or a monster of the dead? (Neither, you fools!) Fortunately or unfortunately, I've never been sure which, Thérèse was with them and rendered their speculations academic. Reaching into the bloodied matrix, she helped me to be born. I was now heir to the family fortune, and Thérèse took me back to America. She was extremely resourceful in this regard, arranging with a sympathetic and avaricious lawyer to become the trustee of my estate. This required a little magic act with identities. It required that Thérèse, for reasons of her own which I've never questioned, be promoted from my mother's maid to her posthumous sister. And so my Aunt T. was christened, born in the same year as I.

Naturally all this leads to the story of my life, which has no more life in it than story. It's not for the cinema, it is not for novels; it wouldn't even fill out a single lyric of modest length. It might make a piece of modern music: a slow, throbbing drone like the lethargic pumping of a premature heart. Best of all, though, would be the depiction of my life story as an abstract painting: a twilight world, indistinct around the edges and without center or focus; a bridge without banks, tunnels without openings; a crepuscular existence pure and simple. No heaven or hell, only a quiet haven between life's hysteria and death's tenacious darkness. (And you know, what I most loved about Twilight is the sense, as one looks down the dimming west, not that it is some fleeting transitional moment, but that there's actually nothing before or after it: *that that's all there is.*) My life never had a beginning, so naturally I thought it would never end. Naturally, I was

89

wrong.

Well, and what was the answer to those questions hastily put by the monsters who stalked my mother? Was my nature to be souled humanness or soulless vampirism? The answer: neither. I existed between two worlds and had little claim upon the assets or liabilities of either. Neither living nor dead, unalive or undead, not having anything crucial to do with such tedious polarities, such tiresome opposites, which ultimately are no more different from each other than a pair of imbecilic monozygotes. I said no to life and death. No, Mr. Springbud. No, Mr. Worm. Without ever saying hello or goodbye, I merely avoided their company, scorned their gaudy invitations.

Of course, in the beginning Aunt T. tried to care for me as if I were a normal child. (Incidentally, I can perfectly recall every moment of my life from birth, for my existence took the form of one seamless moment, without forgettable yesterdays or expectant tomorrows.) She tried to give me normal food, which I always regurgitated. Later Aunt T. prepared for me a sort of puréed meat, which I ingested and digested, though it never became a habit. And I never asked her what was actually in that preparation, for Aunt T. wasn't afraid to use money, and I knew what money could buy in the way of unusual food for an unusual infant. I suppose I did become accustomed to similar nourishment while growing within my mother's womb, feeding on a potpourri of blood types contributed by the citizens of Aix. But my appetite was never very strong for physical food.

Stronger by far was my hunger for a kind of transcendental fare, a feasting of the mind and soul: the astral banquet of Art. There I fed. And I had quite a few master chefs to plan the menu. Though we lived in exile from the world, Aunt T. did not overlook my education. For purposes of appearance

90

and legality, I have earned diplomas from some of the finest private schools in the world. (These, too, money can buy.) But my real education was even more private than that. Tutorial geniuses were well paid to visit our home, only too glad to teach an invalid child of nonetheless exceptional promise.

Through personal instruction I scanned the arts and sciences. Yes, I learned to quote my French poets,

> *Lean immortality, all crêpe*
> *and gold,*
> *Laurelled consoler frightening to*
> *behold,*
> *Death is a womb, a mother's*
> *breast, you feign —*
> *The fine illusion, oh the pious*
> *trick!*

but mostly in translation, for something kept me from ever attaining more than a beginner's facility in that foreign tongue. I did master, however, the complete grammar, every dialect and idiom of the French *eye*. I could read the inner world of Redon (who was almost born an American) — his *grand isolé* paradise of black. I could effortlessly comprehend the outer world of Manet and the Impressionists — that secret language of light. And I could decipher the impossible worlds of the surrealists — those twisted arcades where brilliant shadows are sewn to the rotting flesh of rainbows.

I remember in particular a man by the name of Raymond, who taught me the rudimentary skills of the artist in oils. I recollect vividly showing him a study I had done of that sacred phenomenon I witnessed each sundown. Most of all I recall the look of his eyes, as if they beheld the rising of a curtain upon some terribly involved outrage. He abstractedly adjusted his delicate spectacles, wobbling them around on the bridge of his nose. His gaze shifted from the canvas to my face and back again. I'm not sure whether my face helped him understand something in the picture or vice versa. His only comment was: "The shapes, the colors are not supposed to lose themselves that way. Something . . . No, too much —" Then he asked to be permitted use of the bathroom facilities. At first I thought this gesture was means as a symbolic appraisal of my work. But he was quite in earnest and all I could do was give him directions to the nearest chamber of convenience in a voice of equal seriousness. He walked out of the room with the first two fingers of his right hand pressing upon the pulsing wrist of his left. And he never came back.

Such is a thumbnail sketch of my half-toned existence: twilight after twilight after twilight. And in all that blur of time I but occasionally, and then briefly, wondered if I too possessed the same potential for immortality as my undead mother before her life was aborted and I was born. It is not a question that really bothers one who exists beyond, below, above, between — triumphantly *outside* — the clashing worlds of human fathers and enchanted mothers.

I did wonder, though, how I would explain, that is *conceal,* my unnatural mode of being from those people arriving from France. Despite the hostility I showed toward them in front of Aunt T., I actually desired that they should take a good report of me back to the real world, if only to keep it away from my own world in the future. For days previous to their arrival, I came to think of myself as a certain stock character in Gothic stories: the stranger in a strange castle of a house, that shadowy figure whom the hero travels over long distances to encounter, a dark soul hiding his horrors. In short, a medieval geek perpetrating strange deeds in secret sanctums. I expected they would soon have the proper image of me as all impotence and no impetus. And that

would be that.

But never did I anticipate being called upon to face the almost forgotten realities of vampirism — the taint beneath the paint of the family portrait.

The Duval family, and unmarried sister, were arriving on a night flight, which we would meet at the local international airport. Aunt T. thought this would suit me fine, considering my tendency to sleep most of the day away and arise with the setting sun. But at the last minute I suffered an acute seizure of stage fright. "The *crowds,*" I appealed to Aunt T. She knew that crowds were the world's most powerful talisman against me, as if it had needed any at all. She understood that I would not be able to serve on the welcoming committee, and Rops's younger brother Gerald (a good seventy-five if he was a day) drove her to the airport alone. Yes, I promised Aunt T. that I would be sociable and come out to meet everyone as soon as I saw the lights of the big black car floating up our private drive.

But I wasn't and I didn't. I took to my room and drowsed before a television with the sound turned off. As the colors danced in the dark, I submitted more and more to an anti-social sleepiness. Finally I instructed Rops, by way of the estate-wide intercom, to inform Aunt T. and company that I wasn't feeling very well, needed to rest. This, I figured, would be in keeping with the facade of a harmless valetudinarian, and a perfectly normal one at that. A night-sleeper. Very good, I could hear them saying to their souls. And then, I swear, I actually turned off the television and slept real sleep in real darkness.

But things became less real at some point deep in the night. I must have left the intercom open, for I heard little metal voices emanating from that little

91

metal square on my bedroom wall. In my state of quasi-somnolence it never occurred to me that I could simply get out of bed and make the voices go away by switching off that terrible box. And terrible it indeed seemed. The voices spoke a foreign language, but it wasn't French, as one might have suspected. Something more foreign than that. Perhaps a cross between a madman talking in his sleep and the sonar screech of a bat. The voices chittered and chattered with each other in my dreams when I finally fell completely asleep. And they ceased entirely long before I awoke, for the first time in my life, to the bright eyes of morning.

The house was quiet. Even the servants seemed to have duties that kept them soundless and invisible. I took advantage of my wakefulness at that early hour and prowled unnoticed about the floors of the house, figuring everyone else was still in bed after their long and somewhat noisy night. The four rooms Aunt T. had set aside for our guests all had their big panelled doors closed: a room for the mama and papa, two others close by for the kids, and a chilly chamber at the end of the hall for the maiden sister. I paused a moment outside each room and listened for the revealing songs of slumber, hoping to know my relations better by their snores and whistles and monosyllables grunted between breaths. But they made none of the usual racket. They hardly made any sounds at all, though they echoed one another in making a certain noise that seemed to issue from the same cavity. It was a kind of weird wheeze, an open mouth panting from the back of the throat, the hacking of a tubercular demon. Or a very faint grating sound, as if some heavy object were being dragged across bare wooden floors in a distant part of the house; a muted cacophony. Thus, I soon abandoned my eavesdropping without regret.

I spent the day in the library, whose high windows I noticed were designed to allow a maximum of natural reading light. However, I drew the drapes on them and kept to the shadows, finding morning sunshine not everything it was said to be. But it was difficult to get much reading done. Any moment I expected to hear foreign footsteps descending the double-winged staircase, crossing the black and white marble chessboard of the front hall, taking over the house. Nevertheless, despite my expectations, and to my increasing uneasiness, the family never appeared.

Twilight came and still no mama and papa, no sleepy-eyed son or daughter, no demure sister remarking with astonishment at the inordinate length of her beauty sleep. And no Aunt T., either. They must've had quite a time the night before, I thought. But I didn't mind being alone with the twilight. I undraped the three west windows, each of them a canvas depicting the same scene in the sky. My private *salon d'Automne*.

It was an unusual sunset. Having sat behind opaque drapery all day, I had not realized that a storm was pushing in and that much of the sky was the precise shade of old suits of armor one finds in museums. At the same time, patches of brilliance engaged in a territorial dispute with the oncoming onyx of the storm. Light and darkness mingled in strange ways both above and below. Shadows and sunshine washed together, streaking the landscape in an unearthly study of glare and gloom. Bright clouds and black folded into each other in a no-man's land of the sky. The autumn trees turned in accordance with a strange season as their leaden-colored trunks and branches, along with their iron-red leaves, took on the appearance of sculptures formed in a dream, locked into an infinite and unliving moment, unnaturally timeless. The gray lake slowly tossed and tumbled in a deep sleep, nudging unconsciously against its breakwall of numb stone. A scene of contradiction and ambivalence, a tragicomedic haze over all. A land of perfect twilight.

I was in exaltation: finally the twilight had come down to earth, and to me. I had to go out into this rare atmosphere, I had no choice. I left the house and walked to the lake and stood on the slope of stiff grass which led down to it. I gazed up through the trees at the opposing tones of the sky. I kept my hands in my pockets and touched nothing, except with my eyes.

Not until an hour or more had elapsed did I think of returning home. It was dark by then, though I don't recall the passing of the twilight into evening, for twilight has no edges. There were no stars anywhere, the storm clouds having moved in and wrapped up the sky. They began sending out tentative drops of rain. Thunder mumbled above and I was forced back to the house, cheated once again by the night. But I'll always remember savoring that particular twilight, unaware that there would be no others after it.

In the front hall of the house I called out names in the form of questions. "Aunt T.? Rops? Gerald? M. Duval? Madame?" Everything was silence. Where was everyone, I wondered. They couldn't still be asleep. I passed from room to room and found no signs of occupation. A day of dust was upon all surfaces. Where were the domestics? At last I opened the double doors to the dining room. Was I late for the supper Aunt T. had planned to honor our visiting family?

It appeared so. But if Aunt T. sometimes had me consume the forbidden fruit of flesh and blood, it was never directly from the branches, never the sap taken warm from the tree of life itself. But here in fact were spread the remains of such a feast. It was the ravaged body of Aunt T. herself, though they'd barely left enough on her bones for identification. The thick white linen was clotted like an unwrapped bandage. "Rops!" I shouted. "Gerald, somebody!" But I knew the servants were no longer in the house, that I was alone.

Not quite alone, of course. This soon became apparent to my twilight brain as it dipped its way into total darkness. I was in the company of five black shapes which stuck to the walls and soon began flowing along their surface. One of them detached itself and moved toward me, a weightless mass which felt icy when I tried to sweep it away and put my hand right through the thing. Another followed, unhinging itself from a doorway where it hung down. A third left a blanched scar upon the wallpaper where it clung like a slug, pushing itself off to join the attack. Then came the others descending from the ceiling, dropping onto me as I stumbled in circles and flailed my arms. I ran from the room but the things had me closely surrounded. They guided my flight, heading me down hallways and up staircases. Finally they cornered me in a small room, a dusty little place I had not been in for years. Colored animals frolicked upon the walls, blue bears and yellow rabbits. Miniature furniture was draped with graying sheets. I hid beneath a tiny, elevated crib with ivory bars. But they found me and closed in.

They were not driven by hunger, for they had already feasted. They were not frenzied with a murderer's bloodlust, for they were cautious and methodical. This was simply a family reunion, a sentimental gathering. Now I understood how the Duvals could afford to be *sans préjugés*. They were worse than I, who was only a half-breed, hybrid, a mere mulatto of the soul: neither a blood-warm human nor a blood-drawing devil. But they — who came from an Aix on the map — were the purebreds of the family.

93

And they drained my body dry.

When I regained awareness once more, it was still dark and there was a great deal of dust in my throat. Not actually dust, of course, but a strange dryness I had never before experienced. And there was another new experience: hunger. I felt as if there were a chasm of infinite depth within me, a great abyss which needed to be filled — flooded with oceans of blood. I was one of them now, reborn into a hungry death. Everything I had shunned in my impossible, blasphemous ambition to avoid living and dying, I had now become. A sallow, ravenous thing. A beast with a hundred stirring hungers. André of the graveyards.

The five of them had each drunk from my body by way of five separate fountains. But the wounds had nearly sealed by the time I awoke in the blackness, owing to the miraculous healing capabilities of the dead. The upper floors were all in shadow now, and I made my way toward the light coming from downstairs. An impressionistic glow illuminating the wooden banister at the top of the stairway, where I emerged from the darkness of the second floor, inspired in me a terrible ache of emotion I'd never known before. A feeling of loss, though of nothing I could specifically name, as if somehow the deprivation lay in my future.

As I descended the stairs I saw that they were already waiting to meet me, standing silently upon the black and white squares of the front hall. Papa the king, mama the queen, the boy a knight, the girl a dark little pawn, and a bitchy maiden bishop standing behind. And now they had my house, my castle, to complete the pieces on their side. On mine there was nothing.

"Devils," I screamed, leaning hard on the staircase rail. "Devils," I repeated,

but they still appeared horribly undistressed, perhaps uncomprehending of my outburst. *"Diables,"* I reiterated in their own loathsome tongue.

But neither was French their true language, as I found out when they began speaking among themselves. I covered my ears, trying to smother their voices. They had a language all their own, a style of speech well-suited to dead vocal organs. The words were breathless, shapeless rattlings in the backs of their throats, parched scrapings at the mausoleum portal. Arid gasps and dry gurgles were their dialects. These crackling noises were especially disturbing as they emanated from the mouths of things that had at least the form of human beings. But worst of all was my realization that I understood perfectly well what they were saying.

The boy stepped forward, pointing at me while looking back and speaking to his father. It was the opinion of this wine-eyed and rose-lipped youth that I should have suffered the same end as Aunt T. With an authoritative impatience the father told the boy that I was to serve as a sort of tour guide through this strange new land, a native who could keep them out of such difficulties as foreign visitors sometimes get into. Besides, he grotesquely concluded, *I was one of the family*. The boy was incensed and coughed out an incredibly foul characterization of his father. The things he said could only have been conveyed by that queer hacking patois, which suggested feelings and relationships of a nature incomprehensible outside of that particular world it mirrors with disgusting perfection. It is the discourse of Hell on the subject of sin.

An argument ensued, the father's composure turning to an infernal rage and finally subduing the son with bizarre threats that have no counterparts in the language of ordinary malevolence. Monstrous possibilities were implied.

Finally the boy was silenced and turned to his aunt, seemingly for comfort. This woman of chalky cheeks and sunken eyes touched the boy's shoulder and easily drew him toward her with a single finger, guiding his body as if it were a balloon, weightless and toylike. They spoke in sullen whispers, using a personal form of address that hinted at a long-standing and unthinkable allegiance between them.

Apparently encouraged by this scene, the daughter now stepped forward and used this same mode of address to get my attention. Her mother abruptly gagged out a single syllable at her. What she called her daughter might possibly be imagined, but only with reference to the lowliest sectors of the human world. Their own words, their choking rasps, carried all the dissonant overtones of a demonic orchestra in bad tune. Each perverse utterance was a rioting opera of evil, a choir shrieking pious psalms of intricate blasphemy and devout songs of enigmatic lust. "I will not become one of you," I *thought* I screamed at them. But the sound of my voice was already so much like theirs that the words had exactly the opposite meaning I intended. The family suddenly ceased bickering among themselves. My outburst had consolidated them. Each mouth, cluttered with uneven teeth like a village cemetery overcrowded with battered gravestones, opened and smiled. The expression on their faces told me of something in my own. They could see my growing hunger, see deep down into the dusty catacomb of my throat which cried out to be anointed with bloody nourishment. They knew my weakness.

Yes, they could stay in my house. *(Famished.)*

Yes, I could make arrangements to cover up the disappearance of the servants, for I am a wealthy man and know what money can buy. *(Please, my fam-*

ily, I'm famished.)

Yes, their safety could be insured and their permanent asylum perfectly feasible. *(Please, I'm famishing to dust.)*

Yes, yes, yes. I agreed to everything; everything would be taken care of. *(To dust!)*

But first I begged them, for heaven's sake, to let me go out into the night.

Night, night, night, night. Night, night, night.

Now twilight is an alarm, a noxious tocsin which rouses me to an endless eve. There is a sound in my new language for that transitory time of day just before the dark hours. The sound clusters together curious shades of meaning and shadowy impressions, none of which belong to my former conception of an abstract paradise: the true garden of unearthy delights. The new twilight is a violator, desecrator, stealthy graverobber; death-bell, life-knell, curtain-riser; banshee, siren, howling she-wolf. And the old twilight is dead. I am even learning to despise it, just as I am learning to love my eternal life and eternal death. Nevertheless, I wish them well who would attempt to destroy my precarious immortality, for just as my rebirth has taught me the importance of beginnings, the idea of endings has also taken on a painfully tranquil significance. And I cannot deny those who would avenge all those exsanguinated souls of my past and future. Yes, past and future. Endings and beginnings. In brief, Time now exists, measured like a perpetual holiday consisting only of midnight revels. I once had an old family from an old world, and now I have new ones. A new life, a new world. And this world is no longer one where I can languidly gaze upon rosy sunsets, but another in which I must fiercely draw a full-bodied blood from the night.

Night . . . after night . . . after night.   ∇

95

THE LITTLE FINGER ON THE LEFT HAND

by Ardath Mayhar

It wasn't the pain. That was controllable, even without the medication they insisted on shooting into me every time I opened my mouth. I mean, it isn't as though I'd been some sort of marshmallow. In the house wrecking business, you get your share of knocks and cuts, even when you're careful. No, it wasn't exactly the pain. Maybe part was the inactivity.

For a man who has spent his entire life on his feet, when he wasn't actually asleep or making love, this lying flat on my back and staring at the antiseptic white ceiling was making me crazy. For the first time in my life, I was grateful to my Dad for making me graduate from college. Bits and pieces came back to me . . . oddball scraps of literature, formulas, bits of history. It helped to make the time pass, though not much.

Still, it wasn't just the boredom that was getting to me. It was that damned little finger on my left hand. The one that isn't there any more.

With all the broken bones and contusions and whatnot that I got when that cut-stone wall fell on me, you'd think the loss of that finger wouldn't even be noticeable. I mean, it isn't as if you use the thing much. And right now I can't use *anything*, being strung up like a wounded mummy. But that was the bit that was missing from me when they dug me out, and that was the bit that was giving me Hell.

Dr. Yoshida came in, the first day I was out from under sedation enough to tell him what was bothering me.

"Your nerves are still there, in the stump, Mr. Carstairs," he said. "They send signals to the brain, even though they no longer lead to the finger. After such a trauma, they are sending scrambled signals, I suspect. That is why you have that gnawing sensation and the sudden sharp pains.

"After a time, they will heal at the severed ends, and the worst will be past. Though I must admit that I have had patients who had terrible itches in missing limbs for years after losing them. However, right now you can call for sedation, when it gets too painful. You need that for rest, too, I am sure. By the time you are able to move about a bit, the worst will be over."

It made some sense. I believed him. But I'm not one who likes to be doped up, no matter what. I just lay there and felt sharp teeth gnawing away at that finger until I was ready to scream. If it hadn't been for Lola, I'd have gone off my gourd.

She comes in every day for as long as they'll let her stay. I keep reminding her that if she'd said yes when I asked her to marry me she might stay as long as she liked. She grins at that, because she didn't exactly say no. She said in four months, when she has her degree and time for a husband and a new job, both at once.

Anyway, she kept looking at me, those first few days, as if she could sense what I was pretending not to feel.

THE LITTLE FINGER ON THE LEFT HAND

Finally she asked, right out, "Hamp, you're hurting, aren't you?"

I had sworn never to lie to her. I meant it, too, so I nodded. "Some."

"More than some. What is it? The back? The neck? You're so wrapped up I can't tell what's hurt the worst."

I felt silly. I stared up at her, and she fixed me with those big brown eyes that demand the truth and nothing but the truth. "It's that little finger. The one that's gone. The thing's driving me wild . . . feels as if mice with saber-teeth are gnawing it to rags."

"Ghost pains," she said, nodding. "They told me you'd have them, but I don't think they realize how bad it is for you. They're used to people having them in entire arms and legs. I think they don't expect a small bit like a finger to give you so much trouble."

That was probably true, but at least she knew and sympathized. That helped a little. When it got so that I was trying to turn off the TV with thought waves, she read to me or told me funny stories about her classmates and professors, or her boss and the techs in the lab where she worked. It helped.

But when she was gone . . . after dark when the hospital quieted to its nightly routine, there was nothing left in the world but me and the little finger on my left hand.

Rog, the foreman of my crew, came in to see me, once they took the sign off my door. I felt funny about asking him the question I'd saved for him, but I finally got up the nerve.

"Rog, that house. The one that fell in on me. Is it all the way down, yet?"

He looked at me sort of funny. "Not yet. They got the contractor out there and some engineers. It's a funny deal — if we'd had any idea of problems, we'd have gone that route first and waited to start demolition. Maybe we'd have used a wrecking ball.

"That entire house is so unstable it stinks. And it looked solid as Gibraltar, too. It's still sitting there, only that one wall down so far. They can't figure why that one fell or why the rest didn't come down, too. All you did was to chip out an anchor-point for a towline, and whammo! Down she came, right on top of you. I was never so scared in my life . . . we thought you'd had it. No joke!"

Hmm. That brought up my second question. "Did anybody ever look around for my finger? Could it be spotted in all that mess?"

He shook his head. "They won't let us near the thing, now. Once you were out, they put up a fence with padlocks and all the trimmings. Why?"

That was a question I didn't want to answer. "I just wondered. After all, it isn't every day you lose a piece of yourself." I laughed, but it hurt.

After he left, I thought of that loose bit of flesh and bone, lying in all that rubble. By God, mice were probably stripping it down to the bone. And I could, somehow, feel it happening. The thought preyed on my mind.

Then I remembered the motion I had seen, back in the corner when I went in to do my job. Something a lot bigger than a mouse — or even a rat — had been in that old house. I had thought it might be a cat, nosing around, and never thought of it again. But now I recalled the ghost of a growl. Sharp teeth, glinting in the dimness . . .

"Hamp Carstairs," I said aloud, "you will drive yourself completely round the bend, if you lie here making up stories. Go to sleep!"

With the help of a nurse and another shot, I did just that. But the next day I was all nerves. Sedatives just made me worse, until it seemed as if my skin would crawl right out from under the casts and bandages and make off down the hall.

Lola was beside herself. She tried to talk, to read, but I just lay there in a cold sweat, trying to keep from screaming. She could see it in my eyes, which was just about all of my face she could see.

"Hamp!"

I'd closed my eyes, so she could get some rest. I opened them to see her bending over me.

"Hamp, it's that damn finger, isn't it? I'm going down there and dig around until I find it. I'm going to bring it right back here and put it in a jar of formaldehyde on that table, so you can see that nothing's at it. It may not help the nerves, but it just might help the mental strain a bit."

It was hard to talk through the bandages, but I managed. "Lo, listen! That place is a deathtrap. Rog says they locked it up, it's so dangerous. It's not going to help either of us if you get all smashed up, too. I want all of your parts

98

in working order, when I get out of this cast."

She smiled, and I recognized that look. I should have kept that problem to myself. She left, determination in the set of her back.

She didn't come back that afternoon at her usual time. There was no call at bedtime. I began to sweat. I had the nurse call Rog at home, just to see if there had been any sort of commotion out at the work site. But no. The next house was down, and they'd begun working on the one on the other side. There had been no problem at the unstable one.

Lola had early morning class, before her shift at the lab. There was no hope of seeing her before noon, and she hadn't a phone. I kept on sweating.

At ten o'clock, I was surprised when the door opened to let her into my room. She should have been at work. Then I saw a flash of white and stared at her left hand. At the bandage wrapped neatly around it.

In her right hand, she carried a small jar, which she set on the table with a thump. I could see something bobbing around in the liquid it contained. I cut my gaze around and stared. It had been a finger. That was clear, if you used imagination. All the flesh was gone, and the bone was scored with long marks.

I couldn't even raise my eyebrows when I looked up at her.

"Have you felt that finger this morning?" she asked.

I thought hard. I had been so worried that I hadn't even remembered the finger. Now I felt for it, but there was no twinge. Not even the faintest tickle.

"No." I sounded puzzled, even to me.

"Something had it, back in that half-wrecked room. Something furry and bright-eyed and mean. I beat it off with my purse and got your fingerbone away from it. But it . . . got even." She held out her hand. "It took mine, in exchange."

"Lo!" I felt my heart thud soggily. "I told you not to go in there . . . you might have been killed! The thing might even be rabid."

She looked down at me, and I saw deep into her eyes. There was a pain there that I recognized. Oh, did I recognize it!

"You now? It's got yours in place of mine?"

She nodded. "It leaped, when I took the bone away from it, and just snapped off my little finger like a bread stick. But I'm in better shape to cope with it than you are. I can move around, stay busy. I'm not trapped in that cast, wrapped up in ninety yards of gauze. It's . . . it's not such a bad swap, really." She smiled.

I could see the little lines at the corners of her mouth. I knew exactly what she felt. What a girl!

She couldn't stay long, for she was due at the lab. She'd swapped out with another girl so she could come in and relieve my mind.

Once she was gone, I was alone again, thinking about whatever it was living in that abandoned brownstone. Thinking about what Lola was enduring.

It isn't the pain, you see. That's bearable. It's wondering precisely what's causing it.   ∇

MEMORIES

Shall we remember, friend of the morning,
Dusk of the twilight and rose of the dawn? —
Laughing we fared in our youthfulness, scorning —
Mornings as golden shall lift when we're gone.

Oceans are eld and the mountains are hoary,
Ancient forgetfulness leaves them apart,
We shall remember our youth and the glory
We breathed when our race was just at its start.

Soon shall we fade as the twilight's red splendor
Fades to the misting of magical dusk,
Soon to the eons our souls shall surrender —
Ghosts dim at twilight, a faint breath of musk.

We shall remember, our ghosts shall remember
Sunsets of glory and pale rose of dawn;
We shall remember, our ghosts shall remember
Ages and ages long after we're gone.

— Robert E. Howard

KINDRED OF THE CRESCENT MOON

by Gerald Pearce

We had heard that the city called Ras al-Wadi was protected by a tribe of witches. But when we finally came to the edge of the plateau and looked down and saw it off to the right, beyond the dense forest of date palms crowding the valley floor, we found it protected by a defensive wall more than twice a man's height like any small oasis town, as unremarkable as mud.

Behind me on the lead ropes the pack camel and Mujahid's mare stirred briefly.

Mujahid turned in his camel saddle. The effect of his sudden smile was startling. He hadn't smiled since before his father died, weeks ago. Now suddenly he was his old self again, his broad muscular face alight, confident as a child's.

"Now all we have to do is go down there and find him. When we do —"

Slowly, almost lovingly, he drew a hard brown forefinger across his throat just above the collar of his *thaub,* and his smile took on the sometimes irritating assurance of a man who knows he is lucky. He was. Bedouin life was a gamble that Mujahid always won. Before his beard was more than a wisp and a shadow, he had been leading successful raids, bringing back booty in livestock and nubile women. His daring in battle was unmatched; only his luck kept his skin whole. His herds thrived. He had a persuasive tongue and was gifted at poetry and love songs, and his endless success with young women delighted him. Utter confidence could give his smile the arrogant edge I saw now. I had never expected to be glad to see that again, but any sign of the old Mujahid was preferable to the grim, obsessed, silent stranger I had been riding with all these weeks.

"You can't know he's here," I told him. "He didn't have to stop. He could be well on his way to the Red Sea."

Mujahid shook his head, faced the valley, drew in a deep breath.

"What do you smell?" he asked.

"Rain in the air. Oasis smells — moisture, green things growing."

"I smell my luck. It's been hiding from me. Thank you for your patience; I've been a stranger to myself as well as to you. Come on, let's find a way down."

Neither of us would have come to Ras al-Wadi if Kadhim bin Ja'far hadn't fallen in love with old Hasan's young wife. Hasan was Mujahid's father. The young wife's name was Filwa, and she was the prettiest, gentlest girl I had ever seen, with wide eyes as deep as night and lips always on the verge of a smile that was partly humorous but mostly shy. She was hardly any older than I was, and she haunted my dreams. But I was only a servant, with neither ancestors nor tribe, and I probably owed my life to Hasan: so it was loyalty as much as self-protection that made me keep those dreams in check.

Nothing had ever restrained Kadhim bin Ja'far. He had a face like a knife and his eyes were angry. His short black beard was denser than most bedouin beards, and his voice had the edge and cold weight of an enemy's sword. Some said he had the Evil Eye and kept their children from falling under his gaze. Others said he was just a bully that no one had ever stood up to because he was the heir of a rich family of the Numayr clan of the Bani Faris tribe and no one wanted to risk antagonizing him. His approach to Filwa had frightened her into complaining to Hasan.

We were at the tribal center in Hasa oasis at the time. Hasan, the head of a less prominent family of the same kindred, was close to sixty, gray-bearded, calm, with nothing left to prove. He went to Kadhim's tent to warn him away from Filwa and the two were heard arguing. A bit later Kadhim came out carrying his saddlebag. He picked up a waterbag and mounted his riding camel and disappeared south into the Jafura sands.

Toward sunset Kadhim's sister found Hasan in Kadhim's tent with a deep wound under his ribs. Two days later he died.

Grief like a sword bled me of my strength.

When the women had finished their lamentations, the Numayri elders and several shaykhs of the tribal council gathered in Mujahid's tent. They advised, predictably, that he accept Kadhim's permanent banishment and the payment of blood-wit instead of insisting on vengeance, as a blood feud within the clan would weaken it and hurt the tribe. It was sensible advice.

Mujahid only shook his head. No easy flow of words now. His face clenched like a fist, he stepped outside the circle of the impromptu council. He strung his bow, took a single arrow from his quiver, and held it for all to see. The iron tip gleamed dully. The shaft was clean. This would be his arrow of recision, the one thing that could rescind his obligation to avenge a murdered relative. The others, understanding, stood up and followed him outside. I stumbled numbly after them.

Mujahid's tent was pitched not far from Hasan's on the edge of the Hasa oasis. Half-visible through the date palms a huddle of mud-walled houses was the village called Bayt Faris, the tribal center. Beyond the village lay orchards, palm groves, wheatfields, other villages, a marsh where peasants grew rice, even a small walled town. There was a profusion of wells and hot springs. Hasa oasis was an extravagantly watered depression near the shores of the Arabian Gulf, as green and fresh as the surrounding land was desolate.

We went through dwindling palms and a line of tamarisk into the open desert. There, surrounded by witnesses, Mujahid shot the arrow high into the softening empty cloudless sky of late afternoon.

It came hissing back through the dry air, thudding into the sand.

Half its length glistened with fresh blood.

Hasan's spirit, or some God, demanded vengeance.

Unless of course it was magic.

People cried magic the first time I shot a wild dove out of the sky — I was supposed to be a skilled bowman but not *that* skilled. I tried it again later with no watchers and failed and never found the arrow. So much for magic. Later still I had a few successes and a few failures, enough to prove it *was* skill, an intuitive sense of where the bird's flight and the arrow's had to meet, perhaps helped occasionally by luck. Mujahid's luck was reliable. Mine wasn't.

But Mujahid had no skill in magic, and trickery was impossible. We had all seen the clean arrow leave the bow, pierce empty air, and now the blood on it was there to be seen and smelled and touched.

Only one man didn't join in the cries of astonishment. His name was Suhayl, and he was Mujahid's mother's eldest brother. He gave his nephew a speculative stare before adjusting the drape of his headcloth away from his neck and gray-bearded face.

"The tribes have been using this ritual time out of mind," he said mildly. He pointed to the arrow, which Mujahid had plucked out of the ground and was holding between fingertips of both hands. "But I never heard trustworthy accounts of its returning this answer."

Suhayl was known for his skeptical appraisal of men. What he seemed to be suggesting was that the ritual had been dreamed up by cunning shaykhs anxious to reduce the number of blood feuds, and surely that was taking skepticism too far. Most of the council seemed to think so. There were troubled murmurings. Umar bin Auda was scandalized.

"Mother of the Gods! Are you asking for a curse on your family, on the Numayr clan, or perhaps on the whole tribe?" Umar's voice was peppery and his eyes flashed. He was a lot older than Hasan had been; his beard and eyebrows were sparkling white. In recent years he had become increasingly devoted to the study of the Gods and their activities, and though some thought he was sliding into his dotage no one knew enough to argue with him. "Next you'll be denying sorcery, the existence of jinns, the powers of the Gods themselves . . ."

Suhayl shook his head. "No," he said unemphatically, and Mujahid stepped in front of him and held the arrow up before his uncle's eyes.

He said in a quiet, driven voice, "My father was your brother-in-law. You owed him kinship duties when he was alive, now you owe him the right to be avenged. It's my right to avenge him."

Several eager voices offered to help. Mujahid, holding the arrow like a cult object, slowly shook his head.

"I'll take one trusted servant. Talal."

Talal son of no one. Young man with no ancestors. Me.

Anyone of unknown parentage was said to have no ancestors. Ten years ago, when I was five or six, I had been a half-starved orphan who had deserted or been dumped by a passing caravan and been caught stealing plums from Hasan's small orchard near Bayt Faris village. Hasan had taken me in and raised me as a bedouin and his well-treated servant. Mujahid, who was some ten years older than I, taught me to ride and use a bow and was the closest thing

104

to a big brother I would ever have.

I supposed, with distant astonishment, that he wanted me along for my skill with the bow and my loyalty to Hasan. But I thought his refusing other help was silly. Avenging Hasan should be a matter for the whole family, not an occasion for a hothead's bravado.

Suhayl made an impatient gesture. Clearly he thought so too; but arguing with Mujahid at the best of times brought out only his cheerful impudence and stony obduracy, and this was not the best of times. Shaking his head, Suhayl subsided. Unexpectedly Umar bin Auda spoke up.

"Is that wise, Mujahid?" The peppery old voice was almost quiet. "You're a man of experience and luck, we all know that; and though you have no brothers your four brothers-in-law will be eager to help you, and so will others, not because duty demands it but because of their regard for your father, may the Gods have mercy on him. You could scour the desert like an army. But Talal . . . he's only a boy."

"He's a man," Mujahid said, "who hasn't had much chance to prove it. If he acquits himself with honor we can adopt him into the tribe and our ancestors will become his too."

Umar turned troubled eyes on me.

"And you, Talal. You want to go with him?"

As though I had a choice. I was a dutiful servant, a grateful friend, an admiring if sometimes irritated little brother. And Hasan had to be avenged.

"Of course," I said. Filwa would have expected it of me.

After a long moment Umar nodded. He sighed, a dry resigned rustle. "The Gods make plans. No doubt this is part of a pattern we can't see." And on that the council broke up.

Mujahid seemed not to have realized that Filwa was now his by inheritance. All he had to do to claim her was throw his cloak around her. Bani Faris law gave him three days to exercise this right; otherwise she was free to return to her own people. . . .

What she actually said when she heard I was going with him was, passionately, "Are you *crazy?*" I only shrugged and went on loading the pack camel. What mattered was getting Mujahid away before he came to his senses and remembered. The disloyalty made me unable to look anyone in the eye.

We left before sunset, riding after Kadhim into the Jafura sands. Filwa and the honored lady Zaynab, Hasan's first wife and Mujahid's mother, threw a couple of potsful of water after us as a charm to assure our finding water on the journey.

Mujahid turned his camel's head away from Ras al-Wadi and urged the beast southward along the rim of the plateau. His smile still lingered. In the weeks of riding I had never once seen him weep for his father. Perhaps the relationship between fathers and sons was more complicated than it seemed. Of course I could only guess.

All day we had been riding west over barren plains and ancient lava beds and rocky hills where the sun glinted off flints and broken pebbles and a thin, hot, bitter wind whipped grit from the desert floor into our eyes. As the shadows lengthened all this had changed. Now, towering black clouds hid the colors of sunset. The wind had shifted, and had an edge, and smelled wet. And as we came to where the drop into the valley became a negotiable slope by way of a well-used camel trail, rain began falling in slow, widely-spaced drops that splashed dust up from the trail and left wet smears as big as a man's hand on the rocks of the valley wall. For a couple of minutes the air smelled of wet dust, and then it began to rain faster.

I looked up at the low lead-colored sky. Rain caught on my eyelashes. Dust from my lips washed into my mouth.

Mujahid turned and threw me his lucky smile.

"We arrive with the rain. It'll assure us a good welcome."

The trail took a sharply angled turn, became steeper, then leveled out and almost disappeared on a gradual slope dotted with spiny desert shrubs. It was darker than it had been above; the mass of the palm trees was only an outline against the slightly paler clouds, and even that disappeared when the steady shower suddenly became a downpour. The whisper of the rain became a rattle on the palm fronds, then a roar, until lightning, pale as death, vicious as Kadhim's dagger, blazed into the ground just ahead of Mujahid's camel with a thunderclap loud enough to curdle courage and split stones.

The world became a chaos of frightened animals plunging about in rain and darkness.

For moments I saw only the memory of the lightning. In that time the pack camel, lunging and dragging on its lead rope, dislodged the saddle I was riding; it tilted, both animals I had been leading reared free, and I went over blindly. I landed on hip and elbow and scrambled madly to avoid the trampling hooves of the horse.

As I blundered clear, a safely distant lightning flash showed Mujahid's camel struggling to stand, and over the following thunder's echo I heard a muttered curse. By then I could almost see clearly again. A few paces away Mujahid was picking himself out of a prickly shrub he'd fallen into, bending to disentangle his wet cloak from its stiff twigs and spines.

I said, "Mujahid?" and as though my voice had turned him into stone he suddenly stopped moving. He didn't speak. I don't think he breathed. For a slow count of three he just stood hunched over in the rain until suddenly he jerked to life, gave a strangled cry and reared back, tearing the cloak free.

105

Bending over, he picked up a double handful of wet gravel and broken rock and flung it into the heart of the bush he had trampled.

"*. . . I take refuge with the Mother of the Gods from all evil!*"

I recognized the ritual with sudden dread. Without moving his feet he turned to me like an old grandfather withered by age and old battle wounds. Vaguely he reached up under his headcloth and touched the side of his head above the right temple, lowered his hand, examined the fingertips, stared at me. His face framed by the dripping headcloth was empty, slack, his eyes lost in wells of darkness like a skull's.

"An *ausaj* bush," he muttered. "I fell and trampled an *ausaj* bush . . ."

My mouth was dry as blown dust. I licked rain off my lips to moisten my tongue.

". . . Perhaps you're wrong," I croaked. "It's dark, perhaps you mistook a —"

"You brainless dog turd!" He scooped up another handful of gravel and flung it — at me. I ducked with my arms around my head. Half a dozen small rocks bounced off me painfully. "Next you'll say I need sunlight to tell a woman from a man . . . Gods! — that this should happen when we've practically caught him . . ." He put a vague hand to his head again. "Are you dreaming? See to your animals."

"Are you hurt?"

"Not yet."

None of the animals had bolted, and Mujahid's camel was only ten paces away. As he approached her his knees buckled. He stumbled forward, kept from falling only by catching the decorative strips trailing from his saddlebag.

Perhaps the women's charm to assure us water was working too well. The lightning had moved away, and the thunder had become a distant grumble,

but the rain continued to hiss and rattle, and profligate streams sluiced heedlessly down the steep valley wall. The space between the wall and the palm trees had become a shallow lake.

The difference between an *ausaj* and other stiff, dry desert bushes is this: that only the *ausaj* is protected by jinns. A vengeful jinni's curse can end a man's life in a day or follow it through decades of tragedy and dishonor. No better way to earn such a curse than to violate an *ausaj*, which is why bedouin take care to avoid them, hurling a rock or a pebble and taking refuge with the Mother of the Gods. What power had luck against the enmity of jinns? Maybe the lightning bolt had signalled that the reign of Mujahid's luck was over. . . .

Soaked, weary, beginning to shiver, I sloshed through ankle-deep water, leading all four animals up the valley toward the city. The three camels were linked one behind the other. The horse I led carefully by the sodden wool halter rope attached to her headstall. On her back slumped Mujahid, inert and dejected, without his headgear but with a bandage made from a strip torn from the hem of my *thaub* around his head. I kept expecting him to fall out of the saddle. . . .

We took a jog to avoid a rocky outcrop taller than a man, had just emerged beyond it when a child's voice laughed out of the rain. The laugh cut off sharply. I halted the animals, peered toward it.

A small naked boy pointed at us.

From a patch of deep water near him, an indistinct shape rose and turned to us. I saw a young woman in a narrow dress; I couldn't see details but had the impression of streaming hair falling past her shoulders, two slender braids on either side framing her face. Women often celebrated the coming of rain by joining the children splashing about in the short-lived pools and puddles, and our arrival had caught this pair by surprise. They studied us in startled silence.

But only for a moment. Even as I started formally to wish them peace, the young woman called out, *"Ahlan wa sahlan"* — a greeting with overtones of welcome. Her upturned hands caught the falling rain and tossed it back at the clouds. "A propitious time: your arrival is green! Tomorrow the wells will be full and the whole world fresh."

"May the Gods prosper you, lady." I wished I were talking to a man. A man had more authority. "My master is injured and appeals for your protection."

"You must take your appeal to my mother."

"Not to your father, or perhaps an uncle — ?"

"My fa— ?" A surprised pause. A bubble of amusement appeared in her voice; she quelled it politely. "No. We of *Ahl al-Hilal* do things the old way."

If the men were absent it would of course be proper to appeal to her mother, but somehow I thought she meant more than that. *Ahl al-Hilal* — kindred of the crescent moon. I'd never heard of them. But I had heard the rumor about a tribe of witches. Was it true after all? Might this kindred have no need of men? Might they have the power to call down lightning to guard Ras al-Wadi's approaches? . . .

The young woman said something to the boy. He turned and ran, splashing through the rain and the gathering dark toward the date palms. I thought I saw the outline of a small building up against the trees. Then she was speaking again.

". . . Lead the animals this way." A careful look at Mujahid. She couldn't have seen much. "Follow me exactly. I'll keep you on level ground."

The house was a minute's walk away, a low rectangle of mud brick thickly daubed with mud and straw. The flickering light from a small indoor fire showed an open doorway beyond which I could make out no details, and then someone blocked the firelight, ducking out into the rain holding what was probably a thick wool cloak overhead like a tent.

"Is that the injured one?"

A woman's voice, deep-toned and decisive even when asking a question.

"On the horse," I said. "His name's Mujahid bin Hasan an-Numayri and he appeals for your protection."

"He has it. *Ahlan wa sahlan.* I am Nur bint Hind. Mabruka!"

"Mother?" the young woman said.

"Tell Latifa to move her bedding in with us; we need her room for our guests. And bring in a candle."

Latifa was an aging servant woman with a small skinny old body muffled in peasant wrappings. In a cheerful cackle she assured us that Nur usually put up a tent to accommodate guests but how could you, when the world was under water? She bundled up her bedding with ostentatious good nature to emphasize the hospitality of her mistress's household and scurried out one door and into the other. There were two rooms in the building with no interior door between them.

To my eyes it was pitch dark in Latifa's room. With no will of his own Mujahid allowed himself to be guided inside to what my toes told me was a rug, at one end of which he obediently sat. I heard the settling rustle of clothing as Nur bint Hind sank to the floor beside him. Then I turned back toward the door to go and see about the animals and baggage just as Mabruka came in, cradling the guttering flame of a tallow candle with a careful hand.

Once inside she stood up straight and held the candle to illuminate the room. Or at least the people in it. What it showed best was Mabruka. Perhaps that was the idea.

In the candlelight her eyes were huge and dark and almost magical. I had

107

thought her young but not this young. Two years ago she could have showed no sign of the breasts and hips that pushed against the fabric of the narrow wet dress. New womanhood glowed from her like a mystery, increasingly exciting in its unfolding possibilities. Perhaps she was fourteen. I couldn't imagine anyone less like Filwa. Filwa was taller, slimmer, her beauty quiet and shy. Mabruka's was sturdy and exuberant, as outgoing as laughter, as confident as a spring sunrise.

Her eyes slid past me to her mother, then fixed on Mujahid. Lucky Mujahid. Mabruka knelt at the edge of the rug, brought the candle nearer his face. He turned slightly to look at it, then at her. His eyes below the rough bandage showed no spark of interest. I was suddenly afraid that this was no temporary despondency, that the old ways and the smiling assurance were gone for good.

Something bitter twisted my lips. A flower of remorse blossomed suddenly under my ribcage, bewildering me. No, not remorse. *Guilt.* I was guilty of something, the accusation was unanswerable, but . . . of what was I accused? And once the question was asked the answer came without effort. *You are accused of secretly, bitterly, under a cloak of admiration, resenting Mujahid's good luck.* And hard on the heels of this recognition came the further question: Must it mean that now I actively *wanted* Mujahid's luck changed?

I was appalled. Since I had already been feeling obscurely disloyal to Filwa for the impression created by my first good look at Mabruka, I had to wonder if I had any loyalty at all. *Of course* I didn't want Mujahid's luck changed! — if only for the practical reason that he might need it to avenge his father, and if he did I certainly would too. Besides, though we shared no formal kinship ties yet, circumstances had made me as much a Numayri of the Bani Faris as anyone; he was my brother,

108

and my friend.

Nur bint Hind leaned into the candlelight. She had dropped the cloak that she'd held overhead down around her shoulders. She had a light shawl draped over her hair and wrapped about her neck; a strikingly handsome woman I guessed to be no more than twice Mabruka's age, her face calm under dark level brows, her eyes direct, with a challenging intelligence. Her hands rose to Mujahid's bandage, showing on her fingers silver rings set with turquoise and red stones, on one wrist the wink of solid silver.

"Are you a healer, lady?"

"I have no magic, but I've treated the cuts and scrapes of many children besides my own, more than my share of lance and knife wounds, and seen women through childbirth. If his hurt's beyond my skill we'll take him in the morning to a healer we know in the city." She slipped the bandage over his head, detaching it carefully from the wound, then used a corner to wipe away congealing blood.

Mujahid flinched slightly. He flinched again when she prodded delicately around the edges of the wound, which I couldn't properly see. Then she sat back on her heels, dropping her hand into her lap and giving him a thoughtful stare which, after a long moment, she turned on me.

"I've seen worse head cuts on five-year-old boys playing sword fights with sticks. Did something else happen to him?"

"His camel stumbled." I licked parched lips. My tongue felt like dry wool. "He was thrown and hit his head and trampled an *ausaj* bush."

She finished the explanation for me. "He fears a jinn curse."

I nodded.

She thought a moment, then looked full into her daughter's face. Her brows rose slightly, an unvoiced question.

Mabruka nodded, settling slowly back

on her heels. She lowered the candle and sat with the other hand in her lap, unmoving, not visibly breathing. I only had the space of a heartbeat to wonder what was happening before I felt myself caught in a curious moment of stretched time, like an insect caught in a drop of honey, with the world stopped. My vision was restricted, I saw only the heavy silver bracelet on Nur's wrist, the upturned fingers of Mabruka's hand lying in her lap. The candle flame was unnaturally still, a golden blade glowing in the first red light of some mythic dawn in a desert without landmarks where the only sound came from the collision of one sand grain against another, each *tick* and *click* distinct and separate, slower than the rattle of a kitten's first purr, inexorable as the fall of mountains but more threatening . . .

Who knows under what spell I was falling? Or perhaps it was only weariness and anxiety played on by the candle flame, evoking a waking dream finally interrupted when an impurity in the tallow caused the flame to sputter and flare up. I was instantly wide awake, my heart hammering under my ribs, and I was staring at Mabruka.

She was on her heels, her body tilted slightly forward from the waist in an attitude of attention, her breasts urgent against the wet dress. Desire for her went through me like a sword. My knees dissolved. I almost groaned aloud.

Mabruka met her mother's eyes and shook her head. Mujahid could not have cared less. Nur looked past him up at me.

"Your master is safe. My daughter tells me there are no spirits present."

I said without thinking, "How would she know?"

"She knows. It's her gift."

"And there's no curse," Mabruka said. "A curse leaves . . . a kind of echo."

I stared. Mabruka looked defensive.

She said, "Some people can make poems, or play music. I can do this."

"It's a great . . . skill, gift," I fumbled huskily, hopelessly.

"It's not *fun,* you know. It's frightening."

"Look," Nur said.

Mujahid was returning to us.

Not quickly, as at the snap of fingers. I didn't know what Nur had seen but when I looked he moved his shoulders, like a child disturbed in sleep. Then his throat made a small soft sound, half query, half protest. After a while he blinked. Several times. When his eyes stayed open the lost uncaring look had left them and the slack lines of his face and body were tightening into a semblance of Mujahid living. Staring at Mabruka whose gleaming hair fell past her shoulders, the slender braids framing her face. At the hand holding the candle. At the other still resting in her lap. At her mouth.

When he spoke his voice was as light and dry as wheat chaff.

"Sorceress."

"No," she said.

Relief had begun storming through me at the first sigh of his recovery. Now it subsided, leaving me weak and angry.

"So you heard it was safe and decided to come back," I sneered. "Where've you been?"

I was still standing. He looked up at me wanly. "Nowhere."

Nur said, "Your injury's nothing, a skin wound, hardly enough to take away your senses. Your servant's been worried."

"Sorry, Talal." He thought a minute, and when he finally shrugged it was almost humorously. The old confidence was returning. In a minute more, I thought, he'll be displaying the full panoply that identified lucky Mujahid, warrior Mujahid, courteous and *tender* Mujahid, Mujahid the romantic conqueror . . .

109

I almost snarled, "He thought a jinni was after him and it scared him witless."

His face closed like a fist; he gave me a cold rejecting stare. It got even worse when a spasm quivered in his cheek and one corner of his mouth began lifting in a ghastly half-smile. I tried to match him stare for stare. I don't think I did too well. And then his face began to relax. He sighed.

"A jinni's a hard enemy to fight. You could be right." His voice was getting stronger every minute. He explained my outburst to the two women: "Talal's as much a younger brother as a servant. Or thinks he is. But that's all right, I often think so too."

I felt obscurely apologetic — and too angry to apologize.

I said awkwardly, "Whichever I am, I still have to see to the animals," and went outside.

The rain had stopped. Water dripped noisily from palm fronds in the date garden that was only visible as a looming mass in the dark.

From somewhere the little boy had summoned a man I later learned was a field hand and the servant Latifa's nephew. So at least these Hilali people weren't a kindred of women only. The man and the boy had the pack camel barracked near the house and were unloading her. I joined them and soon we had all three camels unloaded and the gear and baggage and saddlebags carried in and stacked in Latifa's room. The two women had gone to hurry up the meal that Latifa was preparing next door.

To keep the animals out of the vegetable field, the man helped me lead them into a mud-walled pen. I thanked him. He assured me no thanks were due for the performance of a duty, and when I squatted by a deep puddle to wash my face and arms and feet, the little boy told me to hurry and not miss my din-

110

ner because they had killed a sheep yesterday and there was meat in the stew. I said I was sure it was delicious. He nodded solemnly. I complimented Nur bint Hind's hospitality. He proudly told me she was his mother; he was Sa'd bin Nur. I didn't ask about his father.

"Soon," he told me, "I go to my uncle to learn to be a bedouin herdsman and a hunter. I will hunt gazelle."

I told him gazelle meat was tasty eating.

When I got back inside, Mujahid had a fresh strip of cloth tied around his head; he was sitting where I had left him, now wearing a dry *thaub* they had given him. Nur and Latifa were setting out food on the rug in front of him. No sign of Mabruka. A heady smell rose from the dish of well-spiced stew; there was a bowl of curdled milk, dates, dried apricots, a stack of flat circles of bread. It would have been a feast in any shaykh's tent or house at Hasa oasis. To a bedouin just in from a weeks-long journey on a minimum of bread and dates and stale water the sight and smell were dizzying.

From a store of household furnishings stacked almost ceiling-high against the inside wall Latifa brought us a couple of cushions each and grinned and told us to be comfortable and eat well and then left.

I sat down and we started to eat when there was movement in the doorway and Mabruka came in.

She had changed out of the clinging wet dress into a fuller, black one with red embroidery in a band around the collar, and over this wore a light black mantle. In the candlelight, silver and turquoise glinted from her fingers. Around her neck were strings of red and black beads hung with silver ornaments and tiny silver bells and a string of thick oval honey-colored stones that must have come from beyond the farthest mountains. I twisted my neck to gape at her. Her lips parted and the wide bold dark eyes warmed in my direction and my heart pounded like racing hoofbeats as she crossed the floor to join us.

I had to move to offer her a place to sit between me and Mujahid, then scrambled to offer her the cushions Latifa had given me. A servant's automatic response. She thanked me sweetly, settling down to them in a single fluid movement with a faint tinkling of her jewelry and gave one cushion back, saying I was the guest, a far traveler, it was *her* duty to see to *my* comfort. I felt drugged with delight. Also uncomprehending. Therefore suddenly cautious.

Neither woman ate. Urged on by them, however, Mujahid and I ate heartily to show appreciation but not so much as to seem desperate for food. Mujahid seemed pretty much recovered.

I took a healthy pull at the curdled milk.

"Talal," Nur said crisply. "Talal son of whom?"

I set the bowl down, wiped my lips with my fingers.

"Ibn abuh," Mujahid said. Son-of-his-father. "But nobody knows who he was."

"We'd call him son of his mother."

"She's unknown too. He was caught raiding my father's orchard when he was no bigger than a locust. He couldn't tell us much. He'd been traveling with a northbound caravan, who knows where or with whom, or whether he'd run away or been dumped. My father took pity on him and brought him into his household to raise as a servant. He had four daughters and only one son; accepting the orphan gave him another. No one ever claimed him."

Mabruka smiled. "Your father is a good man."

"He was, may the Gods be merciful."

Both women echoed the wish. I chewed on a dried apricot, found Nur regarding me with a question in her fine eyes.

"I wasn't formally adopted," I explained. "When our . . . business is done and we return home, they've said they'll adopt me into the family and the tribe. Until then I have no ancestors."

She nodded. "Among our people," she said, "that would be more of a problem for a woman than a man, since property descends through the female line."

Mujahid looked blankly astonished. For all I know I did too. Then he looked scandalized, but that may have been pretense. Suddenly he had begun to enjoy himself. I hoped he wouldn't say anything to antagonize these people.

"Among us," he said, "property goes to sons who can defend it." He sat up straighter, muscles flexing in the pride of manhood; but his smile was guileless. "Do women of your kindred take up arms?"

Nur smiled. It made her look like Mabruka's not-much-older sister.

Mabruka said slyly, "We haven't the bodies for it."

"I've noticed," Mujahid said happily. "But are you governed by a shaykha, not a shaykh? Is the prince of that city of the valley actually a princess?"

"Oh, Ras al-Wadi isn't ours," Nur said. "It's the tribal capital of the Bani Ghassan, and its prince is a man named Salah bin Mansur."

"Your kindred isn't part of the Bani Ghassan?"

"No. We were originally from further north. But there were . . . difficulties, and we separated from our own tribe and migrated with all our tents and livestock. This happened five, six generations ago. The details are in many songs and stories, and we've almost become a tribe of our own since then, but in those days our numbers were too few to displace a tribe or take over its range by force. But the Goddess is kind to her devotees, and our ancestors met an ancestor of Shaykh Salah when he was preparing to meet a traditional enemy in battle, and he made an offer: in exchange for help in battle, some land and the use of the Bani Ghassan range for our flocks under his protection. We agreed, the enemy was routed, and this has been our base ever since."

"Have you had to defend it often?"

"Not too often. Often enough."

"But you haven't become part of the Bani Ghassan?"

"No, we're still under their protection."

"Do they follow your customs of inheritance and tracing descent through the mother?"

"Oh no, I'm sure they're just like you."

"How about intermarriage?"

"It happens, of course. My own sister married an outside trader and left the valley. Others of our women have chosen to marry Ghassani men and into the Bani Ghassan tribe, which means into its jurisdiction and customs. When they do they forfeit their property to their sisters or other female relatives, and become their husbands' property."

"Why would they do that?"

"For some it's all for love, some expect to live more comfortably in the house of a rich foreign husband, some simply want a life of more limited responsibility. And sometimes of course one of our men will marry one of their women. But neither will bring more than personal possessions to the marriage, the man because it's all he owns, the woman because only a poor Ghassani gives his daughter to another poor man: he just wants someone else to take care of her. Such marriages we discourage as much as possible. They tend to expand our unpropertied numbers, and force people to live wedged into a corner between the two societies."

"And when a Ghassani man marries one of your women, under your laws?"

"Our marriages are contracted for specific lengths of time, usually five years. He gives her a gift, she gives him a tent and a lance. He takes care of her

112

flocks and fields. She sleeps with him, rides with him, cooks for him, but is not his property. If both want to, the terms of the marriage can be extended for a further period. The children carry her name and are of her family, not his . . ."

"Then he's no better than a servant!" Mujahid protested, and though he was smiling I thought he was dangerously close to insulting the man or men who had fathered Nur's children. We didn't *know* these people, or what they might consider a serious offense.

"Hardly," I said. "Whoever heard of a servant with a property-owner for a wife?"

"Spoken like someone with no ancestors," Mujahid said airily. "We've tried to make a bedouin out of you but you're just a peasant at heart, Talal. What of your pride? Your freedom?"

"You're confusing pride with property. And what freedom? Freedom to do what?"

Mujahid grinned broadly, glanced at the two women in turn. They watched him expectantly.

"I do anything I please," he said simply, turning back to me. "Raid, make love, travel. You won't be a servant forever. You can do the same."

Like the rest of us, most of his traveling was in search of pasture for his herds, a search that controlled and conditioned every bedouin's life. Not even Hasa oasis could support a whole tribe's livestock. I'd never thought about it, but it seemed to be that a bedouin's wide skies and open horizons gave only an illusion of freedom, that he wasn't really any freer than a village carpenter or farmer. And both raiding and making love assumed like-minded partners . . .

His grin widened. "Of course, if you've decided to settle down with a lady of Ahl al-Hilal. . . ."

I said, with a modest smile, "I never aspire above my station," and to my relief everyone laughed. Mabruka turned those great dark eyes on me for a long appraising look that turned my spine to candle-grease. I forgot to breathe.

"If you adopt him into your tribe," Nur told Mujahid, "that glib tongue will make him chief councilor in six months and shaykh before he's forty."

"Does the sorceress confirm that prediction?"

Mabruka hadn't taken her eyes off me. She said without interest, "I'm not a sorceress."

"You mean you can't even tell whether he's going to be a great leader, or just a farmer?"

Nur said unexpectedly, "You're looking at him closely enough. What do you see, if not the future?"

"A lean young man with careful eyes and a face that's thin and still, like a good blade, waiting."

"Anyone can see that," Nur said softly. "What can *you* see?"

Mabruka tensed, started to speak, then changed her mind. She sighed, paused, reached for my hand. It felt rough and uncouth between both of hers. My heart thudded. I stared into her eyes and watched the reflection of the candle flame, twin golden splinters in the mysterious black depths of her pupils.

She shook her head — in surprise. Her eyebrows contracted. She turned her face to look uncertainly over her shoulder toward the wall by the doorway where I had stacked our gear. Her hands slid away from mine.

"You keep trying to get me to do more than I can," she told her mother; then to me, in a puzzled voice, "You brought something in from outside . . ."

"Our baggage."

"Of course!" Mujahid pushed himself to his feet. He moved carefully but seemed steady enough as he crossed to his saddlebag and dug into it.

He produced a slim bundle wrapped in cloth, which he brought back to the rug's edge. He knelt and unrolled the wrapping, revealing the arrow he had shot into the sky the afternoon Hasan died. He picked it up almost reverently, holding it close to the candle. Dried blood discolored half its length.

"With this arrow," he said almost wonderingly, "the spirit world ordered me to avenge my father's murder. Is some spirit following the arrow . . . to see if I obey?"

Mabruka shrugged. "I don't think so. I don't know." Her expression was resentful.

He leaned toward her. The golden glow from the candle met a pale sick light flickering deep in his eyes. His look was still wondering, almost childlike, but his voice was relentless; tension made it almost unrecognizable.

"Last time you tried, the arrow was outside. I have to know if the spirit of my father is following the arrow, *the spirit of Hasan bin Nasir an-Numayri . . . !*"

"She'll tell you what she can," Nur interrupted, straining to keep her voice gentle, "but she's neither sorceress nor seer. You mustn't expect too much of her, even if I sometimes do."

Mujahid ignored her. For the space of one gasping breath he seemed about to attack Mabruka to force an answer from her. I was appalled. None of this made sense. I thought wildly of jinni curses, of delayed effects from his fall from the camel. I tensed to launch myself in a preventive attack — just as he paused, startled recollection coming into his eyes.

After a moment he sat back on his heels. The tension began draining out of him, and a look of deep embarrassment settled on his face. He began an unconditional apology for behaving badly while enjoying protected status under the rules of sanctuary and hospitality.

I knew just how fully he had recovered when, in the middle of the **113** apology, he rediscovered his smile, which he soon turned with growing warmth on Mabruka. It was supposed to melt her bones and turn her brain to buttermilk. I couldn't tell if it was working. Nur smiled faintly. Mabruka overrode the apology with a clucking tongue and a fluttering hand, insisting that he had done no wrong, was distraught from his bereavement and shaken by his fall, which prompted him to tell the story of our search for Kadhim bin Ja'far.

No bedouin ever forgets a traveler seen along the way. Even in the wastes between the wells, people meet and share news: of migrations, marriages and alliances, raids and warfare, acts of chivalry and treachery, who rode to meet whom for reasons known or rumored, even news of lone travelers complete with meticulous descriptions of dress, accoutrements, animal or animals and the tribal brand showing on their flanks. Even someone who had not seen Kadhim might remember hearing about him from someone who had. And so we had followed the fugitive almost to the edge of the Great Sands to the south, lost him, doubled back and met a party of Khalidis moving east; they had seen Kadhim two days before, riding west as though harried by demons. We followed. Three days' ride beyond the Dahnaa — the curving belt of red dunes that flares northward like a flame to burn, it is said, into the tribal range of the distant Shammar — the trail turned north until we came to a well with the single tent of a Bani Tha'lab family pitched nearby. They told us that Kadhim had stopped to fill his waterbag two days previously, then ridden west toward Ras al-Wadi, about which we knew only of its rumored guardians and that it was a small city of no importance off the main trade routes.

Neither Mabruka nor her mother recognized Kadhim by name or description.

"In the morning we'll look for him in the city," Mujahid said. "If he's already left, someone may know in which direction."

Latifa came in to clear away the remains of the meal. From the stack against the inner wall Nur and Mabruka produced bedding for us, and on her way out Mabruka threw me a secret smile, the tiny silver bells on her necklace making a small sweet clash of sound every time she moved.

I closed the lightweight palmleaf door. Mujahid spread his borrowed quilt on the rug and wrapped himself in it. He looked stronger and healthier than at any time since the lightning strike.

He grinned broadly, kept his voice low.

"Admit it: you thought I was going to say the wrong thing to our hostess. You thought my brain was scrambled."

I spread the second quilt on the woven grass mat they had given me.

"Yes! When you got into that business about your father's spirit . . ."

I thought his voice acknowledged some embarrassment, though it wouldn't have been obvious to anyone who didn't know him well.

"All right, that was a weird idea I had. I got carried away, I admit. Let's just say that the crack on the head and the *ausaj* business mixed me up for a while, all right? But it got us protected status — though what good it does to get the protection of a couple of women I don't know."

That would depend on the respect that they and their menfolk were held in.

"Women, one of whom," I reminded him, "you kept calling a sorceress."

"I was mixed up. What she is, is a beauty just aching to lose her virginity."

"How do you know she's still got it?"

I punched out the candle, took off my headcloth and *thaub*. At least they had

had time to absorb warmth from my body. The quilt was as cold as a winter's dawn wind. I wrapped it tightly around me, suddenly impatient for sleep. The packed earth floor felt like solid rock. I wouldn't ever be warm again.

"You develop an instinct about these things," Mujahid said. "You noticed how she got dressed up in her feast finery, with jewels . . ."

"Careful. Maybe these people expect their unmarried girls to be chaste."

"Then I'll steal her in a raid."

"A fine way to repay their hospitality."

"Hospitality," he said airily, "is an obligation in the desert. No payment is expected. My instinct also tells me her thighs have the texture of rose petals."

My throat tightened on a sudden urge to yell at him.

"What about Filwa's thighs?" I whispered violently. "Why didn't you claim her while you had the chance?"

I heard movement from his direction. Perhaps he was coming over to kick me in the head. I wouldn't have blamed him. Obviously he hadn't claimed her because bereavement and the need for vengeance had driven all else from his mind. But he was only adjusting his position. When he spoke it was without rancor, his tone dry, a little amused.

"I just didn't, that's all. I didn't even stop to figure out whether I wanted to." A pause. I heard voices from the next room, the words indistinguishable. Perhaps he was thinking how much more desirable he found Mabruka. Unexpectedly he said, "She'll be there waiting when we get back."

"Why should she be? She told me I was crazy to be going with you. She doesn't sound like one of your uncritical admirers."

"So what? Why should she want to go back to her own people? Her father would only marry her off to another old man."

"And of course she'd much prefer a vigorous young man like you."

"Of course!" The smile in his voice shone through the darkness, but under the smug tone I heard a note of weariness. "Respectable married women have been known to sigh over me, you know."

"How do *you* know?"

"Their younger sisters have told me. They've also told me you're shy. Or is it unadventurous?"

"I'm a servant," I reminded him.

"That wouldn't have bothered some of the young women. Perhaps when we get home I'll give you Filwa."

"You didn't claim her, she's not yours to give. Why, anyway? To get back at her for not being an uncritical admirer?"

"Don't worry about the motive, just enjoy the gift." As though he had already given it. "Mother of the Gods, shut up and go to sleep, can't you?"

"Wake in goodness," I grunted, burying my head under the quilt.

Warmth had begun to gather in my cocoon. My eyelids quickly became heavy.

His voice said out of the darkness, "I'm sorry you were worried."

"I was afraid I might have to avenge Hasan myself, is all."

He grunted. I heard him turn over. I hoped he was through talking. I was more than ready not to have to respond. In a few moments I wouldn't be able to.

He said cryptically, "Maybe it would be better you than me. I might not be . . . acceptable."

I sat bolt upright, staring into the darkness.

Acceptable to *whom?*

The usual scurrilous epithets leaped to mind cataloguing alleged vices, impugning ancestry. Instead I said, "You shit — are you trying to frighten me?"

After a pause I heard his head turn suddenly. His voice was blurred, vaguely surprised. "— What? . . . For all the Gods' sake, Talal, are you crazy? Go to sleep. . . ."

Either he was faking, or he had spoken before more asleep than awake, uttering nonsense or perhaps giving unconsidered words to some secret concern that gnawed at his heart like the disease of the crab. In which case his well-being must all have been sham, put on for my benefit.

"Mujahid?"

No answer.

I lay back down and wrapped the quilt tightly around me, apprehension a cold stone in my belly.

It was still there when I woke up at daybreak, nagged at by already-forgotten but disturbing dreams.

Mujahid breathed deeply, regularly, almost snoring. I crawled out of the quilt and pulled the *thaub* the women had left for me over my head. It was worn but clean, and its hem brushed the ground. I got a thin length of cord from my saddlebag and belted the garment up to ankle-length before opening the door and stepping out into the morning.

The air was cool, the sky a soft clean blue. The sun must have cleared the edge of the desert but wasn't high enough to shine over the rim of the valley, so everything lay in uniform soft shadow, washed clean and dustless. No sign of the sheet of water that had hidden the trail last night except the healthy color of the earth between the valley wall and the dense mass of the palm trees.

A patch of ground planted in what looked like onions stretched away to a clutch of peasant huts and a bedouin tent of brown goat hair, and in this space I saw Nur bint Hind conferring with a tall thin man who had the hem of his *thaub* picked up and tucked into his belt to shorten the garment to knee length, working peasant style. Somewhere, distantly, a man's voice rose in a half-shouted conversation. Closer by, chickens clucked and squawked.

116

I went in among the palm trees to relieve myself, returning by way of our penned animals. Someone had already fed them. Nur's hospitality was thorough. The camels were barracked and looked immovable; the mare was standing, drinking in the morning air, her nostrils making a soft snuffling sound when she saw me.

The chickens were quieter now. As I walked back toward the house, Mabruka came from behind it carrying a basket of eggs. No mantle or shawl this morning, just a plum-colored dress with embroidery at the neck and a decorated gazelle-skin belt, no jewelry except a necklace of agate beads and a couple of silver finger rings. Enough to remind me that she was no peasant or servant girl, as out of reach as the crescent moon itself.

But not nearly so cool. She saw me and smiled. My heart lurched.

"Morning of goodness, Talal."

At that moment the sun's edge looked over the rim of the valley, already losing its gentleness, the last of dawn's gold warming her cheek and turning her hair into a gleaming fall of black water. I felt hollow as chaff and about as much use. I bit down hard on empty jaws before returning the formal response to her greeting.

"Morning of light," I said stiffly.

Her smile vanished. The wide dark eyes blinked once, twice, became suddenly opaque.

". . . I'll . . . send in Latifa with breakfast if you're ready."

"I'll make sure my master's awake."

Mabruka turned away and I stuck my head into Latifa's room. Mujahid was propped up on one elbow, his free hand poking cautiously at yesterday's scalp wound.

"Breakfast's coming."

"I heard."

"How's the head?"

"Hurts a bit. Nothing to worry about."

"Good," I said, and turned back outside.

Mabruka had disappeared. Two horses with riders, cantering from the direction of the city, swung off the trail and approached.

One of them, a small gray, slowed and stopped in front of Nur's house. The rider carried a lance; he was a young man with a cast in one eye, wearing the unadorned clothing of a servant or a groom. The other horse, a rangy roan, shifted without pause into a thudding gallop when its rider drove his heels into its ribs. This pair charged past Nur's house to the mud-walled pen, where the rider hauled savagely on his halter rope and pulled the horse into a barbarous pirouette to face back toward us, prancing and curvetting while the man took a long look at our animals. Then he came galloping back. The other rider moved the gray out of the way so the roan could be stopped in a storm of stamping hooves and empty bravado.

The rider was no herdsman. His clothes were too good and too clean; despite his lean hard look something in his face said settled comfort. A narrow-bladed dagger in a decorated leather sheath was attached to the belt around his waist and he looked somewhere between Mujahid's age and mine. His nose curved like a scythe. He had full lips that dipped in the middle and tilted up at the ends, like the wings of a bird, like a smile gone wrong. Small disdainful bright eyes regarded me with unpleasant speculation. Then their focus changed and I realized that Mabruka had come outside again.

"Peace be unto you, Mabruka." The man on the roan smiled, his fastidious, delicately curved nostrils curling up as though he found himself downwind from something dead.

"*Ahlan*, Zuhayr." She stood a half-step outside the door, now folded her arms loosely across her middle. She was polite, withdrawn, disinterested. "Will you eat with us?"

"I have already eaten. Have you reconsidered my offer?"

"Nothing to reconsider."

"I'd give you sons to make history."

"You mean *I'd* give *you* sons. And daughters for you to sell to the highest bidder."

His smile deepened. "I'm chagrined, of course, but all that can wait. I have a message from the shaykh to all the kindred."

"Which shaykh?"

"Ours. Shaykh Harith. He wants it known that yesterday a traveler came as a suppliant who placed himself under the protection of Salah bin Mansur of the Bani Ghassan. Out of regard for Shaykh Salah, we are to regard this man as being under our protection too. He is Kadhim bin Ja'far of an eastern tribe, the Bani Faris, and he's in flight from a band of cut-throats because of a dispute over the ownership of a strip of land at the Hasa oasis."

Nur had come in from the field and was joining us. Mabruka's face had stiffened at the names of Kadhim and the Bani Faris but nothing more. She waited as though expecting him to go on, nodded politely when he didn't. The reptilian eyes of the young man she had called Zuhayr flickered briefly in my direction, and Mujahid came out of the room behind me.

He was wearing his headgear, the drape of the *kaffiyya* hiding his scalp wound. I guessed he'd taken the bandage off. He wore the borrowed *thaub* with his leather belt, the dagger in its worn sheath attached in the horizontal position at the right side of his belly. He looked untroubled, relaxed, his broad face trying not to smile.

Then Zuhayr noticed that Nur was among us. He directed a deep smile at her. His nostrils performed their unintended commentary.

"Morning of goodness, Nur."

Her smile was everything politeness demanded and not a hair more.

118

"Morning of light, Ibn Zahra."

Zuhayr laughed.

"You never miss a chance to remind me that we Hilalis trace descent through the mother, do you, Bint Hind? But things are changing, I promise you. I see you have guests. Suitors of Mabruka's, no doubt."

"If they are they haven't announced it," Nur said. "They arrived last night, at the height of the storm, asking protection. Which I gave. One had been injured."

"I trust he has recovered."

"I have," Mujahid said. "The Great Goddess is kind."

" 'Goddess,' " Zuhayr murmured. "And yet I hear that beyond these deserts the chief Gods are thought to be male."

Mujahid laughed.

Nur said, "That would be blasphemy if it weren't so funny. As I presume you learned when you examined the brands on their animals, our guests are Bani Faris. This Kadhim did familiarize you with the Bani Faris brand, didn't he? But there are only two of them, no party of cut-throats. If any harm comes to them, my kinsmen will hunt Kadhim down and I'll see the council goes after Shaykh Harith. They're not too happy with him anyway because he's grown complacent and slack."

"Who says so?"

"I do. Last month again, some herdsmen from the Bayt Ali clan of Bani Ghassan tried to dispute one of my herdsmen's right to water his animals at Ghazala well. This has been happening for over a year and Harith has done nothing. He should get the behavior stopped or get the Bani Ghassan council to declare the old policy of cooperation and protection rescinded."

"And suppose they did that?"

"Then we'd move. But they won't. Alone they're not strong enough and they know it."

Zuhayr thought a moment, then smiled faintly.

"The Bayt Ali are hooligans," he acknowledged. "They wouldn't bother you if you or Mabruka had a powerful husband."

Nur's face softened, her eyes warmed, and her lips parted suddenly in the disarming smile I had seen take years off her last night.

"Why Zuhayr, I believe you've been behind these harassments all along!"

Zuhayr jerked visibly, as though poked with a sharp stick, his hard young face slack with astonishment and chagrin. But he recovered quickly enough.

"If I'd thought of it, I might have." He had no gift for levity; even this light humorous concession made him uncomfortable; he backed away from it sharply, turning to Mujahid. "I am Zuhayr bin Zahra, aide to Shaykh Harith bin Mit'ab of Ahl al-Hilal."

"I'm Mujahid bin Hasan an-Numayri of Bani Faris," Mujahid said mildly. "This is my servant, Talal."

Zuhayr gave him a long look. He couldn't ask Mujahid his business in the valley; the implied suspicion would be a discourtesy to Nur. Mujahid, half smiling, the picture of bland innocence, wasn't about to tell him anything.

Zuhayr sighed, and switched his attention to me.

"Talal . . ." he said thoughtfully, as though the name bothered him. The small eyes were bright as polished brown agates but less friendly. His brows contracted faintly. "Not Talal the bowman, who brings down wild doves in flight?"

So Kadhim had mentioned me.

I shrugged.

"Sometimes."

He looked surprised. Perhaps he expected someone older. Then his expression shifted subtly.

"Don't Goddess-worshipers hold the dove sacred?"

I shrugged again. "The Bani Faris don't."

He looked slyly at the two women.

"I told you things were changing." His nostrils described their faint insulting curl. Abruptly he turned the roan's head toward the trail. "More people to see. Peace unto you."

The two horsemen thudded away, turned down the valley, and picked up speed.

Latifa began carrying our breakfast from one room into the other. Hunched and scowling over a bowl of curdled milk, she paused to stare after Zuhayr.

"Cockroach!" she spat. "Traitor! And he wants to marry the baby, my darling, and make a foreigner of her."

"Isn't he one of you?" I asked.

"He is," she admitted, "but he's picked up the notion that women should have no power at all, even over their own selves or property. He thinks we'd be better off like Bani Ghassan. So he wants to marry Mabruka under Ghassani law."

"At least he can't get his hands on the property she'll inherit," Mujahid said.

"He's working on it, you can be sure!" Latifa broke into a cackling laugh. "He's ambitious, young Zuhayr. I think he dreams of combining the Ghassani and Hilali peoples and becoming prince over everyone and making us all worship his piddling male Gods."

"Oh, he's just a nuisance," Mabruka said.

The laughter vanished from Latifa's old face.

" 'Just a nuisance!' — who's making himself indispensable to Shaykh Harith and who knows who else! What do *you* know? You're only a child. . . ." The flare of anger died in her eyes. Her snappish voice became a mumble. "Oh. The breakfast . . ."

"I'll help you," Mabruka said, and Mujahid and I were soon seated on either side of the breakfast they had laid out on the rug in Latifa's room. The old woman wished us health and ordered Mabruka in to her own breakfast next door, would she bother the men at their meal, did she want her mother to eat alone?

When they had gone Mujahid grinned broadly. No sign of the vacillation and despondency of last night. He seemed confident, and very much at ease.

He tore a round of fresh warm bread in two and gave me half.

"So Hilali women are strong in the council too, are they? That's probably one reason why they're not happy with Shaykh Harith: *he's* not happy with *them*."

"No shaykh can go against his council," I said. "Not for long, anyway."

"But when the council includes women . . . ? Women think with their bellies. And what do *these* women give us for breakfast? Why, curdled milk and honey, of course — a combination long trusted to sustain virility. The dates and bread are only to make the intent less obvious. I wonder whose idea it was?"

"Latifa's. She wants to make sure you have something left for her when the other two are through with you. Too bad we have work to do."

He started to laugh but it died in his mouth. After a moment he sighed, a disconsolate sound, and stuffed a piece of bread between his teeth. He chewed without interest, his face abstracted. Vaguely his hand went up inside his headcloth, fingers poking at the edges of yesterday's wound.

We ate in silence.

He muttered finally, "What that snake-eyed bandit Zuhayr said makes it harder."

He meant Kadhim's protection by the two shaykhs. Killing Kadhim within their reach would not only shame them and invite swift retribution, but would also blacken Nur's face because Kadhim was considered under the protection of all Ahl al-Hilal and *we* were her guests and under her protection too. We might escape the valley, but who knew

120

how far the shaykhs' men — and doubtless Nur's kinsmen too — would follow?

"You'll find a way," I said. "With your luck you're bound to."

"That's the trouble with luck. People expect great things from you."

"I'm confident," I assured him.

"Good."

He delivered the word with something of the old glint. His head tossed as though he were about to let go a peal of laughter. He didn't but his lips stretched and the grin flashed, the one that scattered doubts and lifted the souls of the faint-hearted. The trouble was I remembered my doubts of last night: he could still be faking it. I was beginning to suspect that behind the laughing eyes and the self-assurance lay a stranger no one had ever been aware of. Mujahid was my brother, but after all the years I simply didn't know him.

We finished breakfast and went back outside. Old Latifa was shaking out a skimpy quilt. She saw us and called Nur, who came out of the other door with Mabruka close behind her. Still withdrawn and distant, Mabruka stayed by the entrance, leaned one shoulder against the wall, folded her arms. . . .

"So the man Kadhim has powerful protectors," Nur said crisply. "Powerful hereabouts, anyway. You'll be making new plans. Until you know what they are, you'll be my guests."

Mujahid thanked her. "How do I get to see the Ghassani shaykh?"

"You go to the palace in the city and ask for an audience," Nur said. An idea struck her. "Except today might be different. I think he's holding a public court of justice. You might present yourself and make your case against Kadhim there. For what good it'll do."

Mujahid nodded. "That's this morning?"

"We could go to the city and find out," Mabruka said unexpectedly. "We know enough people, we might learn something useful."

Nur gave her a sharp look but said nothing. Mabruka stood unmoving and indifferent, her arms still folded.

"There's no danger, mother. No one wants to risk violating anyone's protection."

"Our guests don't. Can you be so sure of Kadhim?"

"Does Kadhim want more enemies than he has already?"

Nur tilted her head thoughtfully.

"I suppose not."

"It's settled, then."

Mujahid asked, "Are you to be our guide, Mabruka?"

"Would you rather go alone?"

He gave her the slow smile, assured, gently mocking, shook his head and said, "No, no!" in a voice like honey. He was beginning the campaign he had announced last night. He had to be feeling more like himself after all. Well, that was what I'd wanted, wasn't it?

I threw Nur a quick glance. She looked back with ironic eyes.

I ducked into Latifa's room and got my bow and strung it and hung the quiver of arrows across my back.

There was little talk as we walked to the city. Mabruka was so aloof she seemed hardly aware of us. Why had she suggested coming along? Maybe she just wished me elsewhere; which a good part of me did too.

The farmland and the great date grove beyond it ended; the trail curved left and we found ourselves crossing barren trampled ground toward the city wall. The narrow southern gate stood open between low towers with sloping walls and no guardsmen on top.

Once through the gate the trail became a dusty street advancing crookedly into the city between monotonous mud-plastered walls inset with occasional doors and windows and sometimes interrupted by narrow alleys. A knot of kids played in the dust. A few

people of no great wealth went about their business, some carrying bundles or baskets. Donkey and camel droppings caked the street. The air baked and smelled of smoke and cooking and refuse, as though no clean desert wind ever penetrated the defensive walls.

We came to a small temple to the Goddess on the corner of a narrow street leading west, and the street we were on took a jog and opened into a market square. Neither rich nor particularly busy, it was small enough to be crowded by half a dozen barracked camels being unloaded by bedouin caravaneers under the critical eyes of local merchants. Two streets entered the square on the north. Mabruka led us past the camels and a few shops and stalls and the entrance to a covered bazaar toward the street on the right, which proved to be short and to lead into a second and bigger square.

Also busier, but not much. At the far side the city's northern gate stood open, showing tethered horses outside, an expanse of cultivation, and a broad trail leading up the valley to where it sloped sharply up to the level of the surrounding desert. Through the gate came a woman driving a couple of scrawny donkeys loaded down with something in sacks toward another entrance to the covered bazaar. Two fine riding camels knelt in the center of the square.

Open trading stalls under ragged awnings lined the square's east side, and a high, mud-plastered wall with an impressive double door set into it ran down the west. The doors stood open. A burly man, with a sheathed sword at his side and a dagger in his belt, stood guard but allowed a group of peasants to enter with a word and a nod. They joined other people standing or sitting on the ground inside.

Beyond the walls a couple of tall date palms reached into the sky, nodding over a considerable building, two deep stories to the crenelated parapet surrounding the flat roof. A wind tower pushed even higher to catch the breeze to cool the interior. Overhead, a scavenging kite hawk with wingtip feathers like extended fingers wheeled and dipped.

"That's the palace." Mabruka nodded toward the double doors. "Nur was right about the court, it's the only time they let the crowd in."

Mujahid's face looked suddenly older, thinner.

I asked, "What's the plan? You won't get him to revoke his protection."

"I might keep him from extending it." His sudden smile was thin as a knife edge. "Anyhow Kadhim knows a shaykh's protection won't deflect a well-aimed bowshot."

"We can't ambush him here without betraying Nur."

"He doesn't know he can rely on that. He'll worry. Maybe he'll run. Here, I'd better go in there unarmed."

He unbuckled the belt with the dagger on it and took it off and gave it to me. "Put it on. You look silly with that string around your middle."

"I'd look sillier falling down because I tripped on my robe."

"Not much," Mujahid said, and started for the double doors while I buckled on his belt and followed with the silent Mabruka.

The burly guard had a muscular neck and a beard with gray patches and a knife or sword scar that ran from his forehead to his cheek, just missing his left eye. It could have made him look sinister but didn't. When he answered Mujahid's greeting his voice was almost friendly but thin and husky, as though at some time he'd taken a bad wound in the neck.

"I seek the shaykh's judgment," Mujahid said.

The guard's eyes went from Mujahid to Mabruka and me — and quickly back to Mabruka. Then reluctantly returned to Mujahid.

122

"Your witnesses?"

"I need no witnesses. These are friends."

"Go in and give them your name and wait your turn," the guard said. "Your friends had better wait outside till some of the disputes are settled and the crowd thins out."

"I would rather they were with me."

"Wait outside with them until there's room, then you can all go in together. But then you'll be later in line; who knows when the shaykh'll hear you?"

Through the double doorway I could see past the crowd in the yard to half of the building Mabruka had called the palace. Two guards with lances stood at either side of a big door with nothing fancy about it. Near the door a faded cloth awning cast a patch of shadow mostly on the wall, but when the sun rose higher it would shade an area of rugs and cushions that would presumably be occupied by the shaykh and members of his staff and council. This was the city version of the desert *diwan*, the court of justice at which every tribal member could petition the high chief in person. Accusations ran from murder to theft, petty fraud to harassment. A shaykh who met his obligations as judge with skill and insight saw his name for wisdom grow and assent to his chieftaincy flourish. . . .

Mujahid looked at the crowd briefly, then turned back to the guard. "No, I'll go in now." He poked a forefinger at my chest. "Look around, see what you can learn. Come back later, or I'll see you at Mabruka's house."

I agreed. He went through the archway and disappeared into the crowd.

"How long will it be?" I asked the guard.

He tore his eyes off Mabruka long enough to shrug. "Noon. Before noon. What can I tell you?" He hawked and spat, scratched delicately at the corner of his eye where the scar ran. "Sometimes these *diwans* last all morning, sometimes longer." The husky voice was still affable, probably because the longer he talked the longer he could go on looking at Mabruka. She ignored him. I gave him a thin commiserating smile. He gave it right back.

With a small nod she drew me away in the direction we had come. When we were beyond the guard's hearing she stopped and faced me. Her forehead was beginning to shine with sweat.

"What does Mujahid want you to learn?"

"The ways out of the city, into and out of the palace, where the main streets go, where Kadhim's staying, things like that."

"Where Kadhim is won't be hard, there are people we can ask," she said impatiently. "The rest I can show you. First I want you to meet someone."

"Who?"

"His name's Salman. The healer my mother mentioned last night."

Why did she want me to see a healer? It wasn't worth asking: her mood had made me cautious. After a moment she went on, "Only a part of his skill has to do with setting bones and knowing what herbs and oils have medicinal qualities: the rest is magic. He's a powerful wizard. He has a way of freeing his spirit and sending it out. . . . Maybe you'll see. He was my teacher."

"All right."

She started away, changed her mind, glanced back at the palace, then stared at me with baffling antagonism.

"Is he your lover?"

"Is who . . . *Mujahid?* Goddess, no! Mujahid loves only women."

She kept me impaled on that disturbing gaze for a long moment, then shrugged faintly. Did she believe me? Did it matter?

"Let's go to Salman's," Mabruka said.

The light was dim in the covered bazaar, the air stale. A hard incessant hammering came from the copper-smith's. There were few shoppers. Perhaps the place got busier on established market days.

Mabruka took a sharp turn past the sandal maker's. I followed her to a crookedly-hung door. She pushed through it. Harsh daylight flooded in. We stepped into a narrow alley between sun-bleached, mud-daubed walls. I closed the door behind me. We were between two rows of back-to-back dwellings strung together like clay beads on a string until an alley opened on the left. Around the bend was a wooden door, the only one in sight.

Mabruka rapped on it. It rattled in its frame. A light sharp voice said something and the door opened. A wedge of brightness fell through the opening. Beyond it was darkness.

"Morning of goodness, Salman," Mabruka said.

"Mabruka! *Ahlan wa sahlan!*"

The door opened wider, showing someone who seemed thin despite a voluminous unbelted *thaub*. Salman? The name was masculine but the voice had neither virility nor weight and less indication of gender than a rustle of dry leaves. Under the gray *gutra* twisted around the narrow skull the face was thin, bloodless, beardless, almost unlined except around the eyes and where sharp furrows hooked down from nostrils to mouth. "Come in, come in out of the sun!"

Mabruka stepped through the doorway, beckoning to me. I followed her into fragrant shadow. I thought my nose detected cloves and sandalwood and costly cinnamon from India. The room was small and furnished with a couple of heavy chests and a bare wooden bench; there was a worn rug on the floor and one corner had cushions and a roll of bedding. Jars and bottles crowded a shelf that ran along two walls. Strings of clay beads curtained a doorway into a back room.

"Salman bin Najma," Mabruka in-

123

troduced. "This is our visitor, Talal."

"*Ahlan*, Talal." Salman closed the door, darkening the room. He took Mabruka's hand. "And you, child: are you ready to resume studying?"

"No, Salman. I'm not meant for sorcery. Perhaps when I'm older, a grandmother."

"Develop it young or a gift often dies." He turned to me. For the first time I saw that his eyes were pale: not the milky white of blindness but a color I couldn't quite make out in the dim room; it seemed to combine green and gray and some other color in the bequest of a foreign ancestor. His look was at once piercing and expressionless. "Talal son of whom?"

"Son of my father," I said.

"His parents are unknown," Mabruka explained. "He was raised by strangers."

"Ah." Salman smiled faintly. "Don't let it go to your head, Talal. There are always orphans. It's quite humbling to know how few turn out to be lost princes or the rightful heirs to great wealth."

My irritation was bitter as bile. What was I doing here?

"I'm just a bedouin," I said.

"How modest. It's ostentatious to undervalue yourself. It fools no one." To Mabruka: "You want to know his parentage?"

"Is it possible?"

"Probably not. Does it matter?"

"No, but it would be nice for him to know his real ancestors before he's adopted into a family of Bani Faris."

"You agree, Talal?"

To a whim of Mabruka's? I rebelled, but couldn't think of a way to say so politely. So I shrugged.

"Why not?"

"Stay still, then."

I did as I was told. He took a slow breath, released it just as slowly, and I saw the angles and edges of his abrasive personality dissolve into the shadowed air. The slatey eyes were as

still as a windless dawn, as water in a cup, and I felt myself trapped within his stillness as last night I'd felt myself an insect trapped in honey. The experiences were similar but this was a lot more powerful. And yet I breathed. My lungs kept filling, fuller and fuller without discomfort, in a giant leisured inhalation that brought a growing sense of well-being while paradoxically my sense of identity as Talal-bowman-without-ancestors, brother-friend-servitor to Mujahid bin Hasan, retreated to the vanishing point. I found this vaguely disturbing; but even though a thread of apprehension began to writhe and loop itself around and pierce my well-being like a living silver wire, it was not enough to jolt me loose from Salman's spell —

And then abruptly it was over. I think my knees sagged. I heard myself gasp slightly and was instantly embarrassed. I didn't want to seem weak, or ignorant of how to deal with these things. But of course I *was* ignorant, and sensitive about it. A lot of settled people think bedouin are little better than savages, and I didn't want these two laughing at me.

I looked at Mabruka. She looked back with huge dark eyes in a grave, intent face.

"Better sit down," Salman said crisply. He was back to his old self, all abrupt angles and that thin hard genderless voice.

"I don't need to sit down."

"We'll get you some water. Stay here. Mabruka, come with me."

I started to protest but they ignored me. The strung bead curtain rattled as he led her into the other room while I stood where I was like a little boy unable to argue with an arbitrary grandparent. I raged in silence. They took their time. I heard Salman's voice murmuring rapidly but couldn't make out the words, then the scrape of an earthenware jug against a cup's lip, and

124

water being poured. A moment later Mabruka came through the bead curtain with Salman right behind her.

She held out the cup. "Drink some, Talal."

I started to refuse, but when does a bedouin refuse a drink? He seldom knows where the next one's coming from. So I took the cup. It was rough and grainy against my mouth. Apparently Salman didn't go in for luxuries. The water was cool and tasty, as though it had come from a container porous enough to sweat and cool the contents. My body was glad of it.

I gave the cup back. Mabruka drank what I'd left. Salman gave me a probing stare.

"Feeling all right?"

"Of course."

"Most people find the examination disconcerting."

"How long did it take?"

Mabruka tilted her head and half smiled.

"As long as it took you to sigh one deep, peaceful sigh."

It had seemed longer. I asked Salman, "What did you learn?"

"That you have a sound body, that you're not under a spell or curse or haunted by any kind of spirit. Superficial stuff."

"Nothing about my parents?"

"No. Your mind is closed like a fist around your present business. I couldn't get past that determination. I would need time to get you properly relaxed, perhaps an infusion of the poppy . . ."

"I have no time," I said stiffly, and gave formal thanks. "We should leave."

Mabruka began, "But don't you want to ask him — ?"

"What is there to ask? My parentage remains a mystery. I never thought it important anyway. As he said, there are always orphans."

"Yes, but . . ."

"I've imposed on Salman enough."

"Most orphans are just orphans," Salman said abruptly. "But you didn't just lose your parents, you lost your whole kindred. How did you manage that?" A sharp, angular gesture; he didn't expect an answer. I shrugged. He went on, "Even if your mother was simple *badawiyya,* a herdsman's daughter, imagine the complications if her people were like Ahl al-Hilal, tracing descent through the mother's line, and if one day she were taken in a raid by a man of patrilineal tribe to whom the father's name and lineage were everything."

This time he waited. Involuntarily, resentfully, since I didn't want to say anything, I heard myself mutter, "Complications?"

His stare was intense. I expected to feel the transporting influence of sorcery again.

"What happens to women taken in raids? They become wives or concubines. Imagine this happens to your mother. You are born. Your father naturally expects her to raise you according to her traditions, as a member of her kin instead of his, quite likely to grow into his sworn enemy. So he plans to kill you. To save your life she gives you away, probably to a childless woman of another tribe."

"What I've always imagined," I told him, "is simpler and more likely: my mother sold me or gave me away because she was too poor to raise me herself. I probably changed hands a few times before I was taken in by a Bani Faris family."

"Good. The simple answer is usually the right one." A vigorous nod. Then without change in voice or inflection he spun the apparent sign of approval into grounds for criticism. "Habitual diffidence often hides an arrogant personality. Don't let modesty become just a bad habit."

There was no answer to that. Irritation erupted in anger I fought to hide.

"Which hasn't much to do with my ancestry," I said stiffly. "Thank you for your efforts, but I have work to do. With your permission I'll be about it."

I turned to the door and pulled it open. The blast of sunlight from the dusty alley and the mud-plastered walls made me hesitate with my eyes almost shut. I stepped outside and turned to close the door and bumped into Mabruka. I hadn't expected her to follow. I was at once startled and left feeling stupid. My anger slipped its bonds and I had the awful feeling I was going to make a fool of myself and couldn't do a thing about it.

Salman, who was right behind Mabruka, said goodbye and told her to hurry back, then shut the door with a dry clatter.

She blinked while her eyes adjusted to the light. I turned and strode back to the alley we had taken from the bazaar and heard her hurrying after me.

"What did you bring me here for?" I tried to yell as she caught up with me. My throat was tight and my voice a whispery rasp. "What have I done to deserve this hostility?"

Her face went slack with surprise. Her left hand wandered to the agate necklace at her throat. Silver shone harshly from her fingers.

Her mouth had dropped open like a bewildered little girl's. Her head shook vaguely.

"Well?" I demanded.

Her voice was disbelieving, no louder than a murmur.

"Were we wrong about you? Maybe you're not like Mujahid, maybe you don't love women . . ."

"Mujahid, Mujahid! What's it to you whether I love women or little boys or sheep? You don't wear jewelry and pretty clothes for *me*" — I hooked a fist into the loop of the agate necklace — "except to remind me that your mother has land and herds and I'm just a servant —"

"No, no!" Her head shook again,

catching the morning glare. "What's Mujahid to me? He's a lost man who wears despair like a cloak . . ." Hurriedly she fumbled at the back of her neck, under her hair. The necklace came away in my hand. She grabbed it and threw it into the dust. "That wasn't to keep you away, it was supposed to . . . to *attract* you. . . ."

The word was as meaningless as the rattle of pebbles rolling down a hill. *Attract.* Of course it *had* a meaning. It meant *draw. Lure. Entice. Decoy . . .* And what was that nonsense about Mujahid?

"Is that improper among the Bani Faris?" she went on after a quick breath. "I just meant to remind you of the comforts I can offer . . . enough good food . . . a fine riding camel . . ."

Half comprehending I yelled, "Am I something in a bazaar you can *buy?*"

She stamped her foot in the dust.

"Who's trying to *buy* you? I don't want to *own* you . . ."

Her eyes glistened. I bent down and snatched up the necklace.

"This doesn't entice me." I shoved it into her hand. "Try this."

What I did then I would never had had the nerve for if I hadn't been so furious. It was part attack and part expression of hopeless longing and the first was clearly excessive and the second as foredoomed to failure as desperate inexperience can be.

I reached for the front of her dress and covered her breasts with my hands and began fondling them.

An extraordinary thing happened. She made a small sound of surprise and clapped her hands to the sides of my face and kissed me on the mouth, the necklace grinding into my jawbone. I didn't know much about this kind of thing and I don't think she did either but lips and teeth and tongues came together with a life of their own.

For the longest time I didn't believe any of it. I didn't even enjoy it much.

126

It was too full of desperate hurried clutchings and gropings, too frantic, too clumsy. My heart raced. There was a noise in my ears like a flash flood rushing down a *wadi*. And then a stream of sweat slanted across my temple into my eye and stung sharply. I paused to blink and heard in my head Mujahid's gusting laughter, his cheerfully derisive advice, *Wait, idiot — it's finally happening; take time to enjoy it!* and had the wit to realize that Mujahid was nowhere near, the advice quite imaginary but probably sound for all that, and had the further wit to disengage one hand to touch her cheek. Our mouths parted briefly then settled back together again. The last shred of my anger dried up and blew away. I trailed fingertips across her chin and down her neck and back onto her breast, caught the nipple under the cloth between two fingers. Her mouth slid away from mine.

"I think I know a place we can go. . . ."

Mabruka, looking sweaty and disheveled and pleased with herself, sat up and pulled her dress down over her shins. I was euphoric to my fingertips, invulnerable as a stooping falcon, as strong as a young lion of the Omani foothills.

For a moment she looked almost shy, as though protecting some remote corner of her privacy.

"Salman approves. When we got you the water he told me not to let you get away."

The place she had taken me to wasn't much, hardly more secluded than the sun-blinded alley had been: just a ruined stable with two mud walls left standing. Part of the matting roof, frayed and bedraggled, sagged to the ground forming an accidental lean-to that threatened to collapse at every touch. The sun found its way through cracks and loose places in the weave of the matting and threw little jewels of light onto flesh and floor and clothing. Dust jumped at every movement.

Even being reminded of Salman couldn't diminish my well-being.

"He disguises his approval well," I told her.

"Don't mind Salman. He's always testing people, especially when he's curious about them. I thought he might have some ideas about your . . . mission here, but you never asked; you were too eager to get away. But he likes *me*, you see, and I'd always promised him I'd seek his approval when I found someone . . . and then today I thought that if you knew who your real ancestors were, you might not feel you had to get some others by adoption. . . ."

She paused. Her expression showed the first flicker of hesitation. Even before she went on I felt my life begin to take a great dizzying swing. When she spoke I tried not to gasp.

"Then you might be inclined to stay here with me. Would you? Want to, I mean?"

"Of course I would. . . ."

"Only for as long as you want. It wouldn't have to be for a full five years. And of course you have the other thing to do first, and you can't do it here, you have to wait till Kadhim's beyond the two shaykhs' protection, so it'll take time. . . ."

"Even after it's done," I said, "it would be ungrateful of me not to go back to Mujahid's family, whether they adopt me or not. But as soon as I can I'll be back."

I slid a hand up past her ankles. Mujahid's rose petal comparison was barely adequate. She gave me a small conspiratorial smile and pulled her dress up. We wouldn't always have to do this in the cramped corner of a ruined stable at the edge of a city street. An extraordinary shared future stretched ahead. For as long as it pleased her I would be Mabruka's, the father of her children. It didn't bother me at all that they

127

would be Hilalis rather than . . . what? Numayris of Bani Faris? Well, possibly, by adoption. It didn't really matter who I was; it never had, though I imagined there was comfort in knowing where you fit into a sequence of people that stretched back time out of mind and off into the future — a particular people, with a center in a particular spot, with a tribal name and ways that went with it. Well, my children would be the sons and daughters of Mabruka the daughter of Nur the daughter of Hind of Ahl al-Hilal, and they would know my name and I'd make sure they'd remember me. And they would say, *Once he was a servant till Mabruka saw him and said, 'There is a man with a face like a good blade, waiting'* . . . What it was waiting *for* remained to be seen, I'd have to make sure it was worthy. Whatever it was might take some doing but I could do it. I was brimming over with confidence and self-renewing male strength and I was making love to the most desirable young woman in all the tribes and there wasn't anything I *couldn't* do.

Eventually, reluctantly, I remembered all the things I was supposed to be doing. So Mabruka and I crawled out of our refuge and dusted ourselves off. She checked the hang of the agate necklace and the position of the gazelle-skin belt, I slung my bow and quiver across my back, and she took my hand and led me off to learn the geography Mujahid had demanded.

It wasn't hard. The narrow road past the little temple to the Goddess led to the city's western gate. It too was narrow, unguarded, held shut by massive bars whose angles were filled with dust and cobwebs. This gate had had an eastern counterpart, Mabruka said; but it had been walled up long ago. The only other gates were those I had already seen.

On the north, only an alley separated

128

the city's defensive walls from the wall surrounding the palace. There were two ways into the palace grounds: one, the entrance Mujahid had used to join the crowd seeking the shaykh's justice; the other, directly across the compound and through the palace stables. This one gave onto a street that wandered crookedly south to become the northwestern exit from the first market square we had come to this morning.

We wound up back at the square next to the palace. It was quieter. The sun beat down; the air baked, trapped between walls. The two riding camels were gone and in their place a string of pack donkeys waited for someone to come and lead them away somewhere. The gate to the palace grounds still stood open; near it, squatting in the dust with his back against the wall, was the scar-faced guard.

A fly buzzed near his eye. He brushed it away, looked up and saw us approaching hand in hand. After a long fixed stare at Mabruka, whose plum-colored dress was rumpled and sweat-stained and looked as though she'd worn it to work a harvest, he gave me a conspiratorial leer.

"Your friend's still waiting," he said with satisfaction, nodding toward the gate.

"Can we go in?"

"You can't take that bow in with you."

Was he just being obstructive, or had someone identified me as dangerous?

I shrugged. "I'll wait here, then."

Mabruka stepped past the guard and looked through the entrance.

The crowd had shrunk to a thin scattering. Over their heads I saw a big man — tall, black-bearded, of impressive girth — sitting in the middle of the patch of shade provided by the awning. The men with the lances, looking sleepy, stood nearby on either side of him. Six other prosperous-looking men sat in a rough crescent behind him. A man in peasant garb was before the shaykh with his back to us, presenting a case with many gestures toward someone in the crowd whom the black-bearded shaykh eventually invited forward to be heard.

"That's Shaykh Salah of Bani Ghassan, who's also prince of the city," Mabruka murmured. "Behind him, second from the left, older and thin with a gray beard, that's Shaykh Harith of Ahl al-Hilal. The others are all members of the Ghassani tribal council, in case Salah needs help or more information in making a judgment."

"Who decides disputes involving your people?"

"Our Shaykh Harith, of course."

"And when they involve Hilali against Ghassani?"

"Shaykh Salah of Bani Ghassan."

"That's risky for him, isn't it, giving judgment against one of his own in a dispute with an outsider? Doesn't every judgment in a dispute between a Hilali and a Ghassani become a *political* judgment instead of a just one, on its merits?"

"He wants a name for fairness and wisdom. We've learned we can trust him."

"But he doesn't want to go against the Bayt Ali in your mother's case — and even your friend Zuhayr calls them hooligans."

She dug her fingers painfully into my waist just under my ribs.

"Don't call that cockroach a friend of mine! . . . What case? She hasn't brought a case. She doesn't want a public controversy."

"And *that* sounds like a political decision! She doesn't want to risk tilting some balance somewhere. So she appeals to your Shaykh Harith, but he can't get Shaykh Salah to restrain the hooligans. This morning your mother implied it's because Shaykh Harith hasn't the skill or the will, but . . . suppose it isn't that at all. Suppose . . ."

I hesitated. My mind was racing but suddenly came up lame.

"Yes?" Mabruka prompted.

". . . I don't know. Some reason why Shaykh Salah is afraid of the Bayt Ali . . ."

Mabruka was silent. What was left of the crowd looked bored and uncomfortable. The shaykh interrupted the voluble petitioner in a voice too quiet to be heard. Mabruka sighed, "If only we'd thought to ask Salman . . ."

"Ask him what?"

"What you asked me. Why Salah may fear the Bayt Ali."

"What would he know?"

"More than most people, silly. He's a famous healer, he gets about and knows everyone." A sudden decision. "I'm going to talk to him again."

"Where will I find you?"

"Either at Salman's, or I'll find you here, or we'll meet at my house."

She kissed me briskly and walked with determined stride toward the entrance to the covered bazaar.

The guard watched her go with vacant eyes, then turned to me and sighed and shook his head pityingly. It was supposed to convince me he knew something I didn't, to plant seeds of doubt. Nothing could. I responded with my best imitation of Mujahid's demoralizing self-assurance, grinning cheerfully, and for the space of a heartbeat the guard's face went slack. Then his eyes narrowed, his jaw muscles tightened. I almost heard his teeth grinding. I was having a morning of little triumphs as well as big ones. It was obscurely sad that an imitation of a smile should win one for me, but if Mujahid could fake being Mujahid, why shouldn't I?

I turned away to watch the shaykh at his *diwan*.

He disposed of the case before him and two others followed. He continued to speak too quietly to be followed from this distance. When he gave his judgments no one capered with glee or broke

129

into lamentations. Time passed. The sun was high in a sky of molten silver. Walls and ground threw back the heat.

And then it was Mujahid's turn.

The silent shadow of the circling kite hawk slid down the mud-brown walls of the palace and skittered over the assembled people as Mujahid took his place before the shaykh. Behind me now, the bird gave a short angry trill. I shaded my eyes and looked up. Two birds circled low over the market square. The newcomer was a small white scavenger eagle and the two were unhappy to see each other . . .

From the shaykh, a permissive gesture. In a clear bold voice Mujahid gave his name and tribe. The shaykh became still as a great stone, his eyes hidden in the shadow of his headcloth.

Between the shadow and his beard his lips pursed thoughtfully.

"You're a long way from your tribal range, Ibn Hasan," he said at last. "Do you petition for judgment against one of my people?"

Perhaps Mujahid's name and the anticipation of trouble made the shaykh speak more loudly.

"No, lord, not one of yours," Mujahid answered. "And judgment has already been given — against a man called Kadhim bin Ja'far of Bani Faris, who now enjoys your protection but is known to his family and tribe as the man who murdered my father."

Shaykh Salah shifted position on his cushions, scratched the edge of one nostril with a little fingernail. When he didn't say anything Mujahid went on without heat:

"I'm told that this Kadhim represents himself as being in flight from a band of cut-throats. In fact he's in flight from me and my servant. We've been following him since the afternoon my father died and witnesses saw my arrow of recision shot into a clear sky and return bloodstained."

130

The shaykh was startled. Perhaps not very, but enough to show.

He said, "Witnesses?"

"My kin, and Kadhim's, and members of the tribal council."

Salah was unmoving and thoughtful for long moments; then he looked off to one side and beckoned. A young man hurried over. He bent to receive whispered instructions, then straightened and hurried to the palace door and disappeared inside.

The shaykh turned back to Mujahid.

"So, Ibn Hasan: the arrow didn't release you from your blood obligation. I wish I'd been there. But why bring this matter to me?"

"Only to assure you, lord, that I am no cut-throat."

The shaykh smiled faintly.

"And perhaps to get me to rescind my protection?" He shook his draped head. "Even if I knew that what you tell me is true I couldn't do that."

"Nor would I ask it," Mujahid said, and the palace door opened.

The messenger came back out with someone who wore a clean white *thaub*, a light, brown, sleeved cloak, and a headcloth adjusted to shade his face. But I thought the dagger belt around his middle looked familiar, and when he moved toward Salah and the light fell differently I had a glimpse of the knife face and dense beard of Kadhim bin Ja'far.

He was half way to the shaded area under the awning before he recognized Mujahid. He stopped. Mujahid slowly raised his arms and held them straight out from his shoulders.

"You see I'm weaponless, Kadhim."

Kadhim said harshly, "Does Shaykh Salah prepare this kind of surprise for all his guests, or am I the favored exception?"

"You recognize this man?" the shaykh asked.

"He's the one I told you about, a hired cut-throat."

"You're a liar, Kadhim," Mujahid said. "My father told you to stop bothering his young wife and you killed him. My arrow of recision insisted on blood for blood."

Kadhim laughed shortly.

"With members of your own family as witnesses," the shaykh told him, though I wasn't sure he believed it.

"A trick," Kadhim sneered. "Does he expect us to think the spirit world is within reach of any dung-eater with a bow?"

"It is," Mujahid said.

"Then prove it or shut your stupid lying mouth."

"Would you trust me with a bow, Kadhim — and you so close?"

Kadhim hawked and spat into the dust between them.

"I wouldn't be afraid of you if you had a bow and a sword and I had nothing but my teeth —" He stopped abruptly. "Where's Talal?"

The shaykh asked, "Talal? Who's he?"

"My servant," Mujahid said.

"His skill with a bow's unnatural." Kadhim began scanning the crowd intently. "I told you about him yesterday."

"Of course — the servant who shoots doves on the wing." I wasn't sure Salah believed that either.

Kadhim had found me. He pointed an accusing finger.

"That's him!"

A hand gripped my arm. I felt the tip of a blade touch my neck. The voice that spoke from behind my ear was thin and husky but still had power to carry.

"Shall I disarm him?"

A question to Mujahid satisfied the shaykh that the guard had the right man. He nodded. "Take his bow." He offered Mujahid a reassuring gesture. "— Temporarily. Servants have been known to get . . . too zealous."

I didn't resist as the guard took the bow.

He murmured derisively, "On the *wing?*"

"Not always," I admitted.

"Then what good are you?"

I had missed an exchange between Shaykh Salah and the two antagonists, and the shaykh was calling for something. Someone brought him a bow and a single arrow. Drawing his dagger he cut a nick in the arrow a finger-width from the fletching, resheathed the dagger, had both bow and marked arrow given to Mujahid.

Mujahid had accepted Kadhim's

challenge. Of course. The spirit world itself would condemn Kadhim and Shaykh Salah would witness it.

The sparse crowd had been silent and intent since the confrontation began. A brief protest rose as the two men with lances began urging everyone to move back, which they did, clearing a broad strip of dusty ground running all across the palace yard. The crowd settled quickly into a new silence.

Nothing could possibly go wrong; but Mujahid, stepping slowly into the cleared area, nocked the arrow stiff-fingered, as though he'd never held one before. He tilted his head back, looked into the sky. His face with the sun full on it was tormented and rigid as wind-scoured rock. Then he raised the bow and drew the arrow back to his temple and let fly almost vertically into emptiness.

Anyone else would have got out of the way in case a vagrant puff of wind returned the arrow on a dangerous path. Mujahid shaded his eyes and followed its flight without moving.

It plunged to earth between him and the shaykh.

For the time it takes to count the fingers on both hands no one moved or spoke. The shaykh's voice rang with the iron of authority.

"No one touches it."

He shifted his bulk, got his feet under him and stood up, crossed out of his patch of shade to the arrow and plucked it from the ground.

A murmur went up. Even I could see the glistening red wet smear along most of the arrow's length.

Salah looked at the nick he'd cut into the shaft; then, holding it by its feathered end, raised it to his nose. His nostrils flared briefly. He nodded, then held the arrow up for the crowd to see.

"It's the one I gave Ibn Hasan," he told them. "His hands are clean, the bow is clean, but the arrow has blood on it. If anyone tells you that the arrow of recision is just a trick to reduce blood-

shed . . . remember what you saw today."

Perhaps he was surprised to find himself saying that. He turned and stared thoughtfully at Mujahid, then signalled an underling to take away the bow and the blood-smeared arrow. At last he faced Kadhim.

Kadhim's face was lost in shadow. He made a disparaging gesture.

"Perhaps someone did kill this man's father." His voice was stiff and cautious. "But it certainly wasn't I."

"Then why did you lie to me?" the shaykh demanded. "You also challenged Ibn Hasan — and you lost. You have my hospitality for three days, starting now. After that I'll give you an escort anywhere you choose within reason. That's where my protection ends."

Kadhim muttered something and turned and stalked to the palace door and disappeared inside. The shaykh said something to Mujahid which I couldn't hear either, then turned to the people clustered beyond the cleared area and beckoned them forward. They rose and surged to the front.

Mujahid came striding around the edge of the crowd. I had expected to see him elated at getting Kadhim's sanctuary limited but his face was anguished.

I went through the double door to meet him. He gripped my arm painfully, almost dragging me back outside the palace compound.

"Get your bow."

"The guard has it." I shook my arm free. "Mother of the Gods, Mujahid, what's the —"

"Get it, will you?"

He shoved me at the guard who was watching us carefully, holding my bow with both hands.

"You'll get it back when you're outside, fellow."

I gestured at the compound entrance. "I'm already outside."

"Outside the *gate!* Beyond the wall! There'll be no trouble while I'm on duty."

Mujahid demanded in a grinding voice, "Are you another of the Bayt Ali bodyguard?"

". . . What's it to you?" The guard herded me toward the northern gate. "Yes, I am."

"Are all Shaykh Salah's bodyguard of the Bayt Ali?"

"Not yet. You're wasting time."

Mujahid's feet kicked up fine dust as he strode the distance to the city gate. I followed, trying not to let the guard rush me. Beyond the gate a horse was tethered to a wooden peg and another team of scrawny donkeys waited sleepily for the stunned discomfort of midday to pass. The cultivated fields looked wilted. Against a sky as bleak and shining as a polished blade the kite and the scavenger eagle described their separate paths, wheeling out over the fields, then banking and stroking the exhausted air with their wings once or twice and sailing back across the market square.

The guard held out the bow. I took it.

"Don't bring it back inside the walls, sonny."

I almost assured him that if I did he'd be dead before he saw me: a childish threat: actually I'd never loosed an arrow at a man. But Mujahid, impatient as though driven by a demon, snarled something under his breath and jerked my sleeve and set off at a pace just short of a run, following the city wall westward. So I swallowed my empty retort and chased after him.

The wall angled south, taking us out of sight and hearing of the gate and the guard. Mujahid stopped.

"The spirit world's getting impatient, Talal. If I fail this obligation I'll wish a jinn curse *had* fallen on me."

"You won't fail it," I said reasonably. "He's got three days to clear out. We'll follow till the escort leaves him and then —"

"We'd risk losing him on the road, or being attacked by the bodyguard in a careless moment. We have to kill him the moment he's outside the walls."

"That's crazy. We'd have to kill the bodyguard too."

"How many can there be? Three? Two? They'll probably leave by the side gate when the main gates are closed at sunset — maybe even today. We can do it! — with no one to see or raise the alarm."

"The side gate hasn't been opened in years —"

"The shaykh could order it opened. He's protecting Kadhim, he'd want him to leave secretly —"

"We'd blacken his face. He'd hunt us down."

"He'll never know. We'll bury the bodies and take their mounts. Salah may wonder when the escort doesn't come back, but what do we care what he thinks? He has the honor of a maggot, his justice is corrupt. D'you know why he won't act against the Bayt Ali in Mabruka's mother's complaint? Because he's in collusion with them. I heard the crowd talking before the *diwan.* Most of his personal bodyguard are Bayt Ali warriors."

"What abut Nur?"

"What about her?"

"We'd blacken her face too. Kadhim's under the protection of all Ahl al-Hilal . . ."

He shoved me in the chest with both hands. I slammed back against the city wall.

"What do you care? The Hilalis are strangers. Nur's just a woman . . ."

"You're her guest. You owe her . . ."

"I owe my father more!"

"You'd do Hasan justice by dishonoring him?"

He shoved me again, more violently. I tripped over my feet, twisted, hit the wall with the point of my shoulder. The

133

wall took it well but I yelled in pain. This was more than brotherly roughness.

"Are you trying to tell me my duties to my *father*? You don't even *have* a father. What do you know?"

"Are you trying to break my arm? D'you want to go against them alone?" I hugged my shoulder. The arm below it had gone numb. "Great Goddess, you've been following Kadhim for weeks, you've just caught up with him, how can you talk of the spirit world getting impatient?"

"Didn't you see how much blood was on the arrow this time? Goddess, almost the whole shaft, as thick and fresh as if I'd just pulled it out of the heart of a gazelle." His eyes widened. His voice dropped to a wondering whisper. "Whose blood, Talal?"

I stopped kneading my shoulder. I forgot to try working the paralyzed fingers at the end of my paralyzed arm. I just stared at him, and he stared back, waiting for an answer.

"Mujahid! I'm not Umar bin Auda. What do I know about the spirit world?"

He asked hoarsely, "Is it mine? My own blood?"

Which was no sillier than the rest had been but something was clearly wrong. He'd never been one to fret about the invisible world. He avoided places known to be haunted, until yesterday had managed to stay clear of *ausaj* bushes, and carried a she-cat's or a fox's tooth to protect him from demons. Who didn't? The world beyond the world was inhabited by arbitrary and capricious powers, and you had to defend yourself against them with what you could. Mujahid's luck probably meant the continuing influence of some hidden power which might now be extracting hideous payment: anyone could guess, but who could know? I doubted even Umar bin Auda really knew, for all his knowing talk about the Gods having patterns to create. So I swallowed hard, made what I hoped was a calming gesture, and tried to sound reassuring and ordinary.

"I only know this, Mujahid. Hasan was a good man. Nothing in either world could force him to make unreasonable demands of anyone, especially you. You were his only son."

"But I betrayed him. I should have gone with him to see Kadhim . . ."

"How were you to know? If he'd thought it necessary he'd have asked you to —"

"Don't understand, do you? I wasn't available. I was doing something more important. When he went to talk to Kadhim I was in the village in the gardener's hut, doing what Kadhim only wanted to do — lying with Filwa myself."

I didn't say anything. Neither did he. We just stood there, sweating.

My brain had congealed like tallow at the base of a candle, muffling thought and feeling, sealing off shock and disappointment which, if felt, might have proved too painful to bear. It would have yesterday. Yesterday Filwa had dominated my dreams. Not that I wanted her to. She was as far above me as the evening star was above the empty plain. As Hasan had been my father, she was my father's wife. As she had been Mujahid's father's wife but he had apparently not let that bother him and that, curiously enough, was the greatest disappointment. Not that slender, lovely Filwa had played the wanton behind her husband's back but that Mujahid had been the one to take advantage of it. The brother I loved had betrayed the father I loved.

I felt a distant surge of pity for Mujahid — and a simultaneous urge to hurt him.

So I said calmly, "How was she?"

Slowly the fire of anguish left him. His sigh was an echoing emptiness. He shrugged.

134

"Reluctant. What would you expect? But I am Mujahid: charming, good with words . . . and above all *lucky*." His mouth twisted on the word. "Don't I always get what I want? And what I wanted was Filwa, on a sudden whim when I walked through the orchard that afternoon and found her talking to the gardener in charge. Suddenly she was just another man's pretty wife. So I sent the gardener off on an errand, and then I was never so amusing, never so persuasive, but I think she only gave in to keep us friends, because I was Hasan's son. I took her on the floor of the gardener's hut, expecting her to relent, expecting her to admit she loved it, and me. My luck wouldn't go that far. Maybe that's when it started dying."

My turn to shrug.

"Your luck's all right or we'd have lost Kadhim long ago." Which might even be true. "You simply asked too much of it that time." Plain now why he hadn't claimed Filwa for himself. . . .

He said, as though he hadn't heard me, "That's why Hasan demands vengeance of *me,* not an army of relatives — and no more waiting."

"No."

"Talal . . . *why?*"

"Partly because Hasan wouldn't make this demand, mostly because I won't blacken Nur's face. Or Shaykh Salah's. I have to be able to come back here."

"What for?"

"For Mabruka."

After a short pause he laughed.

"What makes you think she'd welcome you?"

"She already has."

He looked briefly startled, then gave me a slow bemused look.

"You young thief. You've decided not to be any use at all, haven't you? Give me back my knife belt."

I unbuckled it. He took it impatiently.

"All right, Talal. I don't need you."

"You can't do it alone. . . ."

"Watch me." He started back toward the northern gate.

"Mujahid —"

"Who are you, son of no one? If you follow me I'll crack your head open. Leave me alone."

"He'll kill you. Then *I'll* have to do the job alone."

"It's not yours to do."

That wasn't what he'd said last night.

He disappeared around the bend in the wall.

I was so much of two minds I was almost two people: one a rejected child, the other a furious adult. Unsought responsibility was piling up. Being a brother wasn't easy.

In his present mood Mujahid might do something stupid; I ought to keep an eye on him. The scarfaced guard wouldn't let me in through the northern gate so I cursed and hiked through the glaring torpor of midday the length of the city wall and around and back through the southern gate and the twisted streets and the trapped breathless air to the first market square.

Animals dozed. A few trading stalls were open with vendors nodding off behind their merchandise. No one I talked to had seen anyone who looked like Mujahid. I approached the palace from the stables side, then ducked between the palace and the city wall to see the second square without showing myself to the guard. The door into the palace yard was closed. No sign of the man himself. His replacement was settling down on his hams, leaning back against the door in the narrow strip of shadow the wall was beginning to throw into the square now that noon was past. Still no Mujahid. I ducked back into the alley when the new guard began looking around, went back to the first square and entered the covered bazaar, where no one could remember seeing him either. I don't think anyone was interested enough to give the question much thought. Anyway what would I say to Mujahid if I found him? Supposing he made good his threat to crack my head open? Finally I went back to the sandalmaker's and through the crooked door into the alley that led to Salman's place.

He told me in his hard, genderless voice that Mabruka had already left — and seemed to wait for me to ask him something else. I had no other questions, at least none that Mabruka would not already have asked, and besides I still found his challenging manner unsettling, so I awkwardly took my leave and retraced my steps to the southern gate and back onto the trail that ran between the valley wall and the farmlands.

Out of the glare a horseman came galloping at me. With no one to show off for, he wasn't mistreating the horse as badly as this morning, but he wasn't being gentle either. Zuhayr of the heavy hands, on his big roan.

He thundered past, then wheeled around in a quick storm of hooves and flying dust, too close to ignore. I took a quick look back over my shoulder, met a pair of savage eyes in a face twisted with anger before he dragged the horse's head back toward the city and galloped away.

Nur's place blazed quietly in the afternoon glare but I heard voices. I called to Mabruka. Latifa came out of Nur's room and invited me in with a grin of few teeth but much goodwill. Nur sat at a loom on which a handspan of pale sandy cloth had been completed. Mabruka, still in her dusty plum-colored dress, sat on a carpet nearby with a basket of wool by her knee and a wooden drop spindle in her lap.

Latifa followed me inside. When the outside glare had left my eyes I saw Mabruka's warm secret smile. But Nur looked tense, her face drawn as fine as carved bone, her eyes glowing darkly.

"Well, Talal!" She turned from her loom, setting down her shuttle stick. "I hear that certain things have been settled between you two. I'm pleased. But you've come at a worrisome time."

"Is anyone worried except Zuhayr?" I shed my bow and quiver and sat down beside Mabruka. "I met him on the road. He would've liked to run me down."

"He came to warn us against you," Nur explained. "He said your friend Mujahid was clearly a sorcerer, and that Shaykh Salah was convinced that your skill with the bow isn't natural. He had you disarmed when you disrupted the *diwan*."

"Zuhayr is a liar." I told them briefly what had happened at the *diwan*. "Did he also tell you that Kadhim has three days to enjoy the shaykh's hospitality, then has to accept an escort out of the territory?"

Mabruka's lip curled.

"Mostly he told us how comfortable I would be as his wife," she said. "Under Ghassani law, of course. And that I should be thinking about things like that because Ahl al-Hilal was only tolerated here and the life we'd known could collapse at any time like a tent in a gale. So I told him about us. He almost choked on his own spit."

"I went back to Salman's looking for you."

"I went back to the palace entrance looking for *you*. That guard was closing the doors. He asked me what I was doing wasting time with riffraff like you. I told him he'd never understand."

"He's Bayt Ali. Most of Salah's bodyguard are. Did Salman mention that?"

"Yes. He believes the other clans have been intimidated into preventing their men from taking bodyguard work."

"That's what Salah's afraid of, then! Of becoming a Bayt Ali puppet! He can't take on too many of his own clan: he could be accused of building a personal army to impose his will on the whole tribe. He may feel he can't take on any of them."

"There's more," Nur said abruptly.

"It's a rumor," Mabruka said, "but Salman thinks it's true. It says the Bayt Ali are trying to get the agreement between Bani Ghassan and Ahl al-Hilal set aside. They want us out, our right to water our herds at Ghassani wells cancelled, our lands surrendered. Hilalis who want to stay in the valley can do so — working as peasants on Ghassani land."

"The motive is pure Bayt Ali greed," Nur said. "They say Bani Ghassan are more numerous now, they don't need Hilali manpower for defense, so why shouldn't the Ghassanis have all the riches for themselves?"

I said slowly, "It may be only a rumor but I think Zuhayr believes it. He works for your Shaykh Harith. Does Harith know anything?"

"I'll go and ask him," Nur said. "Where's your friend Mujahid?"

"We had a . . . disagreement."

She looked faintly startled.

"He still has a duty to perform. He won't try to do it alone, will he?"

"He'd better not. All he's got with him is his dagger. Besides, he's a man of honor; he wouldn't violate hospitality and embarrass his hostess."

"No, of course not." Nur stood up in a rustle of clothing. "Child, get this man something to eat. Come on, Latifa, I'm sure these young people want to be alone; you and I will go and see Shaykh Harith. If I don't appear with a servant in train he'll think something's wrong, I've lost status. If he can pretend I'm nobody I won't get much out of him."

A derisive cackle came from Latifa.

"These shaykhs get a little authority, right away they start thinking they're something. Maybe we need a shaykha instead of a shaykh, eh, Talal? What d'you think of *that* idea?" Another cackle of laughter left her wheezing and gasping. "But the traditions say we

tried it long ago. And the shaykhas are no better! Eventually they set themselves just as far above the people, and to make sure other tribes take them seriously they become more warlike than the men!"

"No one said being a chief was easy," Nur said.

The laughter began again, raucous and good-natured.

"The chicken just laid a square egg," Mabruka told me.

"A chicken, am I?" Latifa cackled. "Feed me today, wring my neck tomorrow, I know how *that* goes! But you'll find me tough and stringy! . . . Now where's that mantle of mine? I'm not going out into that sun unprotected. —Ah, there it is. Well?"

"Let's go," Nur said equably, throwing a light shawl over her head and pulling it forward to shade her face.

The two women left, Latifa closing the lightweight door before padding away, chuckling.

Their voices faded into silence.

In the dim light filtering into the room Mabruka turned to me and studied me with calm intensity. I found myself anticipating being trapped in a crystalline moment of stopped time like last night with the candle flame reflected as twin golden blades in the depths of her eyes, or like this morning in another unfamiliar room with my sense of self dissipating like smoke under Salman's magic. But none of this happened. I was seated firmly on firm ground, heartbeat steady and familiar under my ribs, senses alert, thoughts clear, entirely myself.

Mabruka stood up in a single movement, poured a splash of water from a clay jug onto a wadded-up kerchief, came back and knelt and mopped my face.

"Are you hungry, Talal?"

"Not for food."

I took the cloth from her hand, shook it out and washed her face and neck, then moved behind her to reach it more easily inside the embroidered neck of her dress to cool her breasts and armpits. When I withdrew it she stood up and turned to face me, unfastening her gazelle-skin belt, dropping it at her feet.

She wasn't doing anything magical but in that dim room a vagrant thread of light pricked color from the embroidery at her neck and her eyes were dark and enormous and deeper than any well and for a fleeting moment I had the dizzying conviction I was floating above years of unrolling time in the presence of a power to summon lightning and govern whirlwinds and control the destinies of tribes, but it was brief, so brief I couldn't be sure I hadn't imagined it, and didn't even ask about it later; and what she was doing now was pulling the plum-colored dress over her head.

It was late afternoon when Nur and Latifa came back.

The sun had lost its malevolence, the air was like a caress. The sky had softened, to a gentle blue through which the sun was dropping toward the valley's western rim. The late day was soft and pretty as a flower.

I had seen to the animals while Mabruka went to the well to fill a tall water jug. We went back to the front of the house as Nur and the old servant turned toward us from the trail. Mabruka took the water jug inside and came back out. Latifa, scowling and ill-tempered, asked her if she'd started fixing dinner.

"No," Mabruka said.

"What good are you?" Latifa snarled. With a gesture of contempt she disappeared inside.

Mabruka asked her mother, "What did Harith say?"

Nur slipped the shawl off her head. Coppery highlights sparked from her black hair.

"That Salman was right." Her voice was matter-of-fact, her face calm, but her eyes were worried. "The Bayt Ali want us out and have the support of several important families. Shaykh Salah is opposed and so far the majority of the tribal council is with him. If that changes, he becomes a prisoner of his Bayt-Ali-dominated bodyguard. This situation is why Harith didn't want me to bring up the Ghazala well incident at a public *diwan*. If Salah judges in their favor it'll happen more often. If he judges in my favor he'll lay himself open to charges of having some private reason for favoring one of us over one of them. Which could get him deposed, or start him thinking we're not worth the trouble."

Mabruka's face had gone blank, in a kind of little-girl shock. Her eyes snapped suddenly and she stood taller and the little-girl semblance was gone.

"Did you tell Shaykh Harith that his eager young aide seemed determined that we assimilate into Ghassani law and custom?"

"Yes." Nur smiled thinly. "He snapped that Zuhayr was only a messenger boy."

"If we're dispossessed what do we do? Fight?"

"There aren't enough of us. And we can't buy off the Bayt Ali because then we'd have to buy off their friends and we'd end up with nothing anyway. All we can do is hope the council stays with us."

"There must be *something* we can do."

I said tentatively, "What about Salman? Isn't he a sorcerer?"

"He's a healer," Nur said. "He has no magic for this problem."

I felt silly for even thinking of it. Then Mabruka touched my arm and pointed past me. I turned and saw Mujahid leave the trail and come toward us, his face calm and ruddy in the approaching sunset.

He seemed unhurried, purposeful, with no sign of the anguish that had gripped him earlier. Nor of his charm. He greeted the women indifferently and came right to the point.

"You were right, Talal. It can't be done alone."

I agreed carefully.

He went on, "Kadhim's leaving by the side gate as soon as it's dark, taking the north road out of the valley."

"How'd you find out?"

"Zuhayr told me."

"Why?"

"I don't know why! It doesn't matter why!" He made an impatient gesture. "Look, I met him in the city; he'd just ridden in after passing you on the road. He demanded very officiously to know what I was doing, if I was looking for Kadhim I should remember that every man's hand would be against me. I said no, I was just trying to find out when he'd be leaving. He gave that a moment's thought and his manner changed and he said very casually, 'Maybe I can find out for you; wait for me here.' I waited all afternoon, thinking he might be making a fool of me. But he came back with the information."

"I wouldn't believe anything he says."

"Neither would I. But suppose he's right. We intercept Kadhim when he gets out onto the desert or we're back where we started."

"We can't violate hospitality."

"Of course not."

That was all the assurance I needed. In a few brisk minutes we had the animals loaded and were mounted and on our way.

We climbed the rock slope leading out of the farmlands, went over the valley's rim and out onto the desert. We stopped then, and turned to look back the way we had come.

Slender columns of smoke rose from the little mud ovens in which farmers bake their flat loaves of bread. The valley floor was in shadow; thicker shadow oozed out of the hollows in the farm-lands and climbed the walls inside the city. The light on the western horizon was fading and shrinking. The moon, not quite half full, began to glow, washing out the early stars.

The city's northern gate swung closed. Either because of the angle or the thickening darkness, the side gate wasn't visible. We were apparently well ahead of Kadhim.

We moved fifty or sixty paces back from the rim and Mujahid dismounted. Nothing was going to happen; but the distant confusion spreading under my ribs I recognized as excitement tinged with apprehension, which I tried to quiet; while Mujahid seemed seized by an odd calm that made him move slowly, almost dreamily. Without a word he strolled back to where he could watch the road up from the valley and sat on his heels, his back to me, and didn't move a muscle until the sky had darkened and the moon glowed fully yellow and the stars were everywhere as bright as the moon would allow. Meanwhile I waited patiently on my camel listening to the sounds of the night, the howl of a distant jackal, an occasional raised voice from the farmland below, mostly to the sounds of the camels' breathing and the grumbling of their guts.

Then Mujahid stood up and wandered back.

"Three riders approaching, Talal. Have your bow ready."

"We're not going to ambush them."

"Three riders *on horses*, leading their camels. They're expecting an attack."

"So Zuhayr betrayed you."

"Don't tell me you're surprised." He took the back hem of his *thaub* and pulled it up between his legs and tucked it into his belt, turning the long garment into something like a pair of breeches, then unhooked the sheathed sword from his camel saddle and slung it around his waist. Disconnecting the mare's lead rope, he checked her headstall and saddle and mounted.

That alone was almost a declaration of war.

I reminded him urgently, "We can't attack,"

"We won't have to." He spoke in a disinterested murmur. "I suppose Zuhayr saw this as a chance to get rid of you. Be glad you're not lucky, Talal. Luck changes. You never know if you still have it, only that you had it the last time you needed it."

He sighed, a faint whisper out of emptiness. I bent my bow around my saddle's pommel, holding one end behind a knee and slipping the looped string into its notch at the other end.

Three horsemen came over the lip of the hill, followed by four camels on lead ropes. The horsemen came to a cautious halt, the camels moving aimlessly behind them before deciding they'd come to a rest stop and settling down. The three men stared at us.

Even with the half moon behind them I could tell that the one in the middle was Kadhim, and that he was drawing his sword. The man on his left made a series of familiar movements, drawing an arrow from his quiver, fitting it to his bow. Automatically I did the same, without thinking, my mind calm, my fingers on the arrow at once thick and unpracticed, skillful and deft. *This wasn't supposed to be happening!* I couldn't really believe it was. Surely I must be so calm because I was stupefied with fright. I didn't feel frightened, only caught up in something utterly unfamiliar. My bones and muscles knew what they were doing, it was only half my mind that was at a loss, having to resist the urge to look around and go back and find its bearings.

The metallic whisper was Mujahid's sword leaving its scabbard. He turned to me with the big careless confident grin of the Mujahid of old.

"Don't worry, little brother. Shooting a man's no different from shooting a

dove, only easier."

"You promised no violation —"

From fifty paces away Kadhim's voice scraped like millstones.

"Mujahid!"

"I'm here," Mujahid called back easily.

"I warn you, I'm under the protection of Shaykh Salah and Bani Ghassan."

"You could be under the protection of the Mother of the Gods herself and it would do you no good. I'm going to kill you."

"Try it, braggart."

It might not have done any good but Mujahid *could* have answered, "Not here" or "Not yet" and given us an arguable claim of having respected Kadhim's protected status; but that didn't occur to me until too late, and what I actually said as Mujahid started his mare toward Kadhim was, *"Not against three of them!"* As the mare broke into a charge, hooves drumming against the rocky desert, the man on Kadhim's left went into another series of familiar movements. I ducked low against my camel's neck and heard his arrow rip the air above my head. I released my own arrow from low over the pommel of the saddle, a moment later heard a coughing grunt. I thought his bow jumped out of his hands, then one hand clawed the air and he lay back almost onto the horse's hindquarters. The horse dithered and sidled, and Mujahid's charge brought him up against Kadhim and the other bodyguard.

Hitting a man with an arrow in near-dark was nothing. Following blurred action involving three horsemen wielding swords against a background of disturbed camels in the same dark was impossible. Voices came in desperate half-articulated shouts, someone's horse stumbled and almost went down, and then one of the other horses was trotting toward me.

It slowed as it came, was almost half way here before I saw it was Mujahid's horse and that he no longer had his sword.

Behind him one of the two men had jumped to the ground, began with an air of desperation to search for something while hanging onto his horse's halter rope and half dragging the animal behind him.

The approaching horse was walking now. Mujahid's right hand plucked at something near his breast bone, then fell listlessly away. A sword hilt and a hand's span of blade protruded from his chest. He must have been run clear through. He never said a word. He died, I think, there in the saddle. I heard a faint breath dribble from his throat and then he sagged forward and toppled sideways and fell to the ground, as limp and unprotesting as a discarded cloak.

The man on the ground found what he was looking for, picked it up. Mujahid's sword. He jumped back onto his saddle. Kadhim was rearmed. He and the other man rode away from each other to attack from different directions.

I watched Kadhim turn his horse, facing me.

"Do you have a quarrel with me, Talal?"

"Of course I do," I called back, looking around to keep track of the other horse too. "You killed my father and my brother."

A heartbeat's pause. Then the hoofbeats starting Kadhim's charge signalled the other man to attack from the other angle.

Kadhim first. The bow was up, the arrow pulled back to my temple and let fly and I was reaching for another even before the horse's lurch as its rider was hit and shifted weight told me I'd aimed well. Actually I'd hardly aimed at all. Even by half-moonlight a man *was* easier to hit than a dove. I loosed a second arrow at Kadhim, reached for a third arrow and turned atop my saddle when there was a slithering, scrabbling noise

as the second horse lost its footing on a sloping patch of gravel and loose rock and stumbled and threw the rider over its head.

Man and horse were less than ten paces away. Behind me now I heard Kadhim's horse falter, stop, and the inert thud as Kadhim fell from the saddle. His horse suddenly shied away and bolted, while the second horse found its footing and pranced away, scattering the camels . . . and the thrown man got to his feet.

"You don't have to die," I told him, but he was already running at me, sword raised. I hardly got the arrow drawn back enough to have the force to pierce skin, much less bone, but I did. It took him in the middle of the forehead. He fell over backward, knees buckling, the sword still in his hand.

He neither spoke nor moved, except for a while his free hand kept rising listlessly, as though to make some tired complaint, and falling back to the cooling ground. When I slid off the camel and looked closer I found he was the scarfaced guard from this morning at the palace.

Of course Mujahid was dead, as I'd known he had to be. I felt only a contained and far-away sorrow then, as though I were still tensed to fight off attackers and had no time to mourn a brother. Neither had I time to think of Mabruka, nor to examine too closely the suspicion, either sent by the spirit world or dreamed up by an anguished mind in the aftermath of bloody action, that by lying with Mabruka I had somehow ended Mujahid's luck.

It finally struck me how stupid I had been not to realize before Mujahid told me that he had never known if he was still lucky. Of course he hadn't! Luck didn't mark the palm of your hand, or leave a sign like a tribal tattoo on wrist or cheek or chin, to fade when luck left you. How lucky I was not to be lucky!

141

142

There was even a small spark of solace
— bitter and unworthy and shameful
though it was — to be taken from knowing I would no longer live in the shadow
of Mujahid and his luck. Though I
might not live among the Numayris.
Who knew what they would do when
I returned unharmed, alone? I might
get sent back into the obscurity I came
from, forever a man with no ancestors.
. . .

Kadhim had taken one arrow in the
throat and one through the ribs. He
wasn't quite dead, though I never knew
if he heard me saying it was disgraceful
how easy he had been to kill. I retrieved
my arrows and cleaned them on his
cloak, undid his dagger belt and pulled
it free of him and buckled it around my
waist.

The man I'd traded arrows with was
still on his horse, holding himself upright with stiff arms braced on his cloth
saddle. The arrow was lodged in his
side, and his eyes were closed and he
made small moaning sounds with every
breath. Helping him dismount might
injure him worse. I asked what I should
do but got no answer.

Then I heard faint cautious sounds
approaching up the incline from the
valley.

I nocked another arrow, crouched,
waited until a man on a tall dark horse
rode slowly over the valley's rim. Alone.
No lance or bow. I assumed he had a
sword and dagger but couldn't see them.

He pulled the horse to a stop, moving
his head slowly to take in the scattered
animals, the prone forms if not their
identities, straining to see farther into
the darkness . . .

I imagined his fastidious nostrils
curling at the smell of blood.

I stood up.

"Ahlan, Zuhayr. Evening of goodness."

He quelled his surprise and gave me
a long stare.

144

"Did you do all this with your bow?"

"Not all of it. Mujahid's dead. So are
Kadhim and one of the escort, the one
with the scarred face. The other one's
hurt."

Zuhayr glanced briefly at the injured
man then back at me. He had thinking
to do. I wasn't supposed to have survived. That I had was bad enough —
but that one of the escort had, too, I
thought, might really complicate things
for him.

And he already knew that he would
live no longer than a heartbeat if he
tried to bolt.

At last he sighed and shook his head
sympathetically.

"You don't believe in making things
easy for yourself, do you? Kadhim was
under the protection of both Harith and
Salah. They can't let you get away with
killing him. The fellow on the horse is
one of us, a Hilali. If he lives, so what?
The other guard was of Bayt Ali. You're
not rich enough to buy yourself out of
a blood feud with them."

"You're going to advise me to run,
aren't you?" And of course not to come
back. Coming back alone would only be
a suicidal gesture. Coming back with
a raiding party would be pointless too,
because rescuing Mabruka would be no
rescue, only an abduction. And anyway,
how could I recruit a raiding party?

I went on, "Would you let me go without wiping out the disgrace to the two
shaykhs?"

"You're the bowman. I couldn't stop
you."

"What about your friend there?"

"I'll go back down the hill and bring
some men with a litter. He can't walk.
Riding would kill him."

"You're a smooth liar, Zuhayr. You
know very well you'll have to kill him
yourself."

"Are you mad? Why should I kill
him?"

"Because he knows you told Kadhim
that we'd be here waiting to ambush

him. So Kadhim and his two body-guards rode out of the valley on horse-back, ready for a fight, as you'd planned — to get rid of me. You set up a Hilali guard to get seriously injured and a Bayt Ali guard to get killed in a fight that wouldn't have happened but for you. The Bayt Ali won't like that. You think you're in league with them but they're only using you."

Zuhayr laughed. It was raucous and jarring.

"You insulting little shit!" He snatched at the sword hilt I only now saw but had the sense not to draw it.

"Your Shaykh Harith says you're only a messenger boy," I went on, "but you know enough about what's going on to know the Bayt Ali are trying to get the Hilalis dispossessed. But you still want to get your hands on Mabruka's inheritance. It's land she'll own that you want even more than her. There'll be no advantage to owning land, though, unless you've worked out some arrangement with the Bayt Ali to let you keep it. What do you have to do in return?"

He said blankly, "What are you talking about?"

The moon was behind him. His chin came up, his face moving side to side as though he were scanning the desert behind me. His chin came down again. While I maneuvered around so my back was less exposed, keeping my undrawn arrow pointed his way all the time, he said in an oddly bodiless voice, "What dispossession?"

The voice was more convincing than the raucous laugh or the hand-on-sword bluster. Mother of the Gods! — had I over-estimated him?

I said slowly, "The Bayt Ali are trying to get Shaykh Salah and the Ghassani tribal council to rescind the old agreement with Ahl al-Hilal."

"Who says so?"

"Your own Shaykh Harith."

I think his mouth hung open a while.

Then he turned away from me to the open desert, without any attempt at concealment, craning his neck from side to side but not finding what he was looking for.

His head swiveled back.

"I don't believe you!" Breath whistled in his nostrils. Then, in a petulant whine, *"Dispossess* us? After all these . . . *lifetimes?"*

I gestured with the point of the arrow at the fallen men, the blood, the scattered beasts.

"You mean all this was just over Mabruka? All the talk this morning of coming change was just an empty ignorant threat to frighten her into marrying you on your terms — when she wouldn't have you as a *servant?"*

"Oh, she'll have me — in my bed."

"You're forgetting. One of the men your treachery killed was my brother."

I raised the bow.

He stuttered, "Y-you wouldn't dare."

"Count to three. See how far you get."

Instead he tried to call his lance-bearer.

I put the arrow in his heart.

The big horse skittered away from the fallen body and ran nervously into the desert. Somewhere a calm voice spoke. The roan veered toward it. A figure moved out of a patch of deeper shadow and took the horse's headrope.

"Come here," I called. "There'll be no more trouble."

He took a moment to make sure the roan was calm before releasing the rope and approaching me without hurry or reluctance.

It was the man with the cast in one eye who had ridden with Zuhayr that morning. He was unarmed. He looked down at what had been his master and spat disinterestedly.

"His friends may mourn him but I don't know why."

The words were callous enough to make me say, "Didn't you owe him loyalty?"

"Loyalty!" He laughed shortly. "Listen. He had me ride up here late this afternoon with a lance and a sword and find a hiding place and wait. I said, 'If you're so eager to get rid of this Talal, come with me; when he shows up we'll ambush him and it'll be over.' He said, 'Why take chances, we'll let Kadhim do it for us; if something goes wrong we're the surprise reinforcements.' He was supposed to come up the hill right behind Kadhim's party, not wait till the fight was over and everything was quiet."

"You were a great help," I reminded him.

A shrug, eloquent in its spareness.

"Everyone involved in this quarrel was under someone's protection, so it was disobey my master or get an arrow in my liver or get done to death by one of the protectors." His head shook. "Then when Zuhayr finally did arrive, I got very interested in what you two were saying . . ."

He looked around, found Mujahid's body.

"You'll want to bury your friend."

My odd calm, the sense of unfamiliarity approaching disbelief, hadn't left me. It didn't now. I hoped vaguely that it was some sort of natural condition and not a sign of spirit world interference. The spirit world was too arbitrary. I didn't want its enmity, and I didn't want to be singled out for favors that could mean I was being brought onto one side of some game I didn't know was being played nor by what

rules. The spirit world might be as much a place of rivalries and cross-purposes as our world. In which case some day Zuhayr's male Gods might triumph after all, and old Umar bin Auda's patterns of the Gods were no more than accidents, as unplanned as the patterns of flying dust.

"The others too," I heard myself say. "I don't want angry ghosts cursing me."

"Leave them. Someone will take care of Kadhim. Everyone's going to know what happened anyway" — his voice fell to a murmur — "unless you want to kill that one on the horse?"

"Goddess, no! Enough killing."

I took the sword from Mujahid's body and snapped the blade between two rocks and threw the pieces away. Zuhayr's man helped me bury my brother in a scant grave we dug in a sandy hollow hot far off. Then we rounded up the animals. I roped Kadhim's camel to our own and took all the waterbags. Shaykh Salah and Zuhayr's family could have the other animals back. Zuhayr's man thought that was silly; why didn't I steal them as spoils of war?

"I have no quarrel with Salah," I said. "I didn't mean to blacken his face."

"But you did. He and the Bayt Ali hotheads will be after your blood. Even Zuhayr got that part right."

"How long before I can come back?"

"Never."

He promised to get help for the wounded Hilali. I mounted my camel and led the other animals into the night.

▽

Are you a subscriber yet . . . ?

www.ingramcontent.com/pod-product-compliance
Lightning Source LLC
Chambersburg PA
CBHW070556180626
46817CB00005B/1873